ALPHA OMEGA
THE HOLY DRUG

A GATSBY DONOVAN *PARADIGMS LOST* MYSTERY

ELLERY STONE

Verbatim Publishing
Portland, OR USA

Copyeditor: Linda Grimsson

Ordering Information:
Quantity sales. Special discounts are available on quantity purchases by corporations, associations, and others. Orders by U.S. trade bookstores and wholesalers.

Cover: Photoshop art by Terry Journey, Wind Dancer Design

1. Main category—Fiction
2. Other category—Action & Adventure
3. Other category—Mystery, Thriller
4. Other category—Psychological Suspense

First edition: Published 2008 by Big Bang Books/BookSurge Publishing
Copyright © 2008 by Lori Stephens
ISBN13: 978-4196-8925-3 (pbk.)

Second edition: Published 2018 by Verbatim Publishing
Copyright © 2018 by Lori Stephens
ISBN13: 978-0-9658835-6-6 (pbk.)

Manufactured in the United States of America

ALSO BY ELLERY STONE

DEEP STRUCTURE
The Stonehenge Quantum
Where are the mysterious symbols coming from? Why have they appeared in an Egyptian tomb, a Peruvian palace, and a shape created by a fakir's squirming snakes?

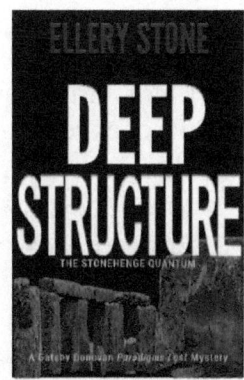

Dr. Gatsby Donovan's career at the British Museum has made her an expert in decoding ancient glyphs, but solving this linguistic puzzle is the greatest challenge of her life. Will her knowledge unearth the answers, or are they secreted within the very source that she dare not decipher? As she spirals into the universal "deep structure," she finds herself dangling from the edge of everything she once believed about reality.

VIRAL GLYPH
The Rosette Rebellion
When Dr. Gatsby Donovan meets a cocky stage magician, Maceo Affiato, he claims that the most mysterious artifact of all human history—the Phaistos Disk—has been stolen, and he needs her expertise in order to find it.

If the disk on display in the Heraklion Museum isn't genuine, where is the real one? And how is it connected to a terrible massacre? Finding the answers means outwitting the female-only syndicate called The Circle. Its global network of agents will do whatever it takes to protect the disk and conceal its true purpose and power, no matter the price. Can Gatsby connect the dots—and overcome her darkest fears—before time runs out?

www.ellerystone.com

ACKNOWLEDGMENTS

My heartfelt thanks go to the following individuals:
- Linda Grimsson, Northwest Independent Editors Guild, for copyediting
- Terry Journey, Wind Dancer Design, who refined the cover art
- Eric Witchey, whose dedication to the craft of writing inspires me
- Elizabeth Lyon and Mike Nettleton, both extraordinary editors and all-around great people

Abban wau
Non an men-gah
sho day too vashla meed
nen-vee von vesh garan
mem vanla padaran
on men-ga
Damaii vash an parate
on men-gan falaji
atan raaloh
Di-wan nassa way an
pash-lo salesh
meed nen-vee von
Travi ash anta rom
chanava ri-ana enfaj
Vasira atan raaloh
nash verey on men-ga

PROLOGUE

The fate of my soul!!

Reymann choked back a cry and the acidic glob in his mouth as he dropped. His kneecaps thumped against the carpet, sending shivers of pain through both thighs. As he tipped back against the bed and pulled the burlap satchel into his lap, the object inside it shifted. Opening the bag, he lifted the Librah Vae-ta out and turned it over with quivering fingers.

I have it in my hands! My salvation! My eternal life!!

The Abba's voice rippled in his mind—

There is only one path to Omega...

—phantasmal, like drifting frankincense: *When you attain entrance, Omega will receive you in the same manner as when it brought you into existence, and when your eyes are finally opened, you will see in not seeing, know in not knowing, and you will escape, dispersing into all TRUTH...*

The Prayer of Devotion pulsed through him like a monstrous heartbeat. His voice cracked as he whispered: "Abbah way non vash ah parateh, sho day too vashla meed neh-vee von besh garah, mem vahla padarah..."

I won't wait any longer! He squeezed his eyes shut, intensely aware of the leather pressing against his palms and the pain stabbing at his temples.

There is only one path to Omega...

One eyelid twitched as he stared at the symbol on the cover:

$$\Omega$$

Reymann glanced around the bedroom, his eyes flitting to the light fixture overhead, the telephone on a folding table beside a filing cabinet. Were there wiretaps? Cameras secreted in the walls? Would the web of lies and bribes that had allowed him access to the Abba's private office protect him now? He felt even more vulnerable than when he'd grabbed the book, raced into the dark asylum of his car, and gunned the engine.

What would the Abba do? How would the discipleship survive without its holy word?

Whatever the hell they do, my path is guaranteed. The book is mine! Not the fragments offered to the pathetic sycophants, the entire Word! My immortality!!

Red and glassy from nights of muttering prayers while the rest of London slept, his eyes now blazed: he had the look of the warrior who bellows into the sky as his foe's bloody head swings from his fist. He anchored his elbows on his knees and held the book up as if delivering a squalling newborn, slippery with blood and meconium, to its mother. *My life has been shackled to the service of the truth, but I will have my reward NOW!*

He pulled on the tab; the snap released with an abrupt pop. A river of ecstasy flooded through him. The devotion, the self-denial, the celibacy would all submerge in shadow as his soul was blessed, as he received what the years of sacrifice had earned him: his immortality. His joining with The Ultimate.

There is only one path to Omega...

He licked his lips and tasted the bitterness of ammonia.

On the first page, he saw lines of calligraphy: Latin, Greek, and hieroglyphics fused in linear but incoherent constructions. As he blinked at it, trying to match the symbols with the syllables of the prayer language he knew well, an irritating buzz began to whine at the back of his head. His forehead bunched into a frown.

"But...these words open the gates of Omega?" he sputtered.

As his eyes darted across the text, Reymann's heart pumped harder and faster. His lungs hitched, as if he were sucking air through wadded cheesecloth. Dagger-points of pain sliced through his temporal lobes. The pain intensified, and he dropped his head into his hands, groaning. The book cartwheeled to the carpet, landing on its spine with a thump.

Realization struck him like a suicide bomb. *I have just said my last prayer!*

"NO! No, dear God!"

The shout sent electric jolts through his eyes. He staggered to his feet, stumbling against a wheeled chair and sending it spinning in crazy circles. As his hip smacked against the folding table, a framed picture sitting on it toppled: Maura's long-suffering smile, the smile that had stiffened like arthritis as their accounts emptied. Hugged next to her, Geoff, then a sturdy adolescent in his football uniform, his expression of *Just fuck off and die—that's what you want, isn't it?*

My job, my money and possessions, my friends—my wife! My child! Rage filled his throat. "I've given everything! Everything!"

A drop welled and splattered onto the page, but it was not the clear wetness of tears.

Blood.

The Abba's face rose before him, a specter of onyx eyes and lips moving in slow motion.

There is only one path to Omega...

Reymann felt himself dripping from every pore, every cell; crimson beads fell onto the Berber carpeting and across his legs. Blood rushed to his hands and feet, swelling each digit. An iron-rich taste filled his mouth. He tried to swallow the metallic saliva, but his throat had locked. Cramps exploded through his stomach, doubling him over. With a bellow of agony, he clapped his hands to his sides, staggered toward the hallway, stretched one quivering hand toward the house alarm panel, and toppled.

Each throb that sucked the blood out of his collapsing veins sent excruciating blasts through his head. He was swimming in fire, drowning in acid. Something demonic howled through his organs and up into his lungs, across his larynx and tongue, thrashing against his teeth. He heard himself screaming, screaming as the infidel on the rack, screaming at the burning stake of faith, screaming at the idolatry of the discipleship, screaming at the assassins of religion, screaming that was now a liquid gurgle, screaming into the inferno of hell, screaming as all hope entered darkness.

CHAPTER 1

On a tall table to her left, The Sargon—a brown clay tablet just under a meter square—lay in its protective acrylic casing. The desk to her right held a full battalion of technology: two Axon PCs that linked to the World Wide Web as well as the British Museum's intranet and servers.

Gatsby Donovan's eyes zigzagged across the work space—the explosion of reference books, notepads, pens, paperclips, empty bottles of iced tea, and half-eaten Toblerone chocolate bars. She thought, *Could all this detritus give future archeologists clues as to how orthographers performed the magic of translation?* She shook her head. *Or will they just think we're unmitigated slobs?*

She shifted back to the tablet. *An eight-point-two earthquake. It took thousands of lives, but the fresh cache of artifacts held this gem.*

The limestone tablet, discovered in what appeared to be a buried palace, was The Sargon. At its discovery, the Iranian Bureau of Antiquities had immediately claimed the tablet as its national property. The conservation team carbon-dated the artifact at 714 BCE—the period of the Persian kingdom of Mannai.

As her eyes moved across the ancient writing, she thought, *One more time. Start with the story. It's the oldest drama of human history: political machinations that end in mass slaughter.*

Heralds sing the song of the mighty Aza, ruler of the kingdom. His firstborn son is Melek.

She pressed a fingertip against the casing and moved it from left to right as the proto-alphabetic Phoenician script revealed the tale.

Prince Melek did love Ru-na, the daughter Of King Sargon of the east.

Assyria, she thought.

```
In the season of the mirah rains, King Aza's
warriors raided the kingdom of Sargon and
killed the multitudes. In his anger, Sargon
sought his just revenge by beheading...
```

Who?

The last glyph secreted the answer. The last *undeciphered* glyph. Its two squiggly sections, one Chinese in its graceful intricacy, indicated two syllables. The second was a vertical stalk that intersected a curving shape reminiscent of breasts.

Who? Gatsby asked herself for what seemed like the thousandth time. *Translators around the world have slaved over this tablet for two years now, trying to decipher a single symbol that appears nowhere else on it and on no other artifacts from the site.*

Across the room, drowning in a precarious stack of reference books and huddled over a parchment of Early Hebrew, Clive Gruedin shifted on his stool and took a long, noisy pull from the Orangina he'd been nursing all morning.

The veteran head of the Department of the Ancient Near East, Gruedin pirouetted between grave seriousness one moment and exuberant humor the next. His demeanor kept Gatsby on her toes: the geeky scholar could poke fun at the most taboo topics with a face as deadpan as a mortician. It was a cat-and-mouse game to keep up with his impishness— a game that, over the last eight years, had made him endearing to her. His professional expertise was translating Semitic texts, and his free time, as he regularly reported to her, was devoted to the comparative analysis of beers of the world.

Gatsby glanced at the clock on her computer monitor. Almost noon. She rubbed her eyes.

Time for lunch. The cafeteria's to-die-for spanakopita? Sounds good. But first let's check this.

She wheeled toward the computer, logged on to the Internet and then her personal ISP, and brought up her email folder. A new message waited for her. As she clicked on it and began to read, her lips curled in a smile.

Subject: Greetings from Boulder
Date: 07 September
From: Definite_Article@linguist-list.roye.com
To: grdonovan@zipmail.net
I dash off a note before attacking this Everest of student papers. I wanted to congratulate you once again on the coup of your latest engagement. The Brits don't know the depth of your talents. Past perfect participles call, gotta run.
As always, I send my best.
Semantically yours, B.

Thanks, Definite Article. You always make me smile. The grin seeped away. *But this pen-pal relationship has gone on for, what, ten years? We keep talking about meeting, someday it has to happen. He might even be someone that I could fall—*

A pang sizzled through her.

Fall in love with? And when is that going to happen, when Mars freezes? Who could take the place of him?

A dark place inside of her began to shudder; a rasping growl, the sound of a beast baring its teeth.

Trust a man with my heart? How can I ever trust a man again, any man? After he walked out on me? And worse, the night that I...

The wound shrieked in protest, but the memories swept over her, and she dropped her head into her hands, squeezing her eyes shut.

Seattle. The dark room, sweat, hot breath, flickering candlelight, rough hands raking over her shoulder blades.

No. Don't! Don't think about it! Don't remember...

Gritting her teeth, she pulled in a deep breath and released it slowly. Another breath. Released it from her lungs with a sound like air sighing from a bicycle tire.

"Gatsby?"

Gruedin's voice popped her back to the room. She looked up. "Huh?"

"You okay? You look upset."

She turned in her chair to peer down at the tablet. "I'm fine. Just lost," she stretched one hand toward the mouse and closed the email, "in the past."

Nodding, Gruedin pushed his thick glasses up on his nose. "Yes. Well. Are you about to go for lunch?"

As she picked through the bones of buried memories and lowered them into tiny mental coffins, she sighed. "Um, in a few minutes."

"Okay." He leaned over his table and began closing books.

She turned in her chair to face The Sargon, and the details of it flowed back into her mind. The rest of the tablet had been successfully decrypted by two world-class orthographers, Clermont and Chozsa, but the blasted final symbol still eluded everyone who touched the artifact.

She rubbed her chin. *What would the rulers of the time feel compelled to dictate to their scribes? What would they pay the most attention to? How would the record-keepers describe the familial and political conflicts in the script most widely used at th...*

(A curving shape reminiscent of breasts)

Breasts?

A connection struck at her.

Wait! What if it...

She whirled toward her PC again and brought up the Museum's storehouse of orthographies from the period, Phoenician, Hebrew, Arabic, and Greek. She accessed two databases that she hadn't worked with in over a year: Linear A and B.

The syllabary of Linear B faded into view on the monitor. Her eyes raced across the rows, and in the last column...

The single line that ended at the midpoint of a curving *w* shape; the shape of two full breasts.

As adrenaline blasted through her, Gatsby heard a roar burst from her mouth.

Still hunched at his table, Gruedin jumped and blurted, "Good lord, you startled me!" He blinked rapidly. "What is it?"

She flapped a hand in his direction. "Come here, quick, Clive, look at this! The last symbol that Clermont and Chozsa were never able to resolve? I've got the bastard!"

He popped from his chair and raced toward her. As he approached to stand next to her, he peered down at The Sargon.

"No one would have thought of it," she said, her words flowing together as she pulled in air, "because we all assumed that it would be the name of Aza, or Melek, or one of Aza's other sons, or a close relative, or some commander of the armies. No one thought to consider that it might be the name of a woman, Sargon's daughter, Ru-na!"

Gruedin's eyes widened. "Jesus!"

"*And* that, for some unfathomable reason, this last word isn't written in Phoenician but in Linear B! The scribe switched to a different orthography at the last moment."

Amazement melted over Gruedin's face. "You've just broken The Sargon, do you realize that?!" Gruedin slapped his thigh and whooped like a lottery winner as Gatsby looked back and forth between his shining face and the tablet.

Gruedin dashed to the far side of the room, snatched the phone perched on the wall, and frantically pressed buttons. He muttered between gulps, "Director? It's Gruedin. I'm in the translation lab. Come down here right away and bring everyone on the third floor. It's Donovan, sir, she's resolved The Sargon!" His eyes widening, he blurted, "Yes, The Sargon!" After a pause, he grinned over at Gatsby. "You're on your way, I'll tell her." He replaced the handset and galloped back to Gatsby's work space.

As they chattered, the door opened. Nelson Clevis trundled into the room. Wearing the tiny glasses, severe grey suit, and pinched look that hadn't changed in eight years, he stepped toward Gatsby, who had regularly imagined him as a slightly taller and decidedly balder version of Veruca Salt from *Charlie and the Chocolate Factory*. He approached her table and, over the tops of his lenses, scowled down at The Sargon.

"Nelson." Gatsby greeted him, knowing full well how terribly the informality of first names pricked at him. She pointed him toward the tablet. "Right here, the last symbol, the one that baffled everyone! It's the name of a woman. And the rest of the tablet is Phoenician, but this lone symbol is bloody Linear B."

She glanced up to see Clevis frowning. He leveled a sideways look in her direction, and then a smile flowered on his face.

"Congratulations, Donovan." He reached out and took her hand in his own, which was too small for an adult and too cold for a mammal.

Gatsby smiled back, whirling through thoughts of what the discovery would mean for her and for the Museum and the stream of consulting engagements that were about to take over her life. "Thank you."

The door squealed again as representatives from four departments flooded into the room. Kleiner from Conservation Science, Ashiki from Ancient Near East, Kortge from Greek and Roman Antiquities, and Jouvet from Ancient Egypt and Japan descended on her, forming a tight huddle. When the crush became threatening, Clevis barked at them to move back. He cleared his throat.

"Please, everyone, your attention?" The group settled as Clevis smoothed his hands down the front of his suit. "Our esteemed consultant, Dr. Donovan, is claiming that she has deciphered the last element of The Sargon, a tablet that has baffled prominent translators and orthographers for several years."

A boisterous cheer rose. When it died to low chatter, Clevis continued, "And in a moment, she is going to explain to us just how she came to this conclusion."

Chuckles and murmurs rippled through the room.

"For now," he turned toward Gatsby, seeming to vibrate with restrained pride, "I believe a generous round of applause is in order."

Gatsby watched her colleagues' excited faces as the applause fluttered around her like confetti.

"Three cheers!" Gruedin shouted as he dove forward to wrap her in a tight hug.

"Thank you, everyone!" Grinning, exhilarated, she looked from Clevis' shining face to Gruedin's sparkling eyes, and around the group, swimming in the applause.

CHAPTER 2

Central London drowned in rain, so much so that it had washed away all traces of pigeon poop in Trafalgar Square. Cabs, buses, and subway cars were soggy with umbrellas and wet irritation.

Her Mackintosh hung where she'd tossed it on the coat rack in the corner; drops running down it were now a puddle on the tile floor.

The tendrils of steam rising from her second mug of Kenyan espresso floated toward her like caffeinated phantoms. Settled at her desk, Gatsby leaned toward her monitor, reading the Web article on The Sargon. Linear B— Phoenician—King Sargon—Melek—Ru-na...Was there anything related to the symbol for which she'd received a warm round of applause just the day before?

The first Proto-Canaanite writings, discovered approximately 2800 BCE, later gave rise to the Phoenician system (alphabetic), which was the predecessor of Greek and Hebrew. Several cuneiform scripts in use around 1200 BCE were mysteriously wiped out by...

An abrupt beep broke her concentration.

The text faded from her mind like the last measure of a love song. Gatsby turned away from the monitor, peered at the phone-com, sighed, and leaned across her desk to press the ANSWER key.

"Yes?"

"It's Mr. Clevis."

"Nelson. What is it?" *He hates it when I do that.* She stifled a chuckle.

A guttural harrumph implied the lecture that she knew was goose-stepping through the Director's shiny head at that moment: *Dr. Donovan, your years of service to the Museum have been invaluable, but you are attached with disturbing persistence to the gauche Americanism of first-name address. This insubordination must cease, posthaste.* Her secret smile widened.

"The gentleman in my office is with the Crown Investigation Service, and he wishes to speak with you."

Her smile drained away. "What? The CIS? What does he want?"

The next harrumph carried an edge of tension. "He has not informed me. Please join us now."

"I...but..."

"Meeting hall five, third floor. Now, please."

Gatsby sensed the urgency in Clevis' voice and felt her shoulders tighten. What the hell would a CIS agent want to talk with her about? Was the British government deporting her, *posthaste,* back to the U.S. for some crime that she hadn't committed? Did it have to do with the Sargon? Did the Iranian government want its property returned?

She exhaled. "I'll be right there."

From her office, she sped down the hall to the bank of lifts at the south end, rode up to the third floor, and emerged into the Hargrove Wing. The architects had seamlessly fused operations with the grandeur of antiquity: the corridors were flanked with tapestries from Mongolia and Morocco. Greco-Roman statuary. Egyptian friezes. Chinese oracle bones. For the staff, researchers, and curators of the British Museum, it was a sanctuary of samadhic serenity, perched silently above the bustle of tourists on the floors below.

She raced past a triptych of Lascaux cave art and pushed open the door to Meeting Hall 5. From seated positions at the massive cherry oak table, two men rose.

In a crisp black suit, the CIS agent had a weight lifter's sturdiness grafted onto the agile frame of a downhill skier. Gatsby felt her mental software quickly cataloging him. Black hair framed a wide face; his dark eyes were busy and probing. Tufted eyebrows, a commanding nose, square chin. Watching how his eyes moved over her, she got the feeling that an ID subroutine had just booted up in his head, recording data: White female, 40ish. Nine to ten stone. Dark auburn hair, green eyes. BLAKE UNIVERSITY sweatshirt with Space Needle logo.

Clevis stepped forward. "Come in." He raised ring-gilded fingers toward the man. "Agent Singer, this is Dr.

Gatsby Donovan. Once a staff translator here at the Museum and now one of our most valued consultants. Yesterday, in fact, she made a translation discovery with a piece that has thwarted many before her."

Warming at the recognition, Gatsby murmured "hello" as she moved round the table.

Singer gave a nod of greeting and sat. "Dr. Donovan." The clipped precision in his voice said OFFICIAL BUSINESS.

She settled into a chair opposite Singer and looked around the room. It was one of the few meeting rooms at the Museum that she had never used. A white board stretched across one wall, a recessed walnut cabinet was packed with audio/video equipment, and leather chairs flanked a rodomontade table.

As Clevis sidled toward the door, his gabardine slacks made rhythmic swishing sounds. "When you are finished, Agent Singer, please check back with me, and I will show you to the private exit." He lifted an eyebrow, turned as if perturbed by the cosmos in general, and exited.

The door eased shut. The snick of the latch bolt sliding home seemed to echo in the silence.

Gatsby peered at Singer. He was a government official, but she couldn't stop herself from commenting, "Very James Bond, wouldn't you say?

He leaned back in his chair and folded thick arms over his chest. "The reasons for contacting you in this way will become clear." The deep, detached tone of authority in his voice made her think of plate tectonics. "There was an incident. It has not been released to the media, nor will it."

She frowned. "What sort of incident?" *And what do I have to do with it?*

"Before I discuss it, I must secure your understanding that everything I tell you is confidential. This information must not be discussed with anyone. Not your family or best friend. You must consent to keeping it completely private." His eyes flickered.

"For how long?"

"Until the case is solved." He held an unblinking stare on her.

Until the case is solved? "Not a phrase a translation consultant hears every day—or ever, I should say." She paused. "Well, you wouldn't have to worry about discretion. Confidentiality comes with the territory in my line of work." Seeing his frown, she explained, "The Museum does get hot artifacts and is sometimes called upon by police forces." She leveled an equally immovable look at him. "So, Agent Singer, will you please tell me what the bollocks this is about?"

Singer seemed momentarily caught by the sheen of the table before he looked up at her. "Earlier this week, an alarm went off at a private residence in Kent. The alarm company was notified. Standard procedure. They called back repeatedly, but there was no answer, so they sent a patrol car to the premises. There was no sign of forced entry. When the guardsman knocked and called the resident's name, there was still no answer. He entered the house and found the body." Singer shifted forward. "There was a trail of fresh blood from the resident's office to the hallway, where he had managed to trip the security alarm and then collapsed on the floor."

Gatsby prodded, "And this has..."

Singer cut her off. "There were no wounds, no suicide apparatus or note. All toxicology tests came up clean. It could have been a heart attack, seizure, something along those lines, but that wouldn't explain the terrible blood loss." He sucked in a breath, his eyes darkening as if witnessing something torturous. "Do you remember the news stories some years back about the African Ebola virus?"

Hearing "African" and "virus" in the same sentence brought up disturbing mental images: HIV clinics, needles, latex gloves, near-death orphans. She nodded.

"Imagine that level of exsanguination. Absolutely unbelievable. Every last drop of blood squeezed out through every pore and orifice."

A knife-tip of fear poked at her stomach.

"But we haven't found viral infection or conditions of any kind, anything that could explain this sort of death. He was a ridiculously healthy man." He held the stare on her, but she saw his eyes narrow.

"That's...um, disturbing, to say the least." Gatsby leaned back and pulled at the collar of her sweatshirt. "But I'm still wondering how it prompts an unannounced meeting with someone who does translation for museums and has never so much as bounced a ten-pound cheque." Impatience sent her Nikes jiggling under the table. "What exactly is it that you want from me?"

Singer shifted his bulk in the chair while clearing his throat. "I'm coming to that. While we didn't find any weapons at the scene, the man was gripping something as he died in a lake of his own blood. A book written, we think, in a jumble of ancient languages."

The story of the man's death piqued a morbid curiosity, but hearing "jumble of ancient languages," she felt her heart jump. "A book?"

"Yes, a handmade book. We're hoping that a translation of it will help us to understand how and why the victim died, but the crypto division doesn't even know where to begin in translating it. It seems to be a combination of living and dead languages. It might be a recently invented language, it may be gibberish, but I want to find out whatever I can about the damn thing and why it was found at the scene of a blood bath in a middle-class neighborhood."

Gatsby ran a hand through her hair, working for a cogent response.

"I spoke yesterday with a Professor Edwards at the University of London, and he suggested that a," he frowned, and his eyes moved toward the ceiling as if searching for the word, "an orthographic expert might be of aid. And I understand that translating ancient scripts is your area of expertise."

She nodded. "Probably sounds pretty dry, but yes it is."

"Then I've found the right person." He folded his hands on the table. "I'd like you to examine this book and see what you can make of it."

"I've never been asked to assist with a crime. First time for everything." She propped one foot on the opposite knee. "Yes, of course I'll look at it, but what else can you tell me? Who was this guy?"

Singer shook his head. "Sorry, the family doesn't want any personal information released, and we do not want the general public knowing about it. People might jump to the conclusion that some biological warfare agent or virus is loose. Mass hysteria." He paused. "I can tell you the code name of the case. RED-MK7."

Red em kay seven. Gatsby frowned at him. *Was the guy murdered? Why should I get involved?* A finger of fear traced a line down her spine. "I'm not exactly a crime fighter, Agent Singer. What happens if I refuse to help you?"

Singer's chin dropped as if he were pondering the question, then he looked her in the eye and rumbled, "I'm confident that you won't."

Or else what? Goons with automatic weapons? She ran her hands through her hair and took a deep breath. "Okay. When can I see it?"

"Tomorrow afternoon. Can you make that?"

I'm set to meet with Clevis about The Sargon tomorrow afternoon. An image of the man rose in her mind as she considered his reaction. Mr. Director was not known for fuzzy receptions to anything that jostled his china teacup schedule or world. "Yes, I believe so."

"Good." Singer stood, his knees popping, and started toward the door. "Would you point me toward the Director's office?"

She held out her hands as she rose. "Wait, is that it? Can't you give me any more details?"

He shook his head. "Not yet. I'll call you in the morning with directions to the facility. I'll tell you what I can when you come in." He shouldered the door open and turned his profile toward the hallway. "Which way?"

"End of the hall, take the lift to the fourth floor. It's the last office."

Singer strode down the corridor, martial and imperial, his black heels clapping against the parquet, oblivious to the marble stares of the naked statues.

As she walked toward the opposite end of the hall and started down the stairs, her mind spun.

Everything I tell you is confidential...a combination of living and dead languages...RED-MK7...a blood bath in a middle-class neighborhood...

Living and *dead* languages.

God, what am I getting myself into?

CHAPTER 3

Blood will flow!

A wave of fury crashed over him as he stared at the open door of the steel box, the vault in which, four days earlier, the Librah Vae-ta—the Book of Life, Omega's holy scripture—had been locked.

Niccolo Rueke paced the length of his private office from the banks of state-of-the-art computers at one end to the library-style stacks at the other.

He glanced toward the far wall and the acrylic case it held. Within it, the set of gleaming knives was arranged against black velvet. Handles of metal, bone, leather, and steel, all with vicious, serrated edges. The voices of his teachers whispered through his mind: *The cleanest cut is the one withheld.*

He thought, *Or the one invited.*

Decades of taekwondo training had sculpted his body into a killing weapon, yet he felt a disquieting weakness twist through him. His legs trembled as he paced to the other side of the room. In the years that he had worked to build the discipleship of Omega—now with fully inducted Damaii groups in ninety-seven countries—he had never known the feeling that clawed through him now. It was anger. An undercurrent boiled beneath it, and he knew its name— helplessness—but he would not say it.

The Librah Vae-ta IS Omega! It's the key to everything! The language keys, the discipleship! The empire!!

Whirling toward the sprawling desk that held an assortment of high-tech peripherals, he slammed his fist against it. Flashes of pain shot through his fingers.

The Elders will arrive at any minute.

He tried to breathe slowly. His hand rose to the silver chain that had hung around his neck for twenty years. As he had done so many times in the past, he fingered its small links, hypnotically, ritually, and his body began to relax.

Crossing the room, he entered the bathroom. After urinating and then splashing his face with cold water, he felt a dull calm. A *ralea* traitor had stolen the book, but the discipleship didn't know that.

It's a setback but manageable. Swift damage control. Tracking and punishment. The reach of the network is stronger than ever. The empire will continue to grow.

He took a deep breath and slipped back into the Officia Abba.

For this Council meeting, he had chosen the black robe and a stole embroidered with two symbols: the rising sun and the sword. One's message was new day, light, hope, glory. The message of the sword was clear. Wrath.

A slight man, monkish in his servile posture, had entered the room. Seeing the Abba, Arthur Enright bowed, his slate-grey robe ruffling. His hands clasped behind his back, he murmured the ritual greeting, "Abbah way non push tah non ah meh-gah." *Abba, the Blessed Guide to Omega.*

"Ah meh gah sho met yah," Niccolo intoned in response. He spread his arm toward the table that commanded the center of the dark wood-paneled room. Six high-backed executive chairs flanked it.

As Enright took a seat, two forms appeared in the doorway: a bear of a man, Ivan Kuznetsov, and then a wiry woman, both wearing the same slate-colored robes. They entered, bowed, and offered him the same greeting.

The woman was the Habareh. Her saffron-colored hair flowed over her shoulders, a wake of living silk. Her cheekbones cut the air, and her hazel eyes seemed to announce an impenetrable determination.

Ahh, Franca Volante. Extremely useful to me since rising to second in command, but her utility is threatened by...

By what? In a moment, he knew. *By the lust she tries very hard to hide: her lust for power.*

The Elders addressed each other in hushed tones as a milk-skinned man stepped through the doorway. John Fitch's body seemed to move at different speeds and directions, as if brain and limbs reacted to opposing signals. A chaotic shock of black hair hung to his shoulder blades. He stumbled into the room, his head twitching as he glanced behind him at the door, then at the ceiling, then at Niccolo.

He clasped his hands behind his back and stammered, "A-a-abbah way non push t-tah non ah m-meh gah."

With Fitch present, only one Elder was missing.

An incandescent image of her breezed through Niccolo's mind. So often his thoughts of her had dragged him to the brink of iniquity. He imagined slipping his fingertips down the landscape of her steel-hard thighs, the sweetness of the breath that must waft from her lips. The curve in the small of her back, the delicate pit of her collar bone. The fire that raged in her eyes—those eyes that were black as the depths of space, unknowable as the reasoning of men, terrible as the first eclipse.

A shudder of desire, shameless in its power, throbbed through his organs. He dug his nails into his palms. The slivers of pain drove him back to the crucial business at hand and the somber faces of the Elders.

A flurry at the doorway. With the force of a charging samurai, Maia swept into the room and toward Niccolo, her robe billowing like a hurricane behind her. "Abbah tah non ah me-gah." Her sonorous voice reflected the crack precision of a finely tuned weapon of war.

She truncated the phrase and ignored the honorific posture, deliberately! She does not fear me, never has...but she will.

The Elders' faces flowered with shock at her words. They spun toward him with furrowed brows and shifting eyes.

Holding a steady gaze on her, Niccolo responded quietly, "Ah meh gah sho met yah," and tipped his chin toward the last empty chair.

She maneuvered into it with a smile, as if she'd engineered a successful coup d'état.

A murmur rippled through the room.

Niccolo stepped to the head of the table, scanning their faces and bodies, noticing a hundred subtle clues that he knew a novice would miss. He pulled in a deep breath, held it, released the air as a slow exhalation, and watched as each Elder mirrored the breath. He drew his hands upward, pressing the palms together. With his head tipped back, he stared slightly above eye level, as if witnessing the entrance of divine entities into the corporeal realm.

Their faces weighted and shaped by reverence, the Elders' eyes rose to the space at which he gazed.

"Let us pray." He murmured the Prayer of Invocation.

The Elders joined, reciting the ritual phrases in low tones, eyes open but fixed in concentration, closing with *nah-maen. It is truth.*

As they exhaled deeply, they turned toward the Abba, waiting for guidance.

As he slid into the tallest chair at the head of the table, he felt his mood shift from transcendence to low-grade impatience. "What have you learned?"

They glanced at each other. Kuznetsov cleared his throat. "There is no doubt. It was the one rising in the Anglican church toward priesthood. The Dama Stephen Reymann."

In the silence, the room beat with tension.

"How do you know?" Niccolo growled.

Kuznetsov planted his elbows on the table. "We found the Dama, Edward Kirsch. Reymann was paying him off to gain access to the Officia Abba and then to the vault. After Reymann took the book, Kirsch followed him, and he saw Reymann entering his apartment carrying a burlap bundle."

My private sanctuary, violated! Niccolo felt his pulse pounding. "But did Kirsch see the book itself?"

Kuznetsov paused. "No, and we have not located it."

"Nor will you." The rumble came from the far end of the table.

All eyes turned toward Maia.

As she leaned forward, her black hair rippled over her shoulders and fanned across her muscular forearms. "Reymann is dead, and the CIS now has the Librah Vae-ta."

Gasps erupted.

Even though Niccolo knew that the information she brought to him was the most trustworthy of all that gathered by the discipleship, he turned on her as if she had stolen the book herself. "Explain!" he snarled.

"Reymann's security alarm went off at twelve thirty-eight. A response team showed up at his apartment, then police. At one forty-five, paramedics loaded his body into the truck. Intercepted radio reports indicate that the police confiscated a leather-bound book at the scene. Because they found no clear indication as to what happened or why, the local police called on the CIS to launch an investigation." She paused. "And they took the book to the CIS Evidence Unit in Kent."

Niccolo felt his body twist with agitation. "Who would kill Reymann? And why?" he sputtered.

Tossing her hair off her face, Maia spoke quietly. "He wasn't murdered, exactly. He didn't commit suicide, and he didn't die from natural causes. Exactly." She probed Niccolo's eyes with her own. "What killed him hasn't been determined."

Niccolo's eyes narrowed. "Go on."

"He suffered extreme hemorrhaging with no clear cause. The only indisputable fact about his death is that he was found in his home clutching the Librah Vae-ta."

Niccolo spun out of his chair as questions flooded him. *The Librah Vae-ta is the key to cementing allegiance, but no disciple has ever died for it!* Adrenaline coursed through his veins. *What does this mean to the empire?*

"The s-weight?" he asked her, referring to the discipleship's truth scale, in which a number represented a verifiable level of accuracy. The Elders watched their exchange with taut faces.

Maia gave him a stony look. "One hundred."

Fitch drummed his feet under the table. Franca Volante stroked her throat with manicured fingers.

Niccolo strode back to the head of the table and slid into his chair, pulling in measured breaths. His face now more composed, he turned to Maia. "Make a list."

"I don't believe that will be necessary."

He blinked. "Why?"

She moved her fists onto the table and anchored them. "Because there may be a breach. I believe the CIS has allowed someone access to the book. Non-enforcement." She held him with eyes as black as assam tea. "If that is the case, the obstructions are significantly reduced."

Volante's body stiffened, and she slowly turned her chair to face Maia. Her voice crackled with derision as she said, "Reduced?"

Maia turned toward her with a stare likely intended to drill the woman into dust. "Yes," she whispered.

Volante returned the look with a scowl that might have emerged if a urine-reeking vagrant had huddled next to her on the Tube.

Finch hiccupped loudly. He covered his lips with dainty hands.

Shaking her head, Volante turned, with regal grace, toward Niccolo.

He shot a look at Maia and then in turn at each Elder. "Find out what's going on. Get on it, immediately. Time is critical. We will then discuss a plan of attack." He picked out Volante. "Now tell me about the Damaii."

She recrossed her legs. "It will be next week. The facility is booked. We have access for the entire day, and it will easily accommodate the Dama."

"All one hundred and fifty?"

She nodded.

"Which sermon have you selected?"

"Salvation in Servitude."

Niccolo smiled. "Excellent choice." His hands cut the air as he spoke. "I want a head count and a detailed report. Late arrivals. What's said and what's not said. What they are wearing. Who sits where and with whom. Who pays attention and whose attention wanders."

"What about the Librah Vae-ta?" Volante asked.

He paused. "Say that the book is missing but the offender has not been found. It may flush out accomplices. Say that the Word of Omega is the most holy writ, it is the path to Omega. Disobedience is sacrilege, and the Librah Vae-ta cannot be contaminated by infidels."

"Is—" Kuznetsov stopped, his eyes darting. "Can't it be reproduced?"

Anger blazed through Niccolo. *You bloody idiot—the keys in the language took decades to develop! There are no copies, the book cannot be rewritten without the original documents, which have never been found, and those who created the language have been dead for a century!* It took all his will to restrain himself and reply calmly, "It is the direct word of Omega. Mere men cannot reproduce the text of greatest truth."

Their heads bobbed like wind-up toys.

Kuznetsov cleared his throat again. "And the contributions?"

Ahh yes, the milk of the sacred cows. The thought brought a sense of calm; his stomach muscles began to relax. "I will notify you as to the times, amounts, and locations. Just reassure the Dama that I am watching over my disciples and that the hand of Omega is with them in infinite blessing."

For the first time that evening, Niccolo smiled.

The Elders squirmed silently.

He dismissed them. Kuznetsov, Fitch and Enright rose and floated away like specters.

As Volante stood, she locked eyes with Maia, blew out a puff of air contemptuously, as if emptying a rank garbage bin, and darkened the air as she strode out the door.

Niccolo swept the length of the table toward Maia. Approaching her, he fought the impulses that throbbed through his mind and body. How difficult—how hard—it was! He had touched her only once. Though he enjoyed full prerogative of sex with any disciple, male or female, he did not call on her. Did not want to distract her from the assignments that he gave her. They were too important to the empire. More than that, he wanted to throb for her, wanted the ache of not taking her.

So soft and hard and beautiful. But I must not touch her. Yet. He stopped at the edge of her chair.

She turned her face upward, taking in his frame as if calculating how easily she could overpower a man of his strength. Seeing in her eyes not obedience but a keen consciousness, he sensed that she knew full well his internal struggle and chose to neither acknowledge his desire nor rebuff it.

"You," he murmured.

She stared at him, calm and quizzical as a lab researcher observing a primate in a cage.

"You know what the Librah Vae-ta is."

"Sho ramil adepya day too shoi nal a-rajla metah." *I know that it serves you like a whore.*

He pulled in a breath. *The arrogant bitch! And her fluency!* Only Volante matched her in the intricacies of the language, the subtle shades of pronunciation and tone, the specific pitches that triggered embedded commands—and only *he* knew the language better than either of them.

She stared as if daring him to tweeze out the submission command.

"Find it. Bring it to me."

Her eyebrows peaked. "If there is resistance?"

His hand impulsively hovered near her shoulder. Out of the corner of his eye, he saw the specter of the knives on the wall. *No, not yet.* He looked down at her hands resting on the table. *I would take those hands, twist them behind your back...no escape, lovely Maia...if I slid the cold edge of a blade, the steel kiss, against your neck, would you shout? Struggle? Shed tears? Or submit to me?*

He laced his fingers and growled, "The wicked have earned their just punishment."

CHAPTER 4

Gatsby switched on the light by the front door. Dropping her shoulderbag onto the couch, she crossed the living room, glancing at her answering machine along the way—its message-indicator eye was dark—and approached a cabinet of liqueurs at the far wall.

Soon, with a White Russian tinkling in her hand, she settled into her home office. It was a noisy coincidence of organization and chaotic levels of collection—the walls crowded with bookshelves, files and filing cabinets, souvenirs, memorabilia, assorted peripherals. She sat at the huge mahogany desk that had been a graduation present from her parents and booted up her iTrax PC.

Her mind whirled with snippets of the unnerving conversation she'd had that morning with Singer. *A combination of living and dead languages,* he'd said.

She gritted her teeth, but there was no stopping it.

Just as she'd been unable to stop herself, at age eleven, from staying awake for thirty-three hours to learn the basics of Egyptian hieroglyphics. Rather than try to stop her, her parents quietly brought fruit juice and toasted sandwiches. They could see that the instinct to investigate and understand languages had their daughter in a powerful trap. The desire had never abated—now it was a hurricane that would not be dammed.

A mysterious death accompanied by a mysterious, polyglot book. Was there a connection?

When people die and there's a book involved, there's a religion involved.

She started at the thought. *A book could contain anything—a traveler's memoirs or the rantings of a lunatic. Why should books have anything to do with religion?*

Sipping, she thought, *When have books* not *been connected with religion? All the major religions are cemented by a holy book that justifies some deity's crusade.*

There was more to the train of thought, an oily subterranean current that did not want to emerge from the dark. *Oh no, Donovan, don't go th...*

What are you talking about, Dr. Volante?

The images flashed, unbidden and furious, and she was at Blake University.

Drizzly, caffeine-soaked Seattle.

Cindy Lauper, Psychedelic Furs, The Cars, The Doors. Meat Loaf, Hunter S. Thompson.

Geraldine Ferraro. Reganomics, AIDS, and The B52s.

Falling insanely in love: first with ancient languages, then with one Woodrow T. Sanderson.

Unending symposia with her thesis committee.

The iron hammer of Professor Volante, who, with a look, turned grad students into quivering goo. The woman's face rose on the screen of her mind: chiseled cheekbones, hair flowing like ripe corn silk. The weapons of her eyes declared that fools would not be suffered and would not survive her. As Gatsby launched her doctoral program, Volante's mentorship had been unwavering. She directed her students like a Russian gym coach, pushing them to levels of excellence that they could not have believed themselves capable of achieving. The price that they paid was the sting of her pedagogic whip.

What was the price that Volante paid?

What about the aborted dissertation?

It had baffled Gatsby at the time and still did, two decades later. When she presented the abstract to Volante, the woman had tossed it into a waste bin, immediately and without explanation.

She remembered standing, blinking rapidly, in Volante's office, choking on a cloying floral smell that made her stomach roll—something vaguely lavender.

Why, Dr. Volante?

Volante's eyes had been frozen gemstones. She had leveled her gaze at the door and mumbled, *Good day, Miss Donovan.*

Gatsby shook her head, shocks of dark hair brushing her cheeks, and wheeled herself closer to the humming computer. A maddening urge struck at her. She navigated to a folder on the hard drive and then a file so archaic that it could only be read in BASIC.

```
Filename: Sword495
Date of first save: 04091985
```

After opening it, she scrolled through the text and read:

```
Across human evolution, and the rise of
civilization and language, violence is a
constant. It is an elemental trait of human
nature, of Darwin's survival of the fittest.
While no language can be charged with a
"responsibility" for violence, could unusually
violent historic eras or social movements be
perpetuated by the writings that have supported
them?

NB: Preliterate cultures, whose ethics were
transmitted through oral histories, show far
less propensity for violence.
Some of the most compelling revolutions of
human history have arguably originated in
politico-religious regimes. From the Code of
Hammurabi onward, the most destructive empires
have spread as their writings have
proliferated, especially those with so-called
holy scriptures: the Muhammadic Koran, the
Christian Bible, and to a certain extent, the
Jewish Torah.

Could the authors of these texts have had any
idea of the widespread and enduring power that
their words held, their capacity to ignite both
ecstasy and global crusades? Or were they fully
aware of the influence that the writing
wielded?
```

She rubbed her eyes until stars sprinkled her vision and then stared back into the monitor.

```
Did the scribes know that they held in their
hands the truest instrument of warfare, the
stylus? While asserting that their scriptures
were the words of God, were they covertly
devising words that incited individuals, or
nations, to bloodshed?
```

The pen mightier than the sword. The pen AS sword.

Combing her fingers through her hair, Gatsby turned away from the computer and stared out the living room window at the warblers diving into the birch trees.

Volante's office on the sixth floor of the Davies Building looked out on a long expanse of lawn. Hunkered at the other end of the lawn was the...

The pang ripped through her. The roof of her mouth tasted like sawdust.

Barricades slammed down, blocking off the memories. Had the mechanism not been there, she would have succumbed to the rage long ago. It still sizzled, like a muscle-memory of burnt flesh.

No. No!!

Her method was mastery. She massaged the emotions with rhythmic breathing, the litany of rationalizations. Zen koans about suffering and impermanence and the Wheel of Birth and Death. Reincarnation makes everything new again. What is mind? No matter. What is matter? Never mind.

The wound shrieked in protest, but memories crashed over her. She dropped her head into her hands, squeezing her eyes shut, her stomach gripping.

The Harstedt Interfaith Center.

After her phonology seminar, she met with him in his office, off campus. Not even ten years her senior, the campus minister moved with energy and stealth. A mission-driven light radiated from his eyes; warm, rounded cheeks gave him a cherubic face. In his quiet voice, he spoke rhythmic words to her, as if reading a story to a yawning child, metaphors that illuminated how the Lord God's pure love washed away all confusion. The Sundays of her childhood spent in Methodist services had prompted her to ponder how the possibility of an omniscient God applied to humankind in general and to a twenty-five-year-old Gatsby Donovan in particular. Was there an eternal soul? She sought answers, and over the course of several months, had stopped by his office to confer with him. She asked him about miracles— wishful thinking or reality? He smiled and invited her to meet with him the following night at the Interfaith Center, where he would instruct her on the miraculous.

The Center's sanctuary adjoined the larger auditorium at the center of the campus. The building was dark and empty, but she had no fear, only a yearning for his guidance...

He leads her to the devotional room, his hands fluttering like wings, warm on her shoulders. As they approach the altar, he leans toward her.

His lips brush her ear.

He whispers a single word, one that she does not remember later or ever.

She is frozen.

Every muscle locks, deaf and dumb to the emergency alarm shrilling through her nervous system, impenetrable, cut off from the voice shrieking inside her. She can't move—can't make a sound—rigid, pliable, mute.

Helpless.

While his fingers roughly explore and probe, while he fondles cotton and lace, while the tissues tear, while he pumps into her, while he explodes, gasping thanks to the Great Divinity that gave him guidance and permission, while his hot breath flows over her back, her bare skin rippling with gooseflesh, while he licks his lips, panting, and straightens his clothing, while he shuffles away and then out of the dark room, leaving the door ajar behind him, inside she silently SCREAMS, SCREAMS IN RAGE...

Rage, in equal measure, against God and man.

As she staggered back to her apartment, her questions about God resolved. She knew that if she ever saw his face—the Interfaith minister *or* God—she'd kill the fucker.

She reported the assault to the SPD. The officers' icy, stubbled faces. Overflowing ashtrays.

The campus security office.

Robotic voices, incomprehensible and muddy in the background, as she rifled through forms. Sign here, initial here.

She then met with the executive director of Blake's Department of Religious Affairs, Paul Jacobsen. Slouched and sodden in a chair in his office, she learned that the only minister on staff was a teetering gentleman that Jacobsen had hired two months ago. Jacobsen had pulled out the file, and she couldn't breathe as she stared at the photo of a man near the age of her grandfather.

Her knuckles digging into her eyes, she felt wetness on her fingers.

She pressed her hands flat against her cheeks, shaking, feeling the hot rush of blood and the waves of hatred that could propel a human being to take another's life. The revelation shocked her but not for the first time.

The images in her mind did slow dissolves from the dark devotional room to the iron in Volante's eyes to the piece of work, noble in reason, that Shakespeare had so poetically described. The epicenter of desire and destiny and romantic courtship, all wrapped in Gore-Tex and faded Levi's. Rapier wit that never skipped a beat, sparkling sable-brown eyes that never moved across her without offerings of love.

Woody.

She sighed out another tear.

She told no one about the crinkled photograph of him that she still carried in her wallet.

Gatsby abruptly pushed back from the computer and stood on shaking legs. Waves of pain derailed coherent thinking. Finally, a ticklish sensation—a tear dangling from the tip of her nose—prompted her to stumble into the bathroom and reach for the toilet paper.

She then found herself in her bedroom, crumpled at the edge of her bed. A few more tears escaped. She spread her hands at her sides, the softness of the comforter crushed inside her fists, and lost herself, down, spiraling, drowning...

The one who got away, who ran when we hit the glass ceiling of love. That night, the broken furniture, broken hearts. And then gone. Forever. Did he know about the attack? And if he did somehow know, was that *really why he disappeared?*

She flopped back onto the bed with a thud, scrubbed her hands across her wet cheeks, and spread her arms. Outstretched. Crucified.

CHAPTER 5

Gatsby trudged up the stairwell of the Tube and headed down the sidewalk. Within a minute, she was at the front door of the CIS building. The Spartan box of concrete and glass was surrounded by mathematically precise rows of rose bushes. She mounted the steps to the entrance and stepped inside a cool foyer of marble. Water flowed down a granite, ceiling-high fountain without making a sound.

As she approached the reception desk, she murmured, "I'm here to see Agent Singer."

The sturdy woman behind the counter eyed her as if examining larvae under a microscope. "Photo ID."

She took Gatsby's ID, studied it, and handed it back while pushing a clipboard forward. "Full name, address, phone number," she muttered, barely parting her lips.

When Gatsby nudged the clipboard back across the counter, the woman bobbed her chin toward the waiting area at the far side of the lobby.

Gatsby slid into a deep, leather armchair. Glancing around, acutely aware of her blood pounding in her temples, she heard Singer's voice: *Imagine that level of exsanguination. Absolutely unbelievable.*

Are cameras recording my every move?

Singer appeared at a glass door and stepped briskly toward her, his demeanor as official as at their last meeting. After murmuring "thank you for coming," he asked her to follow him.

They passed through corridors—sterile, concrete halls, passing glass atriums that overlooked courtyards and blocky modern sculptures. Where each hall intersected another, they stopped so that Singer could slide his badge through a wall device to unlock the gating system. A man in a black uniform passed them with a wordless nod.

He stopped before a frosted glass door and pulled it open. "Here we are."

They entered a cool, wide room where she saw metal tables interspersed with filing cabinets. Hulking steel shelves crowded the walls, and to their left, a keypad flanked a steel-plated window. Singer approached the window and pressed his thumb to a panel, which glowed red and then green. He keyed in a series of numbers and waited, offering Gatsby a *Procedure, you know* look.

A buzz started up behind the wall. The panel inched upward to reveal a recessed niche about the size of a microwave oven.

Very Star Trek, she thought, shifting her weight from one foot to the other, half expecting a tribble to emerge from the opening.

A rectangular item lay on the surface.

The book was wrapped with a leather jacket and secured on the right side by a thick strap.

Singer reached for it, then motioned for Gatsby to follow as he walked toward a table at the middle of the room and reached under the table for a switch. A spotlight popped on overhead.

After setting the book on the gleaming surface, he pulled a pair of latex gloves from his pocket and held them out toward her. "Here. I'm going to go check on the requisition to allow you to remove evidence from the premises. I'll be back in fifteen minutes."

She nodded while tugging on the gloves.

He exited at the door through which they had entered, leaving her in a vacuum of isolation and the sound of her heart thudding in her ribcage. She wondered what watched her in such a high-security space. Would ear-blasting alarms go off if she touched the wrong counter or stood too close to a window?

She forced herself to focus on the book, grit her teeth, and whispered, "Let's have a look at this."

The binding strap, held secure by a brass snap slightly smaller than a penny, fell open as she tugged on it. Grasping the inner cover and the leather jacket at the same time, she eased the book open to the first page. She realized she'd been holding her breath when a metallic click behind her made her gasp and whirl around.

Nothing but tables, drawers, tile.

Geez—just RELAX. She sucked in another deep breath.

As her eyes danced across the lines of symbols, she felt herself easing down into focused concentration as if sliding into a warm sea.

The calligrapher was highly skilled. She saw Latin, some version of Arabic, Greek, angular symbols that might have been an early Aramaic, bits of Square Hebrew, and a clutter of other unrecognizable glyphs. A few marks, jagged and looped, would clarify pronunciation if they were diacritics. There was no obvious punctuation, and she could guess at morphemes but not the syntax.

Like a grab-bag of phrases tossed into a bag and rearranged at random.

It wasn't haiku, or a poetic form, or simple prose, but she sensed deliberate organization. Without following the standard rules of a written language, the lines seemed to *evoke* meaning. Vague, shadowed suggestions, like the patter of a wizened magician, buried within the semblance of coherence.

"But what's the system?" she whispered. "You can't throw morphemes about like confetti and expect them to produce something syntactic..."

Another click made her look up with a jerk. Singer stood at the doorway. He moved toward her, grasping an aluminum case about the dimensions of a notebook computer. She saw two intricate sets of locks beside the handle, one with a keypad. Its shiny aluminum was complemented by black ethylene vinyl acetate. She recognized the EVA; the British Museum often used it to transport fragile artifacts.

He seemed to scan her face and then glanced toward the book, eyebrows raised. "Slithy toves that gyre and gimble?"

She shook her head. "I don't know. So far, not a clue."

He swung the case upward and laid it at the end of the table. "This is a Baber case. You can use it to transport and return the book."

She noticed something on the edge of the case: a plate, bolted to the frame and engraved with three alphanumeric sets.

REBOZO / 502816 / GAHANA
"What's this?"
"EUID. Evidence unit identification code."

He pulled two rolling chairs from a nearby quad of tables and pushed one toward her, waving for her to sit. Staring over at the book, he asked, "You must have some initial impressions? Wild hunches?"

Gatsby dropped into the chair. "Well, the Greek, Hebrew, and Arabic are clear, but they're mixed with Egyptian hieroglyphics, perhaps Latin, and other orthographies that I'm not completely sure of but could probably identify with some digging." She sighed. "But understanding the individual symbols is only the surface level of translation. The semantics, the punctuation, the relationship between phonemes and morphemes," seeing his forehead squeeze into a frown, she explained, "the spoken sounds and the smallest meaningful elements of words? These deeper structures can be extremely complex. Every language has its own sets of rules and exceptions to those rules."

He nodded slowly, still frowning. "Go on."

"Languages have dialects, genders, inflections, and variations that change depending on context and audience, and, as they say, that's just the tip of the iceberg. There may be thousands of other variables. I hope that I can be of some service, Agent Singer, but this book presents a fantastically complex challenge." She looked up, shaking her head. "I don't think I'm telling you anything that you don't already know, right?"

Singer was scowling, but his frustration seemed to be directed at the book, not at her. "Even so, you're the only expert we've got, so do whatever you can. Anything that you can derive from it will be helpful." He rose and reached for the book. "Now watch carefully while I pack it."

She stepped closer while Singer directed her to the keypad beside the first lock. As he entered the ten-number sequence, she quickly devised a mnemonic to remember it. Both locks popped open. Gatsby moved closer and saw that the bottom side of the case was fitted with a foam mold that perfectly matched the contours of the book. A mirror-image mold was recessed into the lid so that when the case was closed, it immobilized the item within.

Very well protected. Packing that tight guards against breakage, heat, and moisture.

After demonstrating how to tuck the book inside the molding and lock the case, he walked her through the procedures for returning the case to the Evidence Unit.

"Pretty straightforward," she said. "I'll take it to the Museum first. I can access all my key databases and reference material there."

"That's fine." Singer turned toward her with a deep frown. "I want to emphasize this again, Dr. Donovan. This book goes with you under strict security. Do not show it to anyone or talk about it with anyone, even close friends or family members. And do not reproduce it—no photocopies, photographs, or scans of any type. Some of the most ingenious acts of terrorism involve hacking secure documents, and even the most diligently protected files or items can be stolen." He paused. "We don't know who wrote this book, what they want, or what they might do besides write these bizarre messages. One person has already died because of it. So do you accept these conditions?"

"Yes, of course." She shrugged. "Who would I show it to anyway?" *Aside from the staff at the Museum, I don't know anyone it would be of any interest to.* A gauzy image of her best friend, Celia Devereaux, slid into her mind. *Celia? Unless it's an updated version of the Kama Sutra, she couldn't be bothered.*

Singer muttered, "Make no assumptions about anyone, Dr. Donovan."

She nodded.

"Let's go. I'll walk you to the lobby."

Grasping the case and lifting it from the table, she flashed to the PERSONAL file on her computer at home: *Did these scribes know that they held in their hands the truest instrument of warfare, the stylus? While asserting that their scriptures were the words of God, were they covertly devising words that incited individuals, or nations, to bloodshed?*

She walked toward the door, feeling Singer's eyes on her back, the case pressed against her thigh. As they made their way down the hallways toward the entrance, she noticed a subtle, aching feeling in her leg muscles. A pins-and-needles sensation sparkled through the hand grasping the case.

She slowed to a stop, shifted the case to the other hand, and flexed her hand a few times. Just as the tingling receded, the world split into two: two hands, ten fingers, slowly curling and uncurling.

She closed her eyes, rubbed them hard, and opened them again. One hand. Muted grey walls. One android-like agent striding toward and then past them.

Frowning, she continued down the hall.

They stopped at the front desk.

"Call me when you've had a chance to review it."

"I will."

As she stepped through the main doors and out toward the Tube, Singer's voice rumbled in her mind. *Make no assumptions about anyone, Dr. Donovan.*

CHAPTER 6

From the grand portico that framed the entrance of the British Museum, Gatsby raced up the marble stairs to her office on the second floor and shut the door. No one would sneak up on her. The only window in the twelve-foot-square room looked out on a courtyard filled with Japanese ferns and water lilies.

As she caught her breath, she settled at her desk with the Baber case.

REBOZO / 502816 / GAHANA

She grabbed a pencil from the Space Needle mug sitting toward one side of the desk and used the eraser to enter the ten-digit code. The locks popped, and there the book sat, nestled within the protective foam molding. With slow movements, she extracted it and set it on the desktop.

A Technicolor image skittered through her head: the Good Witch of the North, squeaking, "Are you a good book or a bad book?"

Ugh...too weird.

Staring intently at the first page, she began to feel the buzz that always marked the start of decipherment. It was like caffeine rocketing into her blood: her pulse jumped, and a tingling sort of tightness grabbed at her brain. She had often wondered if other people got the same kind of buzz from drugs, from sex, from a spine-tingling movie or novel, or from something as simple as a look in their lover's eye. For her, the rush was in the sly undressing, with all the figurative nakedness, of the secrets hidden in languages.

What could be hidden here? And why all the secrecy? What is it that Singer's not telling me about this book?

She scanned across the Latin, Greek, and Arabic and paused over the symbols that resembled Aramaic and Square Hebrew. The Egyptian hieroglyphs were unmistakable. Except for the last, all were language systems in use from about 1700 BCE to the fifth century of the Common Era.

Within that timeframe, the sons of Moses were codifying the laws of Yahweh and scribbling the Dead Sea Scrolls. The apostles were sending letters to the fledgling Christian church, and Muhammad received Allah's messages via the Archangel Gabriel. She rolled her neck and heard it pop. *Let's get this show on the road.*

As she logged on to her computer and Dynasty, the Museum's intranet, she heard two loud raps on the door.

Clevis? Some tedious meeting?

The door handle twisted back and forth. "Gatsby?"

She recognized Gruedin's voice and called out, "Yes, Clive, what is it?"

"Hey! Do you have a moment?"

Shit...

She tucked the book into the molding. Her eyes darted: the bookcase at the other side of the room? There were about fifteen centimeters of space between the bottom shelf and the carpet, just enough to accommodate the height of the case.

"Be right there."

Kneeling, she slid the Baber into the space, rose, and stepped toward the door.

Looking relaxed in his cable-knit sweater and khakis, Clive grinned as the door yawned open. "There you are! We wondered if you'd been abducted by a UFO." He skipped toward her as if he'd tracked down a long-lost relative. "What, are they paying you by the hour now? Y'just pop by to translate a stele or two and then skip off to the Azores with the cash?"

She couldn't help but smile. "You are a wizard of intuition, Clive."

He dropped into the chair at the opposite side of the room. "So much bustle around here lately. We had a goodbye luncheon for Sarah the other day, did you know? She's buying nappies and suing for palimony in the same breath. The woman is unbelievable! Not to spread gossip round, but you know how these things go."

"Uh huh." *I know that right now I need you gone...*

Clive swiveled exuberantly in the chair, flashing the sideways smile that made him look like a stand-up comic who was losing the audience. "We haven't seen you for over a week. Taking some holiday?"

She reeled in an impulse to look toward the bookcase. "No, ahm, I'm working up a white paper for the Epigraphy Society. The conference is in two weeks." She pulled in a breath and glanced toward the door. "Listen, Clive, I'd love to..."

"The life of the for-hire must be nice," he broke in, leaning back in the chair and gazing at the fountain burbling in the courtyard. "Pop in when you're needed, show up for our soporific meetings, work up a report, and head off again, eh? How did you wing this with Clev..."

She held her palms out in a "stop" gesture. "Can't chat, Clive. I'm in the middle of something important."

His eyes widened. "Oh! Geez, sorry, didn't mean to burst in on you like this. Well, will you be at the awards banquet?"

"No problem and, yes, I'll be there."

He rose and moved toward the door. "Capital. Catch you later."

Images of the symbols in the book rose, scotopic, into her mind's eye. Before she could stop herself, she blurted, "Clive? Ahm, just a second."

He turned. "Yes?"

"Have you ever come across a piece that combines orthographies? Say Greek mixed with Hebrew? Or Aramaic with cuneiform?"

He leaned back against the doorjamb as his forehead furrowed. "Combined? Like that buggered Sargon, eh? Let me think." He stroked the dimple in his chin. "Nothing as disparate as clear alphabetic mixed with something pictographic. Within Semitic scripts, there are variations, of course. Earliest Canaanite became Square Hebrew..."

This isn't Orthography for Dummies, Clive, just answer the damn question.

"...which led to the Ashkenazi, Sephardic, and Yiddish forms. Arabic? God, almost two dozen unique scripts there. And Aramaic emerged from the Sargon script, Phoenician." He stared down at the floor. "I've seen plenty of samples that contain different orthographic styles of the same language but none that mix systems." He shrugged. "Then of course there's that pesky Rosetta Stone, hieroglyphic and demotic with a Greek chaser."

I know that!

"Is that the sort of thing you're talking about?"

"No, it isn't!!"

His eyes darkened and leaped from her face to the hallway.

She backpedaled against the belt of anger that had gripped her out of nowhere. "Sorry. I'm sleep deprived and grouchy. It's...I, uh," she stammered, "it's this paper. I want to include data on a Mesopotamian tablet that I came across—this was years ago—that seemed to mix established cuneiform with something else, something unidentified." She felt her cheeks flushing. *Never was a good liar.* "It might have been an early alphabetic script. Or, hell, it might have been a resurrection of the brain cells that I thought I killed in college."

He grinned, but the smile didn't reach his eyes. "No way. Once they're gone—" His hand rose and zigzagged like something migrating toward another continent. "But if you ever come across that tablet again, let me know, right?"

She nodded, intensely aware of her heart beating and the book—under CIS investigation for its link to a grisly death, perhaps a murder—stashed a meter away under her bookcase. "Yep, you bet."

His eyes scanning her, Gruedin gave her a thumbs-up and stepped into the hall.

She walked to the door to close it. *Why would I jump on Clive? Sleep deprived and grouchy? Neither is true. And he would be wealth of information if I could talk to him about the book, but Singer is so adamant about confidentiality.*

In a minute, with the door locked and the book again open on her desktop, she considered the scope of the tasks ahead.

A partial translation won't be possible, or useful, without an understanding of the work in its entirety. Like The Sargon. Just knowing disparate pieces won't lead to the final translation. Even a decipherment in an established language can take weeks or months. There's the peer review and verification. If I can be of any help to the CIS, I'll have to deliver whatever I can without outside assistance.

She cradled her head in her hands and closed her eyes as war broke out inside her.

Unless I ignore Singer's order.

CHAPTER 7

Her eyes crept across the spidery curves of the symbols.

RED-MK7 was reading this when he died—looking at the symbols and creating abstractions. A sound is associated with the symbols and a constellation of meaningful images. We subvocalize the sounds attached to the abstraction. Little of the physiology is required, only the eyes and brain, sometimes the organs of speech for those who move their lips or whisper while they read.

Realizing that she was moving her lips, she set her teeth and pressed her fingertips to her temples.

And though the act of reading does not affect major physiological systems, it can't be denied that the emotions triggered by the content can cause observable effects. You read a horror story or watch The Shining *and feel a heart-pounding adrenaline rush, as if you had just witnessed a murder. You can read about a tragedy and feel tears in your eyes or a lump in your throat.*

She tapped the eraser end of a pencil against the desktop. *This assumes native-language comprehension. If something is written in a language that you don't know, neither comprehension nor emotional response will be possible.*

She heard the metered pad of footsteps in the hallway and glanced at the clock on her monitor. Museum staff members were leaving for the day, pulling on their overcoats for the drizzly commutes back to their boroughs, their shepherd's pies and Hammerhead Bitter.

She tucked the book into the Baber case and thumbed the locks closed. After turning off the overheads and locking the door behind her, she hurried through the hallways to the staff exit and stepped onto Great Russell Street.

As she wove through the wet streets and descended into the bustle of the Tube, the dull throb of a headache ground through her shoulders and into her skull. Once seated on the train and watching the station signs whiz by, the rhythmic bumping that usually lulled her only made the throbbing worse. King's Road was six minutes away.

Her stop rolled into view. She grabbed the case and made her way through the hissing car doors onto the platform.

After a five-minute walk, she was in Chelsea and then inside her flat, checking for email messages and pouring a glass of cold ginger ale.

She threw herself on the living room couch, considered watching the evening news, and then slumped back, closing her eyes with a sigh.

Another fluorohead.

The fluorescent lighting at the Museum—combined with sitting for too many hours hunkered over a manuscript or tablet or staring into a computer monitor—sometimes brought on a mother of a headache.

Guess this is one of those days.

Each throb in her brain seemed to push her deeper into the cushions of the couch and toward the fiery core of the earth. Drawing a long breath, she noticed a subtle twitchiness in her leg muscles and rolling sensations in her stomach. She took another swig of the ginger ale, which relieved the nausea, but the headache ratcheted with each heartbeat.

With her eyes closed, the words whispered through her mind: *Their capacity to arouse ecstasy as well as ignite global crusades of bloodshed...*

It all came tumbling back into her mind: the brick campus plaza, Volante's golden hair and deadly eyes, the practice rooms where she had played the piano between late-night study sessions, Woody's infectious smile.

The Harstedt Interfaith Center.

...and God's pure love will wash away all fear, all confusion...

"No!"

She jumped, astounded that she had actually shouted the word.

There was only one thing to do.

She sat her glass on the coffee table, dragged herself up off the couch, and went to her office to call one of London's most prominent and reputedly horniest hypnotherapists, Celia Devereaux.

CHAPTER 8

Volante leaned hard on the double doors and kicked four metal doorstops into place. She looked around to take in the enormity of the room.

My zashas have done their homework well.

The brick warehouse was in the Waterford district, a greasy clump of warehouses and manufacturing plants. There would be no foot traffic, no curious seekers wandering by, especially this late at night. It was secluded and yet gave the illusion of safety. It was perfect for the evening's Damaii—the gathering of the Dama.

As she paced the parquet flooring, arranged in geometric shapes, she remembered the thrill that had raced through her, years ago, when the Abba had explained Omega's hierarchy to her. In her apartment, squirming on kitchen chairs as the world outside was drowned with rain, she had presented through her many questions, and he had answered them one by one.

Where do we start, Abba?

At Dosa, the level of the novice. The Dosa receive ten weeks of instruction in the devotional language. You learn to speak and think in the tongue of highest truth. With further training in the foundations of the faith, and your vow before witnesses to uphold the precepts of Omega, you ascend to the level of Shoto. Your Ordering begins. The stripping away of illusion, the extinction of attachment to a meaningless world, the pash-lo. You must relinquish the trappings of the old life that is empty and false.

How can we prove our devotion, Abba?

She glanced toward a cluster of stacked, plastic chairs at the other side of the room and thought, *We prove our devotion by providing what is needed.* She shifted her gaze upward to study the cables and lights.

Finally at the opposite wall, Volante turned to look back at the light spilling in through the open doors and around the two-thousand-square-foot auditorium.

Tell me of the Dama.

The image of the Abba filtered into her mind. How wise and strong he had seemed! Beautiful, powerful, truthful, and ambitious: a forceful combination that spoke to her most undeniable and most secreted desires.

When the Shoto is ready to completely surrender existence to the First Creator of all existence, you apply for admittance to the Dama. Only the Dama may attend the Damaii. A battery of tests is given. These reflect the final relinquishment of your prior identity as ralea—an impure nonbeliever, living a life of self-conceit—by bringing your immediate family members to Omega or leaving them behind, no matter how difficult. If your commitments of time, assets, and devotion are not made without reservation, you are not worthy of Omega.

She felt in the pocket of her robe for her notes and reminded herself of the saying that she had used during many of her sermons. The words were passed between the Dama members and whispered into the ears of curious ralea: "Omega does not accept the ambivalent."

These disciples give everything. Body, mind, possessions. Talents. Money. Social connections. Status. Livelihood. Everything.

As she paced the perimeter of the room a second time, Volante thought of another saying that had recently floated through the discipleship: "If you want a Club Med religion, join the Presbyterians. This is spiritual boot camp."

Darwin kneels at the feet of Omega. She smiled. *Only the fittest survive this brand of salvation.*

As she strode back toward the lighting panel and thumbed the sets of black switches, the room flooded with a spooky, half-lit fluorescence. When her assistants, the zasha, arrived, they would set the folding chairs in concentric rows that formed a huge U-shape. At the open end of the U, they would arrange four chairs, two on each side, so that they led away from the outermost row. The most recent inductees sat in the rows farthest from the center, and the more senior Dama filled the other rows. As Habareh, Volante commanded the center.

The address on Salvation in Servitude will stir their hearts, deepen their devotion. Empty their pockets.

"Habareh?"

The voice was that of a young man: Guy Corwin, her primary zasha. As he stepped through the doorway, Volante greeted him.

In the next few minutes, her four other zashas arrived. They began moving banks of the molded plastic chairs into position on the polished floor.

The room filled and warmed with bodies. The newly inducted Dama, attending their first Damaii. Elders who had completed their induction rituals long ago. They wore suits and Levis, miniskirts and tennis shoes, tweed, tie-dye. She heard the scuffling of soles against the floor, whispered conversations, coughs.

As the zashas finished arranging the chairs, people began to sit and stow purses or other carry-alls beneath them. The room was becoming a worming organism of bodies, wiggling into prescribed shapes, all faces intense with emotion.

Soon, almost all hundred and fifty seats were filled.

Volante breezed toward the center of the arrangement of chairs, feeling her linen robe swirling against her ankles. The Prayer of Devotion rose in her mind and then moved her lips as she whispered it: "Abba, the Blessed Guide to Omega. Guide us on the path of eternal truth. We consecrate ourselves in service to Omega."

Relaxation trickled through her psyche but did not pool. For a half-second, she considered the claims of Omega, the golden path toward the realization of ultimate truth. Had it brought that truth to her? Or the surety or acceptance that she'd longed for but never known during a toxic youth? The passages to adulthood that had left their angry scars?

She shook herself, stowing the questions for a less-critical moment.

As she took her place at the center of the innermost row, conversations trailed off. Everyone rose. They stood silently, and all eyes turned to her.

"Damaii, vash an parate oh me-gah falaji atab raaloh!" *Damaii, belief in Omega is service and study.* She called out the ritual greeting, her voice sweeping powerfully over the crowd.

"Mem vahla padarah oh meh-ga!" *We consecrate ourselves in service to Omega.* Their antiphonal response reverberated against the walls of the auditorium.

"Di-wah nassa bay ah pash-lo salesh meed neh-vee von." *We reject the lie of illusion to pursue the Kingdom of Eternal Truth.*

On cue, they responded, "Travi ash ahta rom chahava ri-ana ehfaj!" *This is our holy mission, from this moment until death!*

"Let us pray."

Slacks and skirts rustled as they sank back into their seats and closed their eyes.

With slow, deliberate pacing, she recited the Prayer of Devotion. "Abbah way non vash ah parateh, sho day too vashla meed neh-vee von besh garah, mem vahla padarah oh meh-ga. Nah-maen."

"Nah-maen," they intoned in unison, their voices synthesized into a deep rumble, the sigh of a many-headed beast slouching toward the chasm.

Volante launched into the sermon. She was so familiar with the cadence and intonations that they arose without conscious attention. Her tone rose and fell, and her body swayed in rhythmic patterns that mirrored their collective breathing. She slid to the left to deliver bombastic commands and then to the right to reiterate the scripted, well-known precepts. She saw the cues in their eyes, shoulders, feet, lips, facial muscles, and skin tone, and knew exactly when to pause. Breathe. Stare. Frown. Shout. Gesture. Each syllable and micromovement was targeted for a specific, subconscious response.

The messages were intended to stir their emotions, yet she knew that each listener had been trained to give attention without speaking or moving. In their silence, their bodies and faces shouted how completely they moved in sync with her.

Coming to her final lines, she slowed her pace, deepened her timbre. *Guiding the crafts in for a smooth landing.*

Finally: "Vasira atab raaloh hash verey oh me-gah." *All that can be known comes from Omega.*

She noted how their shoulders, hands, and eyes softened and relaxed.

Now to secure their servitude.

She had weighed the options for delivering the announcement about the Librah Vae-ta. The Abba's instructions were, *Say that the book is missing and the offender has not been found. It may flush out accomplices. Say that the most holy writ is the path to Omega.*

"Now, Disciples, our deeds of devotion that keep us on the path of Omega are needed more than ever. We must stay committed to the truth, rejecting the sin of self-service." She paused for a few moments. "The very sin that one among us has committed."

Their bodies stiffened. Their faces grew tense, eyes wide and darting. Rustling as arms folded. Feet scuffed along the floor. Some cleared their throats.

Reveal the information with the cha-val. With her permission invoked, they would be free to express their emotions without the restraint that was normally required. She knew that the release of tension would work in the favor of the greater discipleship.

"I am given cha-val by the Abba to tell you this, so that we may all know of the sin that one of our own has committed. Committed by one who has abandoned Omega and is now missing. Perhaps by others who helped him. Someone has stolen the Librah Vae-ta."

The audience sat in silence as the words sank in. Then a man shouted, "No!" A woman called out, "The Librah Vae-ta!"

Like a mass orgasm, the audience exploded. Their indignation erupted, sending people to their feet, hands thrown upward, fists curled. The faces of the inner circle of Dama flushed deep red with blood, and their lips curled as they shouted angrily. The newer members tentatively popped from their chairs, their yearning to join in perhaps mixed with uncertainty as to the correct behavior.

At the center of the congregation that was now a mob, Volante raised her arms, and the fabric of her sleeves swung like ship flags in a strong wind. She sharpened her voice with volume and authority. "Keen! Raya keen!" *Listen! Stop and listen!*

Their bodies still pumping and faces flushed, they quieted.

She gazed over them. "I know this is alarming, and you will have many questions, so I invite them in dar-chaliid."

The fresher members would have only fleeting knowledge of the term, but the elder Dama would know it. Q and A. They were free to pose their questions. She would call on a disciple, hear an inquiry, respond, and move to the next one.

A handful of people sank back into their seats like human dominos. The rest of the audience followed with fluttering gestures and whispers.

An older black man raised his hand. "What can we do to help recover it?"

"You can search for clues. If you do not find them in the material world, find them within your own soul." *Always presume guilt within the discipleship itself. A well-proven tactic.*

Another asked, "Do we continue in our devotions?"

Then: "Why did this happen? Is Omega displeased? Or testing our faith?"

She heard a squeal and turned to see one of the main doors opening. Illuminated in a thin shaft of light, a willowy woman crept into the room.

Volante stifled a gasp as alarm flared through her. *What is* she *doing here?*

The Abba's personal zasha was so seldom seen by the discipleship that it was rumored she simply didn't exist. Anne Jillette may as well have been a mythic figure invented for reasons that the Abba did not disclose.

"Anne." Volante managed to anchor her voice with confidence. "Hello. Come join us."

Anne moved toward the rows of plastic chairs. She was auburn-haired and slight with a puckish turn to her lips. The flowing, violet cotton jacket and black leggings accentuated her elfin appearance. Ignoring the throng around her, she seemed to float without touching the ground as she approached the Habareh.

Volante's eyes narrowed. "What is it, Anne?"

Anne reached into the pocket of her jacket and pulled out an envelope. As she held it forward, she whispered, "Our Abba, push tah non ah meh-gah, wishes you to present this to the Dama."

Volante snatched the envelope, feeling even more baffled. A delivery such as this had never happened. Why was it made during the Damaii? And why Anne as the courier? Was it a set of instructions? New information about Reymann or the Librah Vae-ta?

He's strategizing, but to what end?

With one quick motion, she pulled a slip of paper from the envelope, read, and drew a relieved sigh. *Ahhh, the honorum! The pounds and pence of the faithful.* Frowning, she thought, *A zero added to the amount? How will they afford it?*

She smiled toward Anne, who held the impish look on her. "Thank you, Anne."

Volante turned toward the sea of anxious faces and said, "It seems that we have one last piece of business, and then you are dismissed for the evening. I invite you all to come forward to accept your honorum mati. Guy, will you start us off?"

We tell them how much to donate, and they gladly cough it up. How can they prove their devotion? By providing what is needed.

She glanced toward Guy, who sat one row behind the Dama. As he stood and made his way through the maze of chairs toward Volante, the rest of the audience stood to create a single-file line that snaked behind him.

Guy stopped before Volante and turned his head to one side, tipping an ear toward her face. She felt his bursts of hot, rapid breathing as she whispered.

He stepped back, his eyes wide, and ran his tongue over his lower lip. "Padarah oh meh-ga." *Service to Omega.*

CHAPTER 9

Gatsby leaned against the door and stepped inside the cool hush of The Alexis. A doe-eyed woman, wearing a tunic covered with undulating sequins, greeted her. Gatsby said that she was meeting a woman named Devereaux who was probably already seated. The woman beckoned with a "come with me" gesture and herded Gatsby toward a booth at the back of the dining room.

Sensuous as a courtesan, Celia Devereaux sat coiled on the deep leather seat. The pageboy cut to her black hair needed no styling. Long lashes and perfect eyebrows accentuated her mocha-brown eyes. From her cheekbones to her ankles—one encircled by a tattoo of Grecian filigree— everything about her bespoke vivacious beauty. The twinkle in her eyes was only one of the indications of the woman's libido, which had launched into high gear in her thirties and showed no sign of slowing. She exuded all the sass that she had brought to her introduction to Gatsby, eight years ago, and still carried that palpable sexiness.

The smells of pita bread and Celia's rose-water perfume enveloped Gatsby as she approached the table. "Come here often?"

Celia's aquiline nose flared and her painted lips parted as she glanced toward her lap. "Hm, yes, but I pack towelettes." She chuckled. "Sit, babe, drink. Thrall me with your acumen."

"God." Gatsby eased herself into the dark wood paneled booth, a smile spreading over her face. "A city teeming with freezer-burn Badcrumbles, and my best friend is a nympho-maniac who quotes Hannibal Lecter."

"Oh and what would you know about nympho-anything?" Celia shot back, stirring her Tanqueray and tonic with her middle finger so vigorously that it splashed the tablecloth. "I keep hoping, hoping for the day that I open up *The Times* and read the story of the American translator hospitalized after a six-day orgy. I keep my fingers crossed but, sweets, it has not happened." She leaned back, the front of her jumpsuit unzipped just enough to hint at ripe cleavage.

Gatsby tugged a slice of bread from the basket on the table. "Nor is it likely. Not—"

Singer's voice marched through her head: *This book goes with you under strict security. Do not show it to anyone or talk about it with anyone, even close friends or family members.*

"Until I find the guy who can keep up with me."

Celia snorted, drained her glass, and waved a polished fingernail toward the waiter.

They chatted. Celia's private practice was booming; there were more people than ever wanting to overcome their emotional, physical, sexual, or spiritual obstacles through hypnotherapy. She had taken on her first assistant. Her latest romance had self-destructed when the young man had fallen so deeply in love with the exotic Ms. Devereaux that he proposed eight times. After explaining eight times that she had no plans of becoming Mrs. Anybody, now or ever, he had hounded her for three weeks with tragic email and phone messages, some of them quasi-suicidal, and disappeared.

"Pure love addict," she muttered.

Gatsby dipped her knife into the garlic hummus and then spread a dollop onto a pita wedge. "What makes you say that?"

Celia took a sip of her T&T. "Psychologists throw around a saying: A belief is something that you have, an addiction is something that has you. People can turn anything into a drug. Their job, their bodies, a relationship, money, religion. They can apotheosize just about anything into must-have-at-any-cost status." She held her chin in the cup of her hand. "It's unfortunate, but at least some want to change that state and, ergo, I have a well-paying career."

"But if you bring them back session after session, aren't you just supporting their addiction? Enabling rather than curing?"

Celia raised her perfect eyebrows. "You don't cure addictions, darling. That's the first misconception to toss out when doing hypnotherapy or any kind of changework. There isn't anything to cure, because every behavior is useful in some context. It's only when that behavior is invaluable or dangerous in a particular context that something has to change. And cure presupposes that you excise something, like removing a tumor with a knife. What I do is nothing like that."

Given the chance, what would I excise? Gatsby wondered while polishing the knife with her napkin. "Then what *do* you do?"

Celia bit into pita bread. "You never try to eliminate a system, you transfer it. You help the person find a different belief or behavior, one that is beneficial for them. Useful. Then you help them to transfer their old addiction to an unhealthy behavior to a new addiction, that is, the healthy behavior. I help them discover what their destructive patterns are and how to replace them with something more useful. Something better to believe in."

Finishing off her White Russian, Gatsby swallowed, then asked, "You were raised Catholic, weren't you?"

Celia nodded. "Heartily sorry and detested my sins." A frown spread over her face. "And lived to tell the tale. Why do you ask?"

Gatsby stared down at the grape leaf dolmades on her plate. "It's been on my mind. Belief. Religious belief, specifically. Not the redemption-from-sin questions, and not a specific practice, like one of the major world religions, but the idea of belief itself. What is its place in the human condition?" She stirred a fingertip through a pool of olive oil on her plate. "It's beyond Maslow's hierarchy of needs, at a level beyond survival, social community, even beyond actualization. People want bloody enlightenment. Transcendence. They want to feel that there is something above and beyond corporeal existence, some plane of pure being or happiness or knowledge that's unavailable in this world. Why? What's the point?"

Celia studied Gatsby, then wadded her napkin and tossed it onto the table. "You invite me to lunch but want to talk metaphysics? Just when I thought we would discuss something really important, like vaginal versus clitoral. I need another drink."

Gatsby propped her elbows on the table, smiling. "I know, I know. But it's been nagging at me lately, perhaps because my work is language, and language is so intimately connected with personal belief."

A waiter with a dour face arrived to set before them a fresh basket of warm bread and another round of drinks.

Gatsby raised her glass and turned toward Celia. "So what do you believe?"

Celia shrugged. "About what?"

"The big questions. You know, eternal life, sin and salvation. God."

Celia sighed while digging in her handbag. "Listen, darling, I stopped fretting about it all a loooong time ago. Look at the diversity of the world we live in. There are thousands of religious paths, a million different names for God."

Without warning, the night of the big split and the image of Woody's face—angry, guilty, desperate—slipped through her memory. *Did he ever know all million names?* She swallowed, and the alcohol burned inside her throat.

Celia sipped, then continued. "Every culture, practically every generation comes to its own definition of the meaning of life and will spout its own bollocks about why it is AB-solutely crucial to think a certain way or live your life so that when you snuff it—ding ding ding! You win the prize, the big stuffed animal in the sky!"

They both chuckled.

"Going through my clinical training, I came to the conclusion that people will believe whatever they want to believe, whether or not there's an iota of sense in it. They create the reality that suits them." She sucked an ice cube into her mouth and crunched.

"The reality that suits them," Gatsby murmured.

"And for them, whatever that reality is, for godssake don't question it! Here's another universal truth, sweets. A person's beliefs are his personal assembly required spinal cord. They're what keep him standing, or searching. Try to remove one vertebra of that belief system, even the smallest piece, and he'll scream bloody murder." She tipped her glass back for the last swallow. "Or worse."

Considering, Gatsby chewed on bread.

Celia's face brightened as she leaned forward. "Now, puh-leeze, while you work so hard to resolve these burning questions about eternal life, what have you been doing here on planet earth? The usual—spending your weekends holed up in dusty museums rather than tasting even a few of life's pleasures?"

"Afraid so." She longed to tell Celia about RED-MK7, the book, and the mysterious language that evoked religious ponderings. Her nature tugged her toward disclosure, especially with her best friend, but the details would have to wait, at least until she knew more about what she was dealing with. The potential dangers.

"No bloke?" Celia prodded.

Gatsby gave her a weak smile. "I work a lot."

"For fuck's sake." Celia rolled her eyes. "I've known you for eight years, and in all that time, not one notable sexual escapade! Dry bloody sheets!"

"That's not true! I've had..." Gatsby crossed her arms, then sighed. "Okay, it is true." Her voice took a petulant tone. "I have Definite Article. On a regular basis."

Celia flung her napkin onto the table. "The online paramour that you've been emailing for a decade but never met? The wannabe writer with two kids and a tricky sciatic? Your pen pal who signs his letters *semantically yours*?"

Smiling, Gatsby shrugged.

Celia's head flopped back against the seat. "You invest *years* in a person, and what do you get in return? Celibacy! You are incorruptible. I give up."

Gatsby chuckled. "Don't give up. Someday I'll surprise you. You just wait."

"I don't have that long!" Shaking her head, Celia muttered, "Jesus. Well, miss noli me tangere, what are you working on now?"

"I'm writing a white paper for the U.K. Epigraphy Society conference."

Celia caught the waiter's eye and nodded at him. "Uh huh. Delightful. I popped in at the Association of Counselling and Psychotherapy conference earlier this week. What a madhouse. Anyone who puts that many psychologists and psychophysiologists in one place at the same time risks some kind of spontaneous psychic combustion. I did get to meet up with some old friends, but my god the keynote speaker was astounding. One of the most astute men I've ever run across and too bloody handsome to be allowed to live."

Gatsby laughed. "I smell an estrogen strike."

"I wish." She chuckled. "He gave a brilliant lecture on psycholinguistics and transderivational search related to presupposition and behavior." She blinked as if struck by a thought. "You know, the theme of his talk was that language of belief that we were just talking about."

Curiosity clambered onto the back of an odd itch that she couldn't place, and Gatsby reigned in another impulse to mention the book. "Sounds like someone I should have lunch with." She grinned. "What's he look like?"

"Just your type, darling, oh and 3-D, not a cyber pal. Tall, dark hair, even has that goateed look that you used to find irresistible in your past life when you had a libido or at least made claims to one. He had amazing stage presence. Every female in the audience would have eaten crisps out of his hand. Someone in the great Pacific Northwest is spiking the lattes with testosterone."

Gatsby frowned. "How do you know where he's from?"

Celia rolled her eyes. "The CV in the lecture notes, of course. In fact, if memory serves, I think he attended the same university that you did. Where was it? Vancouver?"

Her stomach cramped. "Seattle. Blake University."

Celia relaxed against the leather backrest, smiling. "Yes, that's the one."

The feeling blasted through her, her heart pounding and throat tightening, as data snapped into place at a terrifying rate. She huddled over the table, gasping to catch her breath. "Celia, what was his name?"

Celia peered up at the ceiling and then frowned at the tabletop, seeming to struggle for the memory. "Something *son*. Anderson? Sanderson, that's it. Dr. Woodrow Sanderson. Do you know him?"

The world froze, then crashed like a melting glacier toppling into the Arctic Ocean. Gatsby gripped the edge of the table with white fingers. "Woodrow Sanderson? Are you positive?"

"Yes, I'm sh—darling, you look ill, what is it?"

Gatsby swept her hands to her forehead and knocked over her glass. Milk, Kahlua, and shards of ice flowed across the tablecloth.

"*Shit!!* Woody is in London?!"

Haversham Avenue enfolded them as they stepped out of the restaurant and walked toward Hyde Park.

Gatsby stared down at the sidewalk as shoppers wandered by them. "We met at Blake, during grad school. Began studying together and found ourselves in the middle of something explosive." She exhaled slowly. "It was like nothing I'd known before or have known since. We both knew instantly that it defied mundane description. Romance, desire, need—they paled in comparison to what gripped us. We bounced between working like fiends and acing every project and not working at all. Midnight runs to restock on condoms."

Celia gave her a wide smile. "That's my girl."

Gatsby swerved around a grey-haired woman leashed to a Borzoi. "And then it all went to hell."

As she spoke, she felt her throat tighten.

"Woody was as much in love with linguistics as I was. It was what brought us together: a passion for words and scripts and everything that is human communication. We had so much in common at first, but as we got to know each other, it became clear how very different we were. Were becoming." She paused. "I had burning big picture questions, as we all do at that age. I was just getting started on the path of identity, discovering who I was, what I wanted to do with my life. And what it all meant at the end of the day." She sighed wearily.

"Then what?" Celia asked.

"I could see that Woody's questions burned much brighter than mine. He sometimes wondered if it came from being brought up in a strictly secular family. He wasn't pushed into a specific belief, like some of us, he was pushed away. His philosophic questions turned into a quest. No...a crusade."

"And?"

"We moved in together. A postage-stamp of an apartment in the Fremont district. There was all the euphoria and bustle of setting up house, and we ran all around Seattle, spent entire weekends at Elliott Bay Bookstore."

Celia nodded. "Go on."

"It was glorious, but then something started gnawing at him. He shut himself off from me, he just...left, one bit at a time, focusing entirely on this search for the truth. For enlightenment or salvation, I guess. His hunt was for ultimate answers. Knowing the unknowable. I faded into his private purgatory." She sniffed. "I asked myself too many times to count which was worse, being dumped for another woman or for God."

A Mini Cooper zoomed by and disappeared into the darkness. They turned the corner onto Friars Street.

"That had to be hell," Celia said.

Gatsby stuffed her hands in her pockets. "Celia, I'd fallen so hard that it hurt. Literally. I'd always thought of the term lovesick as absurd until then, but it tore me apart. My heart was breaking while he slipped into a spiritual coma. He read books and bibles and religious credos, he missed classes, he was on the edge of dismissal from his program. His whole world revolved around it. Him. God."

Rage, in equal measure, against God and man...

She turned to Celia, remembering the anger and feeling her face burning. "The shit finally hit the fan. I came home one night to find him crashed in the living room, surrounded by a mountain of religious books, spinning an empty bottle of Jack Daniels. I couldn't get anything out of him but these slurry holy diatribes, and I lost it. I screamed at him. What's it going to be, Woody? The love of the great truth, your eternal pseudo-father figure? The big fucking cosmic clock-maker? Or me? Which is it?!" Her voice caught. "We managed to destroy a coffee table and some other thrift-store crap. I stormed into the bedroom and cried for hours. In the morning, he was gone."

They came to a pair of wrought-iron benches that flanked the sidewalk. Celia dropped onto a bench and waved for Gatsby to sit beside her.

"The next day, I got a voicemail—a fucking voicemail— Kama, I did what I had to do, though I know you won't see it that way. I have no choice."

Her face a well of empathy, Celia whispered, "That was it? Never heard from him again?"

She shook her head. "I've cursed the bastard, each April third, for the last fifteen years."

As Gatsby dropped her head into her hands, Celia wrapped an arm around her shoulder. "Sweetie, I'm so sorry."

Gatsby drew a shaking breath. *And he's in London right now! If...? Oh no no, forget it...but...*

Maybe this time, I have no choice.

She exhaled abruptly. "Celia, you've got to help me. I want to know everything about that conference. What he talked about, who he spoke to, where..."

"Whoa, whoa, whoa." Celia cut her off with a stern look. "Are you going to go on a rampage here? Camp outside the guy's hotel and do your own Nancy Drew espionage? Send your best friend on some scavenger hunt to track down intel on him?" Her look was defiant. "Track him down yourself."

Gatsby recoiled. "I can't! Will you—?"

"No way, babe."

"Celia! Christ, this may be my only opportunity to shut the door on the whole fucking mess. You're a therapist, for chrissake, I don't have to tell you about closure, how important it is t..." her voice caught, "to bury something painful once and for all."

"I won't be your private investigator!"

Her face crumpled. "Okay, then, then...just this? Get the name of the conference coordinator so that I can call him, or just leave him a message or not, but on my own terms. Can you do that? Please? Just that?"

Celia frowned at her for a long moment, then rolled her eyes. "All right, *fine,* I'll get a name for you. Good god. Never let it be said that I stood in the way of a romantic train wreck."

CHAPTER 10

The burly receptionist at the front desk had already called Agent Singer to inform him that Gatsby was waiting to see him. The longer that she had to wait, the more she squirmed. She felt like she had regressed to puberty and had been pulled out of a civics class to speak with the principal. Tapping her toes nervously outside some authority figure's office.

Just settle down. I haven't done anyth...

"Dr. Donovan?"

She looked up. Singer wore his standard black suit and white shirt, but the tie was highlighted with stripes that looked like glowing wires. He tipped his head toward the hallway.

They walked toward his office as they had before, entering each new section of the building through a passcard-access doorway. Turning down a narrow corridor, he ushered her into his office and closed the door.

She had presumed that the office of a CIS agent—especially a male one—would overflow with crates of forgotten memos and paperwork, boxes, the inexorable detritus of bureaucracy. What she saw was systematic organization without obsession. A few potted plants were staked upright with pencils and twist-ties, and a corner of the walnut desk held a caddy stuffed full of papers, but otherwise the space was surprisingly tidy. As she sat in the armchair facing the desk, she looked around to scan the framed photos on the walls. Singer, smiling, holding a CIS award and shaking the hand of a rotund man. In another photo, she saw a female silhouette against the backdrop of a glowing orange sunset—a wide, milk-white beach, palm trees in the foreground.

Singer stepped to the credenza behind his desk, where a coffeemaker gurgled out a fresh pot. "Want some coffee?"

"Sure."

As he poured and then set two ceramic mugs before her, he said, "What have you found?" He sat facing her, eyebrows raised.

She sipped the coffee, found it strong enough to set her teeth on edge, and sat the mug back on the desk. "Bits and pieces. The symbols from living languages are no-brainers, but they're combined with symbols from other languages. I've identified morphemes that translate along the lines of path, holy, light, teach, and life. The hieroglyphics are trickier. Hieroglyphic sets change depending on the determinative that follows, and in this case, the determinatives, if that's even what they are, look modern rather than ancient, so it's almost impossible to even guess at a translation. I had more luck with the Hebrew."

Singer sat forward.

"Now I'm not an expert on Judeo-Christian texts, but I'm guessing that some of the phrases in this book are similar to what might be found in the Torah." She paused. "They look like instructions or commands prescribing expected behavior. Dictums, if you will."

"What kind of expected behavior?"

She shook her head. "I can't say for sure. At this point, there are only two things that I am sure of."

"Yes?"

"First, I'm seeing no obvious references to the popular monotheistic figures. Moses, Muhammad, Jesus, Abraham, the apostles...all conspicuously absent. And no mention of polytheistic or pagan figures."

Singer reached out to grab a pencil stowed on his computer keyboard and fiddled with it. "Would you expect those references to be there?"

She shrugged one shoulder. "I wouldn't know what to expect from a document like this, a priori, but if it *isn't* connected to Judaism, Islam, or Christianity, I'd wonder if someone wanted to write a book that resembles a religious scripture but that is really a red herring or the cornerstone of a designer religion."

He frowned. "Designer? What do you mean?"

"A recently invented belief system. A cult." She paused. "What I believe I'm seeing in this book is the semblance of religious teaching, though what the hell the teaching might be is still beyond me. Someone wants this book to look like a holy bible."

Singer twirled the pencil through the fingers of one hand. "I see. But you said there were two things that you're sure of. What's the second?"

"One clearly identifiable word is repeated on every page. The symbol for the word also appears on the cover."

Singer trapped the pencil under his index fingers. "What is it?"

Gatsby leaned forward and pulled the pencil out of his hand. She reached toward a pad of scratch paper on the desk and drew something on it that looked like a horseshoe: a single curve with outward-facing prongs at each terminus.

"This. The last letter of the Greek alphabet, Omega."

"Does that have any special significance?

Gatsby sat back in her chair. "If I remember back to my Sunday school lessons, there is a reference in the Christian Bible to alpha and omega. Alpha is the first letter of a number of ancient languages, and, as I said, omega is the last letter of Greek. You might know that the word alphabet is taken from the first two letters—*aleph* and *bet*—that began with Phoenician and migrated into the Greco-Roman and Semitic languages."

He shook his head. "I didn't know that."

She continued. "Somewhere in the Christian bible, the Book of Revelation I think, God declared himself the alpha and the omega, the beginning and the end. The uber-deity." She stared down at the desk as she mulled over a thought. "Interesting that omega is synonymous with *end*. The poor bugger who was reading this book met his end in a nasty way."

Singer picked up the pencil again. "I don't think it is a coincidence, considering what we've now learned about him. He had a respectable life. Quite pious. In fact, he was on his way to becoming a priest, but something in his life changed quickly and dramatically. Exactly what set him off isn't clear, but we know that he suddenly left his parish and then a number of social organizations. He began seeing a psychotherapist. A marriage counselor. Seems that his world was unraveling."

I've been there, she thought.

"Then he divorced, lost custody of his son, and left the church entirely. At that point, he got involved with a new organization. Perhaps one that provided the direction he needed in a time of crisis."

Gatsby stared, waiting.

Singer aimed the tip of the pencil as if preparing to launch it at her. "Our intelligence about this organization is very sketchy. The group is completely underground, but we believe it calls itself Omega."

CHAPTER 11

She filled the mug with Kenyan espresso, topped it with cream. Her slippers scuffed the carpet as she shuffled back to her office. The numbers of a digital clock glowed green: 6:28. Yawning, she sipped, turned the switch of the gooseneck lamp, and sat before the mahogany desk.

The Baber case. After opening the locks, she pulled the book from the protective molding and slowly sat it on the desktop.

Driven by a linguist's instinct to categorize, she had searched for a better referral than "the book," but the right substitute had eluded her.

Her eyes moved over the case.

The numeric keypad. The gleaming aluminum.

The black EVA.

The inscribed EUID: REBOZO / 502816 / GAHANA

The last set of letters niggled at her. She booted her computer out of sleep mode and searched the Internet for "gahana," finding one exact match and one near match. *Gahana scopolineus* was an extremely poisonous shade plant that grew in South Africa. The near match was even more interesting: Gahanna.

The Judaic hell.

The Gahana? That'll work. Heady steam warmed her nostrils as she sipped.

She turned to the stack of notes that she'd scribbled the day before. The syllabary that she'd started was divided into a grid for copying, counting, and categorizing the symbols.

Ten Latin letters including T, S, O, E, and I.

Four Hebrew characters: gimel, nun, yod, and lamed.

Seven Greek letters: beta, epsilon, delta, theta, iota, sigma, and omega.

Hieroglyphics of a vulture, viper, reed, mouth, jar, and snake.

Picking up a ballpoint pen, she started into the methodical, tedious categorizing. One glyph, one assessment, at a time.

This must have taken a lifetime to organize.

The numbers on the digital clock changed silently.

Somewhere far away, a clarion called—then called louder, and she realized that it was the phone.

Wheeling her chair to the far end of the desk, she reached out, squinted at the caller ID, saw a Kensington prefix, and pressed the phone to her ear.

"Girls' day out, sweetie!" The voice was far too chipper for nine in the morning.

Gatsby smiled. "Out of what, maximum security?"

"That's one way of describing your world. Come on, Gats, we've got a Saturday of shopping before us. Covent Garden, a raid on Harvey Nicks. We'll get you a makeover and jam the slots of the porn arcades in Soho, maybe scoot off to Citronelle at the Lowndes for tea and biscotti. My treat! Get your Tube pass and your bag, babe."

Gatsby swiveled back and forth in her chair, staring at the Gahana.

Celia moaned, her tone exasperated, "Oh god. You're going to think this to death, aren't you. I can hear it now, I have—"

"Work to do," Gatsby finished. Wailing and profanity made her jerk the phone away from her ear.

"I'm trying to do you a favor, you silly ass!"

"I know, Celia, I appreciate it, but..."

"Prove it. In fact, I'll up the stakes. Promise me, right now, that you'll meet me at Citronelle for lunch...and I'll give you the number of that conference coordinator."

Frowning, Gatsby said, "The Association of Counselling and Psychotherapy? That coordinator?"

"Well, natch."

A series of staccato clicks flickered in the background.

"Okay, I'll see you at three. What's his name?"

"Meet me at the front entrance, three o'clock sharp. You promise?"

"Fine!" She felt her palms growing slippery. "Now will you give me the name and number?"

She heard an almost imperceptible beep, then a series of soft clicks.

"Celia?"

"—four five three five seven two. Theodore Davies Pryce. He's the president of the association and will be more than happy to put you in touch with your Boy Wonder."

She rubbed the earpiece against her temple. *Could I possibly go through with it?*

"Say the number again. The line went out for a second."

"Yeah?" A puff. "That's no surprise. We're having all kinds of phone trouble in this area lately."

While Celia repeated the number, Gatsby grabbed some scratch paper and scribbled. "Thanks, I owe you."

Celia snorted. "Good. Make it a Courvoisier. Meet me at three, or I'll be forced to set the assassins on you."

Lowering the handset to its base, Gatsby swiveled her chair toward the computer. The system had logged her off and slipped back into sleep mode.

She tried to log back into her Internet service provider, but was repeatedly informed that her ID and password were incorrect. Then, the message "Unable to log in user." She rebooted and an unfamiliar, eye-bleeding-violet "welcome" page appeared.

"Damn it," she growled, feeling her blood pressure rising.

She rebooted again and was finally able to bring up her browser, but no functions worked except for the email folder, and a dialogue box said that the folder was full and could not receive any more messages.

I just deleted a slew of old email yesterday!

After trying a clunky backdoor approach, she accessed her ISP, but the system speed had slowed to a rigor mortis-level crawl.

For godssake!

"Time to call the technogeeks. Shit, just what I need right now," she muttered.

She went to a lower shelf of her bookcase, dug through a pile of assorted papers, found an ancient, wrinkled phone book, and thumbed through it until she found "Computer Repair."

After a brief conversation with "Jet" and scheduling an emergency home visit to check her system, she went back to the Gahana. Ten minutes later, the phone rang again, making her jump. She sucked in a breath and grabbed the handset.

"Listen, I told you that I'd—"

"Dr. Donovan? This is Agent Singer."

Her mind spun. "Oh! Ahm, sorry, I was expecting someone else." She imagined the annoyed look on his face.

"I wanted to check on the status of the evidence." His voice was flat yet tinged with urgency.

"I'm still analyzing it."

"What have you determined so far?"

"I've started a syllabary. Once I have a grid of all the symbols, I can tally the number of appearances and start to evaluate the relationships. How many times one character appears before or after another, or which symbol might be added or deleted and in what circumstances." She sighed while combing her fingers through her hair. "It's going to take some time."

She heard breathing, then, "You've had it for a week, Dr. Donovan, and you'll have to return it to the Evidence Unit soon. We can't let these items go unprotected for too long. It's not safe for the possessor or the item."

"What do you mean, not safe for the possessor?" Something dark scratched at the back of her mind.

"Evidence items are targets. You work with priceless pieces at the Museum, so I'm sure you're aware of the risks when a piece is taken off-site. It becomes even more attractive to those who have decided that they must have it."

She knew that it was true. Artifacts en route to the Museum, or taken off-premises for restoration work, were at great risk.

He continued. "We both know that there are always those who will want a valuable item and that sometimes they do whatever it takes to get it." He paused. "Do you have it there, at your home?

"Yes."

"Has anything unusual happened? Any strange phone calls?"

Not unless Celia counts as strange. My computer going wiggy? Hardly unusual. Computers freeze unexpectedly all the time. She shrugged. "No."

"Good. I don't want to make you paranoid, but keep your eyes open. I'm convinced that the RED-MK7 death is linked to that book, though I'm not sure how. There may be much more to it than we realize, so be careful. If you see anything unusual or think that you are in danger in any way, let me know, and we'll put surveillance in place to protect you."

Surveillance? How badly would this cult want to protect its scripture? She remembered saying to Singer, *The poor bugger who was reading this book met his end in a nasty way.* "I'll keep you posted."

"How much longer will you need it?"

"What if I bring it back at the end of the week? The thirty-third?"

A pause. "The thirty-third what?"

Her mind jolted. *What the hell was that?* For a split second, she had known, not guessed but *known,* that it was still September and that there was a thirty-third day in the month.

"God, my mind is somewhere else. The tenth, yes, that's what I meant to say." She swallowed.

"Hm. I'll check. I think the EU will approve the hold, but I'm not making any promises. If it does, we'll need it back then, no matter what stage your investigation is in."

She nodded against the handset. "Understood."

They made goodbyes.

A twinge rippled through her. *Where did that brain-fart come from? Thirty-three?!*

Trying to shake it off, she went back to the Gahana and the growing pile of handwritten notes that she would later transcribe into an electronic file. An hour later, she sat back and rolled her head to pop out the kinks in her neck.

Knowledge of ancient orthographies will only get me to a certain level. Beyond that, I need experts. Though there was no logic of it, the thought pricked at her. *RED-MK7 was gripping this as he died. Could there have been a poison on the pages?* The thought flashed through her. *Could the language itself somehow be a danger?*

The idea was disturbing enough to push her from her chair and hustling into the kitchen. She rinsed out the coffee mug and leaned against the counter while staring out the living room window. Midday traffic buzzed down King's Road. One of London's famous hallmarks, the snub-nosed black diesel taxi, careened by, honking.

"Oh, that's nuts," she muttered.

Crazy, Donovan. Completely.

The idea persisted. It had her in its grip, like a terrier shaking a rat. Like a pernicious virus.

As she dressed for her meeting with Celia, she thought, *I need help. A psychophysiologist, to be precise.*

A bolt of panic raced through her.

There's no other way. I have to. It's impossible! No, it's insanity! I can't!

She closed her eyes against the wave of dread.

But I will.

CHAPTER 12

He tossed the electronic keycard onto the bed and dropped into a padded chair by the window. The thought blazed though his mind: *She'd never know I was here, but still, do I dare?*

Woodrow Sanderson tugged on his goatee and pondered as he stared out the window at the dark London streets. The windows of the adjacent Sydney House Hotel rooms glowed like Yule logs. He pulled in a breath and let it out slowly, as if liberating hallucinogenic smoke.

He turned to the table next to his chair, where his notebook PC sat packed in a black travel case. Pulling it out, he uncoiled the power cord, plugged one end into the notebook, the other into an outlet, and booted up the system.

Then he was reviewing notes from his lecture before the ACP. He hadn't wanted to attend the conference but was pushed—

No, the word is threatened.

—into appearing by the dictatorial regime of UC Berkeley.

The psychophysiologist who went psycho. He recalled the rumblings among his students. A few of them, the bright young hackers, had dug up detailed information about his past—his quest for the holy grail of enlightenment. Some of the students snickered over the secrets they'd unearthed, but some came to him with sincere questions.

We all make our journeys down our own paths. A pang struck dully at his heart. *If only there had been a way...*

The regrets of the past, the nondecisions, the roads untraveled or abandoned, and the future that disappeared one watch-tick at a time pressed on him like stones used for crushing heretics. In his exhaustive reading during that chaotic, pivotal period, he had learned of the *peine forte et dure:* long and forceful punishment. In 1692, a man named Giles Corey had been accused of witchcraft and was pressed to death by stones, not for being proven to be a warlock but for refusing to enter a plea.

He felt that suffocation, his long and forceful punishment, now.

A line from a Wachowski film whispered through his mind: *We make our own choices, we pay our own prices.*

It's the price that I have paid, must continue to pay. Ten years of self-condemnation for the sin of piety. Why do I do it? As penance? As masturbation of the soul? Or as a way to prolong my wickedness? My hope? Or the inevitable?

The thoughts caught in his mind as though they were a cry caught in his throat.

...and all I got is time until the end of time, I won't look back, I won't look back...

Abruptly, he bolted across the room, palms smashed against his hips, shaking his head. It was one of the smaller rooms at the hotel: single bed, dresser, TV/DVD inside a tall entertainment center, mini-bar, floor lamps, a small writing table and chair. Muted earth tones, lacquered wood furniture with carved feet. There weren't enough square feet for him to walk off the ravages of guilt.

He glanced at the spray of ticket stubs and city maps scattered across the bedspread. Dropping onto the bed, he thought, *Just say it, just freaking admit it! You know exactly why you balked at coming, why you didn't want to be within a thousand miles of London.*

Pacing back across the room, he knelt before the mini-bar and pulled out a dark bottle. Newcastle Brown Ale. It felt cold and wet in his hand, like something finned, pulled that moment from the sea.

With the bottlecap spinning on the surface of the table, the bubbles of foam popping in the glass, he pressed his fingers to the keyboard, opened a blank email form, and began to write.

Greetings,

My apologies for the long silence. I am today returned from trainings in the Northeast (remind me never to move there!) and now fly off to Miami. Four years of hard work, and Anthony graduates this month. He would kill me if I missed the ceremony. I will be without email access for a

*week or so but promise to write when I am returned to
Boulder.*

He stopped. *Have I mentioned the son's name?*
Navigating to the documents in a SAVED folder, he
searched for "Anthony." December 1998. There it was.
   Fraud is a dirty business. He shook his head and
returned to the screen.

*In your last missive, you said that your projects were
keeping you very busy, not much time for more pleasurable
pursuits. Then again, for some of us, the work of language is
one of the most pleasurable pursuits.*

He took a long swallow of the beer, coughed, and let his
eyes wander from the keys to the clock-radio on the
nightstand. *When will the day come...*
   The wave that began building in his vitals spread through
his body, bringing a lump to his throat. *The day that she finds
me out and, for better or so much worse, do we turn the last
page of this chronicle of lies?*
   He looked down to see that he had been crushing his fists
against the keyboard; the word "pursuits" was followed by
fcfdsl ksdsmfdfdl kd fskjfdslkfjslk dfsa lkdfjsl.
   Swearing, he deleted the gibberish and replaced his
fingertips on the home keys.
   Yes, the day will come, but not today.
   He typed:

*As always, I send my best and look forward to hearing
from you.*
   Semantically yours, D.

As Sanderson tossed the empty bottle into the trash can,
the lyrics whispered through his mind: *And I know that I've
been released, but I don't know to where...*

CHAPTER 13

She slammed down the phone for the third time, then picked up the handset, dialed to the last digit, and hung up, her heart thudding.

"I can't do this," Gatsby whispered. She dropped into the chair before her desk and tried to prioritize a short list of desperate alternatives.

The president of the Association of Counselling and Psychotherapy, Theodore Davies Pryce, had taken her call. After not-so-patiently listening to her credentials and the referral from Celia Devereaux, he had named the institute at which Dr. Sanderson could be reached.

The psychology department at UC Berkeley gave her the number of the hotel where Dr. Sanderson was lodged for the duration of the London conference, and after two hours of wrangling with herself, she still sat in her office, machine-gunning her foot against the carpet and wondering what the hell she would say if she could actually make the call.

Woody? It's Gatsby. Yes, I still wish you were rotting in a deep grave, but since you're not, what do you think of helping me work out a bizarre linguistic puzzle?

She dropped her head into her hands with a groan. *This is impossible.*

Her thoughts spiraled like leaves in the wind. Would he even speak with her, considering how they'd parted, in rage and chaos? From the stuff he'd abandoned in their apartment to her frantic calls to his committee—the nightmare replayed through her mind and set up an angry throb in her gut.

But this book is important. Very important. There's something occultish, something hidden in the text that...

She shook her head in frustration. *Whatever the something is, I've got to uncover it. So why is it that the man I'm trying to convince myself I need, the same one that I wanted to share every moment of discovery with, is also the one who tore my heart to shreds?*

She swore again, cursing fate and improbability and the brutality of love.

This isn't a matter of choice.

Yes, it is. You can call a hundred other people. Forget it!

Still battling her own motives, she picked up the phone and dialed the numbers. The voice howling in her head edged her blood pressure toward precipitous levels.

No, I can't, I won't. Stop! Don't do it. But I have to, it's the only way. No, it's not, you IDIOT!!

With each ring, she pleaded desperately, *Please be a machine, please, please, please, please be a machine...*

Five rings. The line connected.

A serious voice said, "Hello?"

Her knees buckled, and she collapsed onto the couch. There was no mistaking that voice. Still grappling to shove the ghosts into their closet, she said, her voice thick, "Woody? It's Gatsby."

She heard a sharp inhalation. Each second that ticked by was a lifetime, and she could almost feel synapses exploding like fireworks, almost hear the metal-on-metal screaming of broken hearts.

"Oh my god...I never—" A long pause, and the sigh she heard was all the angst of a destroyed world. "I never thought I'd hear your voice again."

The overtones of his voice instantly brought back memories of his roguish tone, the quirks of speech that were reflected in the smile lines around his eyes, the deep laughter that was lethally infectious—all these joyful memories, white threads in the tapestry of her life, were interwoven with the black threads of bitterness that had pricked at her for more than a decade. The shock that stung her every time she stumbled across something that reminded her of him. A book, a song. A classic movie they'd watched together, wrapped in a comforter. Even the smell of freshly sliced oranges and strawberries: he had brought them to her on a Portofino-yellow saucer on her birthday, breakfast in bed.

She pulled in air, focusing on the diamond pattern in the carpet and the leaves beyond the living room window. When she realized that she was strangling the phone hard enough to set her hand singing, she tried to relax her grip. Speech seemed as impossible as walking through solid glass. At last, she managed, "I never thought that this conversation would happen either, but it is. And...there's a reason."

After a beat, Sanderson prompted, "A reason?" His voice fluttered. "Something's happened. Gatsby, what is it?"

Hearing him say her name brought a surge of the old roller coaster of emotions. "Woody, I have to talk to you. I need your help." She tried to breathe evenly. "It's important."

The Sydney House Hotel's bar was dark oak paneling, soft jazz, waiters in starched tuxedos.

She took a seat in a booth and ordered a White Russian. When the waiter, a Ringo Starr look-alike, brought it, she stirred slowly and kept her eyes riveted on the entrance.

The front door opened, and her heart stopped. A lanky gentleman, early sixties, with a grey Vandyke beard, sidled across the room to the bar where he draped one arm around a woman in a cashmere stole.

She exhaled, tipped her head back against the leather padding, and sensed a flock of muddled thoughts, like birds flying to the wrong pole, fluttering through her head.

How is this going to go down? Shall I do what the New Age gurus talk about and program myself for my desired reality? Or drink heavily and go home and try to put this nightmare behind me?

She heard a scuffling sound and looked up.

He wasn't, and at the same time was, what she'd expected.

The splash of lines around his eyes were all that had been added in the years since they'd shared both bed and dreams. The carriage was different. He held himself more stiffly, though a genteel presence seemed to be misted over him like an English cologne, and the smile and dancing brown eyes had not changed.

While she scrambled for an opening syllable, he said, "My god, you look beautiful."

Hadn't expected that...

He, too, was still beautiful. Still sexy. *Still the man I wanted so desperately but who didn't desperately want me.*

Her heartbeat throbbed in her ears as she stood to face him. Hug? Handshake? Right hook to the kidneys? He seemed to be going through the same line of internal questioning as his eyes darted from her face to her hands and back up.

They saw the waiter approach and both moved back to settle on opposite sides of the booth. The waiter greeted them, planted menus and descriptions, and walked away. Miles Davis's "'Round Midnight" be-bopped around them.

They blurted simultaneously, "I don't want t..." and froze, smiling awkwardly.

She studied his fingers as he ran a hand through his wavy hair. *No rings.*

"Shit. I'm nervous. You?" he murmured.

She nodded. *Don't lose it! Don't give him any clue that you ever wanted or needed him. Let the bastard drown in rejection for a while and know how it feels.*

"How did you find me?"

She raised her eyebrows. "You know. My extensive network of spies."

He took a sip of water. "Jesus. The first time I speak at a conference, and it's in London, and you're here. And then you track me down and call me, and we're...it hasn't sunk in yet."

It's sunk in for me, bub. "Imagine the odds."

"I know precisely what your first question will be."

She sat back and watched him, working to scrub all emotion from her face. "What?"

He sat his glass on the table and looked up at her. "How I could disappear without a trace."

She searched for a workable response while thinking, *Do I really need his help?!* Belaying a statement that would have reduced any cooperative efforts to rubble before they'd even begun, and struggling to keep her voice even, she said, "To say that I've wondered about it for, what, fifteen years would be a gross understatement. Apparently you decided that the best course of action was to just leave. Poof! Like a sperm whale standing too close to David Copperfield?"

He shook his head slowly. "Gatsby, where was I at that time? Gone over to the light side. Immersed in my existential delirium, the God question."

"Uh huh. The almighty God question." The images of their cramped apartment and strolling around the Blake campus hand in hand spun through her, bringing a wave of nostalgia that throbbed painfully, like a broken bone.

"Not how to live a moral life, but the belief and faith and life-after-death questions," he was gathering steam, "all the questions that I never had the chance to ask!"

Go on, Woody, the more you plead this argument of egotism, the quicker you hang yourself.

"You know what my family was like. My parents drove me away from anything that even smelled of religion." He pulled in a deep breath. "You had spiritual guidance at a young age, but I didn't. We all eventually go in search of ourselves, in adulthood, right? The quest for self-knowledge, for identity? For answers to our most ponderous questions, right?"

She stared at her hands:

(hot breath flows over the naked skin of her back)

No! NOT that!

His hands wormed over each other in his lap. "I struggled so damn hard to reconcile everything. My thesis, and being with you, and my compulsion to know why. What humankind is doing on this ridiculous little planet and why anything that we do in one short lifetime makes an iota of difference." He stared. "I had the most astounding woman I'd ever known right there beside me." His voice caught. "But I knew that the agony would continue, and that I was no good to anyone, until I faced those questions...the voices would never be silent until I confronted them head on. I was no good for myself." Tears misted his eyes as he whispered, "I was no good for you, Kama."

Kama. The Sanskrit word for love, reserved for only their moments of deepest intimacy.

She stared at him for a long minute, then muttered, "Oh, Christ, what do you want me to do, Woody, shed a tear over your God crisis? Your spiritual emergency?" It was her turn to erupt; the words boiled out in a rush. "Or see this for what it is, the most inventive excuse imaginable for bolting on me? On *us?*"

"No excuse. I'm giving you the truth in the only way that I can." He looked into her eyes. "It was the hardest thing I ever had to do."

"*Had* to do? What, did your messiah figure hold a gun to your head?"

She stood abruptly and slid toward the paneled wall. The room hummed with gentility: elegant patrons and waiters, sable carpet, candles flickering on the table linen. Bringing one hand to her chin, she saw that it was shaking and stuffed it into the pocket of her jacket. Waves of anger rippled through her. Her brain was splitting into two. She wanted to hammer something heavy and solid against something very vulnerable, wanted to sweep the morass of years of hurt into the depths of a black sea. Under it all, part of her longed for a place of equilibrium, a final resting place that felt peace— or, lacking that, felt nothing at all.

I have to know what it will take to stop feeling this feeling.

She turned back toward him and saw his tight lips and ashen face, his throat working.

Her head tipped back against the paneling, and her arms wrapped themselves around her sides. "God *damn* you, Woody. Just when I was reconciled to the fact that we were ancient history and..."

And I hated you and loved you and wanted to kill you and couldn't bear how you tore me apart...

"And that I was never going to see you again." She raised her chin defiantly.

His body slumped, as if the weight of the air were unbearable. Quietly, he asked, "Were you?"

The word tumbled out before she could stop it. "No."

He rose and moved toward her, but she stiffened. Their gaze connected. They stood rooted. Waiting for a feint. Assessing the risks. Pitting return against investment.

Everything she wanted to say, or scream, scrambled into heart-pounding chaos, leaving her staring stupidly as if aphasic.

Finally, he cleared his throat. "There's something, ahm," he brought his palms together and pressed the thumbs against his chest. A smile tried to emerge. "This will either be the most redemptive or the most disastrous move ever. Come over here. I need to tell you something."

Breathing hard, she hesitated, then slowly moved back to the table and sat. The waiter had brought two glasses of White Zinfandel.

Sanderson rustled himself as if preparing for a speech. "It'll be hard for you to believe me, but leaving hurt me as much as it did you. I knew that you were the only one for me, but I didn't know the me that was the one for you."

She looked toward the bar at the far side of the room, then back at him. Her chest felt like heavy and hot, as if fire burned in her lungs. "Is this the redemptive part?"

He shook his head. "I never wanted to cast you out of my life, Gatsby, ever." He swallowed. "I loved you then, and I always will. I never considered going through life without you. You must know that."

She felt her lips trembling and stopped them by taking a long sip of the wine. "There were a lot of things that I thought I knew back then."

"After that night, I left Seattle. The next day. You knew that, didn't you?"

The frantic calls. "Only what your advisor told me. You'd abandoned your program and left a forwarding address in another city, but he didn't say which one."

He took another labored breath. "I don't think you need all the grisly details right now—I'll tell you anything you want to know, later—but suffice it to say that I went on a crusade. I wound up in a few different cities, and in each one, taste-tested philosophies. I was a Jew, then a Baha'i. A pagan, a Muslim, a pyramid-sitter...I read Tarot cards and the Kabbala..."

"Tarot? Jewish mysticism?!"

He ploughed on, "And I took acid and had visions of my death and past lives and resurrection. I was rebirthed and Rolfed. I saw Reiki masters and gurus who walked on burning coals." He must have seen her eyes widening and paused. "This is a lot to take in. I know."

She snorted. "That's a personal crusade all right."

"And I read like a fiend. All the great religious texts. Then Spinoza, Leary, Dawkins, Aquinas, Muhammad, Watts, Plato, Sun Tzu—I don't know, a hundred others. I was on that ultimate what-is-it journey, the one that would eventually lead me to the answer."

The answer that genuine, tangible, human love—here on this plane—couldn't give you, Woody? She leaned back, her face rigid, "Did you find that answer?"

Holding one palm out toward her, he said, "I learned this. There's a Hindu philosophy that divides all human experience into a hierarchy of four motivations. One of them is kama, the gratification of the senses. The highest is moksha. Liberation. If one state conflicts with another, you must sustain the higher ideal and sacrifice the lower." Tears swam in his eyes. "I was in the agonizing place where liberation was in conflict with kama. The latter had to be sacrificed...but even still, I knew."

The silence became unendurable. "Knew what?" she croaked.

"In all that questing, there was only one true thing that I knew without a doubt. That I would always love you, Gatsby."

It was too much. She dropped her head into her hands, felt the tears burning. "Don't, Woody."

As if he hadn't heard her, he barreled on, his face contorted with pain. "And it took all that traveling to realize that where I had to be was right where I had begun."

She sat back and watched him, feeling her body hardening. Cold as marble. "Well, Sanderson. What a lovely story of unrequited love. What does this mean for me?

Nothing. You split and you pined for me. Boo *hoo*. Fifteen frigging years, and you never once wrote or called. You bastard. I'm leaving." She leaned down to grab her shoulderbag off the floor.

He pounced to grab her hand. "Wait! One question." He looked into her face. "Gatsby...who is Definite Article?"

Her mouth popped open.

Cold sweat. Tachycardia.

When my Internet connection went down and—! Jesus Christ, has he hacked my computer? My email? What IS this?!

"No," she whispered, shaking her head.

"All that email from Definite Article? I found a community site for linguistic scholarship and saw your profile. Joined the site with an anonymous user name...would you have read those letters, a single one of them, if you knew they were from me?" He pressed his lips together. "The only way that I could reach out to you was through an admittedly slippery back door."

What the HELL is going on? Has he been spying on me? Stalking me? Every alarm was going off, every muscle taut, preparing her to bolt. "No. I don't believe you."

He pulled in a long breath. "TESOL instructor, fifty-ish. Working on a book for years but can't finish it. Two children, one in Florida and one in Wisconsin."

"But all those descriptions..."

"Lives in Boulder and travels to Eurasia every now and then?"

Her shoulderbag slipped to the floor with a THUD.

Running her hands through her hair, she leaned into his face, still incredulous. "I...don't..."

He hung his head. "I hated it, Gatsby, hated every minute of deception, hated not being able to reveal myself but knowing that the moment I did, you'd be gone." He drew closer, his eyes round and wet. "It was a lie, I take complete responsibility for all of it, but I had to connect with you! There was no other way, and even though I had found my true self, I couldn't tell you who I really was."

The waiter wafted by, saw their glistening eyes and flushed faces, and floated back toward the bar.

He cleared his throat roughly. "But all that time, I gave you pieces of me. Encoded pieces."

She barely heard him over the booming in her ears and chest. "Encoded? What are you talking about?"

"The last line of each email. Semantically yours—then a letter."

The words flowed into her memory:

(Semantically yours, A)

(Semantically yours, G)

(Semantically yours, B)

(Semantically yours, C)

"The last letter? It's a code?"

He leaned toward her over the table, seeming to buzz with renewed energy. "Yes. A code that I knew would keep the inveterate translator puzzled forever."

Her eyes narrowed. "How?"

He scrabbled for a napkin, then dug in the breast pocket of his suit jacket for a pen. "Something that a die-hard language junkie would overlook. I knew your credentials. I knew that you were well on your way to a high level of renown in the field of ancient script translation. And I knew that a logophile like that wouldn't go to her grave until she had deciphered the message that I sent to her, one letter at a time...if she knew of its existence."

It was coming way too fast—her brain was reeling, trying to come to grips with it all. How many years of lies? Intimate knowledge of her life, prying into her mind through fake emails, each one secreting a piece of a hidden message?

This is all just some elaborate ploy...for what? Absolution?

"Did you ever look for a pattern?"

She crossed her arms. "I found a pattern."

"What was it?"

"They were constrained to the first seven letters of the English alphabet. A through G. Five consonants, two vowels." She sniffled and wiped the back of her hand across her nose. "Hard to send a message of much significance with such a limited base."

Sanderson sat taller and smiled. "I knew that you would do just that, and you would overlook other possibilities." He spread the napkin before her, the pen hovering over it. "You probably don't remember the first dozen or so emails from Definite Article, but if you did, and if you had started to keep track of those final letters, you would have seen this." He wrote a long series on the napkin, then turned it around for her to read.

What kind of game is he playing?

She peered down at the letters, sifting through the linguistic data in her mind, looking for prefixes, abbreviations, acronyms. "It's...I don't know, it's nothing! Stop toying with me!"

Sanderson's smile widened. "Perfect. It worked. Now...don't try to read the letters. Sing them."

Her eyes darted from his face to the napkin. "What?"

He drew something at the far edge of the napkin, just before the first letter. A treble clef. "Sing them."

After a few seconds, her eyes widened.

He reached across the table, his elbow rumpling the napkin, looked into her eyes, and whispered the lyrics. "If I had it any sooner, you know, you know I never would have run away from my home."

"That ancient vinyl album, the one we played a million times?"

"The song we sang to each other. Our song. You know the one."

She squeezed his hands, her heart pounding, flying, and whispered, "Heaven Can Wait."

Everything inside of her tipped upside down. Crashed. Too much, too late, too soon. Too glorious. Too agonizing.

He was pressed to her, arms wrapped tight around her body, choking and whispering against her neck, "This time, I won't let you go, Kama."

They stayed together, joined and trembling, for a long time. Finally, Gatsby sat back with a shuddering breath. "What are we going to do?"

He paused. "We can start by telling each other the truth."

A spark flared in her. *Did he know about it? Has he ever known? How could I possibly tell him that? No no no no...*Old rage sizzled through her veins like acid. Her stomach flip-flopped. In her mind, she saw candles, red fingerprints streaking her steering wheel. VISITOR PARKING signs at Good Samaritan. Felt hands locked on her shoulders. Warm blood oozing down her thighs.

"Gatsby?"

"The truth." She swallowed. "Woody, I never told you...what happened about eight weeks before the night you left."

He stared at her with glassy eyes. "Eight weeks before?"

After she told him everything, no details withheld, she felt like she had just watched something beautiful die a slow death.

Sanderson's face had crumbled. When he could speak, he whispered, "Christ, Gatsby, why didn't you tell me?!"

She hung her head. "Post-traumatic shock. Denial. Humiliation, rage. All that, but mostly because we were already on a downhill slide. You were slipping away from me, and I didn't want to say anything that would tip the scales." A tear rippled down her cheek. "When you did go, at least I knew that it wasn't because of that."

Abruptly, Sanderson spun out of the seat and slammed his fist against the wall. Patrons' heads swiveled, their mouths agape. He pulled his fists up to his eyes, then collapsed back into the booth, eyes blazing and wet. A stream of anguish flowed from his lips as he cradled his head in his hands, panting in hard, irregular bursts. Finally, he blurted, "Is that all? Is there anything else?"

"There's this."

Almost more tormenting than the assault at the Harstedt Interfaith Center was what had happened in the months afterward.

She described how her body swelled and her periods stopped. Her moods rocketed up, down, sideways. She found herself eating entire packets of celery sticks dipped in strawberry jam. Every morning, she retched into the bathroom sink, running water into the sink to cover the sound. After four months, the symptoms dissipated and her body returned to normal, but the questions had always remained.

They'd stopped having sex many months ago.

Multiple visits to Good Samaritan Medical Clinic and a full battery of tests determined unequivocally that it wasn't a miscarriage. Conception had never occurred.

She moved to his side of the table and fell into him, weeping as she had never wept before. Death in admission. Every pain she'd ever felt—from a stubbed toe to a nose broken by a titanium racquet—melded together, detonating and then trickling out of her like milky bile. Her fingers pressed against his cheeks, and they too were hot and slippery.

The waiter crept up to kneel by their table. He cleared his throat, and whispered, "Madame, are you all right?"

Sniffling, she sat back. "Ahm, yes, thank you."

The waiter stood slowly, his lips working silently, eyes rifling over Sanderson, seeming uncertain of what to believe. "Let me know if you need anything." He quietly slipped away.

They tried to breathe, to keep breathing.

Sanderson said softly, "No more skeletons?"

Gatsby shook her head. "No."

"Me either."

He raised his glass of Zinfandel and took a long swallow, then sat it back on the table: light pink beads trickled down the inside of the glass. "No one should do this much self-revelation at one sitting."

She stared at the paneling, her eyes fixed, her muscles cramped, and didn't want to think or say or feel anything.

"And the most puzzling part, we haven't even talked about yet. Why you called me in the first place. You said it's important, that you need my help."

Her heart still hammering, she dragged herself out of the whirlpool of emotions and toward the questions of the book. The Gahana.

Singer's voice whispered through her mind: *Have you had anything usual happen? Any strange phone calls?*

After a long beat, she said, "It's a translation project. A book that...no. I can't tell you any details, or I'll have the CIS on my ass."

"And then I'd have to fight off the competition." Sanderson gave her the lopsided grin that, like the hushed song of the ocean, like flickering firelight, had always managed to draw her into its warmth. "The CIS? Tell me more."

CHAPTER 14

Niccolo stepped through the door and into a square, beige room. A messy collection of literary journals huddled on the coffee table. He heard the click-click-click of a computer keyboard, coming from down the hallway.

The receptionist looked up at him, her eyes wide, and pushed a button on her console. "Dr. Volante? Your appointment is here." She tipped a slender nose toward the hallway.

As he moved past her, he caught a waft of a skin-smell that reminded him subtly of *her*.

He turned into the third doorway to find Volante encamped behind a dark cherry desk. As she rose, the panels of her black suit flared and waves of her flax-colored hair spilled over her shoulders. She fixed a calm expression on him and murmured, "Abbah way non push tah non ah meh-gah."

"Ah meh-gah sho met yah," Niccolo responded. *At all times, she preserves the formalities.*

He spotted the leather chair before him and slid into it. While readying himself for her report on the Damaii, he studied her. Her attire betrayed deliberately conservative choices. Was she hoping to impress him with her attention to detail? Her hair was fixed to the last strand. Where an ornate ring had once rested on her hand he now saw a plain band of white gold. Her smell was exquisite: lavender with hints of rosewood and honey.

The most telling signs were on her face. The muscles at the edges of her mouth strained as if trying to expand and contract at the same time. He saw her pupils dilate as her eyes moved over his face.

She's taking great pains to create the effect.

"Eight were missing. A handful arrived late, by about five minutes."

Looking past him, she rose to sweep around the desk and close the door. He heard the snick as the latch snapped into place, and the fabric of her skirt—wrapping her legs and hips, which he knew were as firm as those of a woman half her age—brushed against his forearm as she strode back to her executive chair.

"A sixty-forty split of women to men. Dress more causal than usual. Two Dama had new tattoos."

"Where?"

"The ankle and the back of the neck."

He listened as she described the details: the lighting, where and how members had positioned themselves in their seats, who had asked questions, what the questions were, who stayed after being dismissed and how long, the level of language fluency, their verbal and nonverbal expressions.

"The honorum mati. Who came forward first?"

"My zasha, Guy, but I had called on him."

He nodded. "The zasha have their uses."

Volante pulled in a slow breath. "I was not informed that she would make an appearance."

He kept his face stiff, blank of expression, as his mind raced. *Of course you were not informed. Anne brings deeper levels of mystery to the drama, played out for an audience already piqued.* He said, "And you told them about the Librah Vae-ta?" At her nod, he asked, "The reaction?"

She leaned back in her chair and gripped the edge of the desk with one hand. "Chaos, as might be expected—as if their oxygen line had been cut."

It has. "Any indication of accomplices?"

"Not that I have seen."

He rubbed his fingers against one cheek. "Who have you selected?"

In her eyes, he saw a flicker of hubris. "The most fluent of the Dama. Rauscher and Isma'il are obvious choices. Polensky has always proven valuable. Bunch and Nguyen, definitely. Ivan Kuznetsov and myself." Her tone went flat. "And, of course, Maia."

Of course, Maia. As soon as her image arose, he struggled to push it away.

His eyes narrowed as he leaned toward Volante; almost imperceptibly, she leaned back. "Status?"

She crossed her arms. "Come tonight, and I will show you."

This is not a safe location, Niccolo thought as he followed her up a flight of concrete stairs.

Volante's loft suite was tucked in the exclusive neighborhood of Caynhall. It offered an airy living space with open hallways to the kitchen and dining area. He saw that a set of oak wood stairs, almost as vertical as a ladder, led to an upper level where he presumed there were bedrooms, perhaps a library or office.

Expensive real estate for a teacher at a small college. How does she afford this?

They entered the living room. As they moved toward a Victorian sofa, huge black-and-white photographs—portraits of tragic faces, bordered with black frames—stared from the walls.

Folding tables had been set up around the room, each covered with pens, reams of paper, and mobile electronics.

Approaching the nearest table, he leaned down for a closer look at the work in progress. As he slid a finger across the lettering, he muttered, "Partials, phrase fragments...this looks like a section from The Words of Appointment."

Volante moved nearer to stand beside him. "Yes. It's Isma'il's work. He can recite the entire chapter from memory and promises to have scribed by the end of the week The Words of the Fountain and The Words of Sanctity."

Striding toward another table, then another, glancing at the scattered sheets, he turned toward her and growled, "This is all you've got?"

"Yes, so far, but there's something else that you should see." Her body seemed to shout, *Something crucial has happened.* "Come this way."

Frowning, he followed as she led him across the space and into a pantry-like room outfitted with wire shelving. Each shelf contained a number of boxes about thirty centimeters square. Volante pulled one of the boxes down from a shelf, carried it to a table, and turned toward Niccolo.

"What is this?"

"The network recovered these from a Dama in Rome."

"Rome?" He felt his mind scanning quickly. *Omega's connections to Rome are deep but very well hidden.* He made a mental note to speak with the Elders in Rome. "Does this explain your travel time over the last three weeks?"

"Yes." She pointed to the box. "They have eluded everyone in the empire: the Dosa, the Shoto, the Dama, even the Council of Elders. We all assumed that they were destroyed long ago. They weren't. Only with the theft of the Librah Vae-ta have they come to the surface."

"Have what?" Niccolo barked, preparing to grab for the box. "You are trying my patience, Franca!"

With a smile, she wrapped her fingers around the lid of the box and murmured, "Be prepared, Abba." She lifted the lid.

He saw a stack of sepia-yellowed papers, covered with spidery writing that looked as if it had been created with quill and ink. Thumbing through the sheaves, he saw page after page of notes, diagrams, citations, and grid-like charts.

As realization flooded him, his mouth dropped open. "Jesus Christ!"

Volante's smile widened. "Better. Omega."

"But, but these are..."

She nodded with calm deliberation. "MCF. It's their notes. The original formula."

Niccolo forced himself to breathe as he tried to grasp the enormity and the implications of what he was seeing.

Volante turned and dragged two chairs toward them. "According to Omegan history, these have been lost for over a century. We don't know where they were hidden. It could have been a basement, a private library, a safe deposit box, a million different places." Her lips curled. "We're not yet sure. Our source has cooperated with great...reluctance."

He dropped into the chair, leafing through the papers slowly, almost unwilling to touch them, feeling his breath course in and out of his nostrils. "Unbelievable."

"The ink, style, content, cross-references, signatures, they are all confirmed. There is no doubt." A look of triumph arched over her face. "These are the originals. The lost Omega scrolls."

Niccolo read late into the night. He knew only the drive to submerge himself in the documents—like the imperative need to stare at something horrific yet ineffable.

Volante brought a drinking glass and a pitcher of water, sat them next to him, and disappeared down a dark hallway.

He discovered the full history of Omega and the workings, the beating heart, of the meme.

The creators—MCF—were Jean-Paul Martine, Joi Chang, and Merta Frohike. Omega's holy trinity.

A journal of almost daily entries, each initialed "JPM," detailed the birth of the group. A young attorney named Noel Greyson began to meet with some friends in his Soho apartment. At first, their gatherings of about a dozen radical thinkers revolved around drinking beer and complaining about politics, but the discussions took a turn toward philosophy and religion. Then the inseparability of politics and religion. Together, they began to study the works of Sun Tzu, Machiavelli, and Hitler, as well as the best-known religious writings: the Koran, the Torah, and the Christian Bible.

The group gave itself a name: Omega.

Rubbing his chin, Niccolo wondered, *Why choose Omega?*

Over the course of the late-night meetings, three attendees discovered their common interest in languages.

Jean-Paul Martine's field was anthropological linguistics. An honor graduate of Lancaster University, he was paying off his loans by writing grants for nonprofit agencies.

Joi Chang had studied Eastern and Middle Eastern languages at the University of Koln and then took over management of an import-export firm.

Merta Frohike was wrapping up her doctorate in comparative linguistics at the University of Cambridge.

Omega has not since seen such a collection of language experts. Niccolo sipped water from the glass and kept reading.

In Greyson's basement, huddled before tables that they scattered with notepads, they sketched out a radical idea: the creation of a language. It had to meet three criteria: it should be incomprehensible to all but the initiated, it should be extremely persuasive, and it should effect in the reader, speaker, or listener deep emotion. Awe, mystery, majesty, deference, fear.

As they began to craft the language, they compiled their writings into chapters, each titled *The Book of—*. The books were then organized into an "Omega bible," which they called the Librah Vae-ta.

The Book of Life.

Greyson established a hierarchy and formalized his role as leader. Martine, Chang, and Frohike taught him the intricacies of the language so that he could read it, speak it, and teach it.

With the mystique of the new language, and buoyed by a code of precepts, the group grew by word of mouth. Once a handful of rag-tag defectors from other faiths, Omega began to attract members from all levels of society, from the barely middle-class to the bourgeoisie.

Those with scientific, linguistic, and statistical skills were quietly recruited.

Niccolo read: *New converts are taught the language but are forbidden to handle the Librah Vae-ta.* He thought, *Only the Abbas, five generations of them, allowed to touch the Librah Vae-ta. Never the membership.* He shook his head. *More deeply reinforcing the aura of sanctity. Mystery. Rank.*

MCF's theories mutated into documented evidence as they discovered that their objectives were becoming reality. It was clear that the new language slipped across neurophysiological barriers, like a fast-acting chemical, in ways that they themselves did not fully understand.

They began to test the language on unsuspecting subjects. About seventy percent of those regularly exposed to the language became "addicted," showing all the textbook symptoms of drug dependency. The notes described evidence that, when put through a battery of psychological tests, this segment showed deep insecurity, high suggestibility, strong attraction to paranormal belief, and "creative delusion."

He read: *Once fluent in the language, they slide out of society, quitting their jobs, abandoning their families, devoting themselves with every fiber to the glory of Omega.*

And thought: *Conversion brings zeal, the mission of highest purpose. Like soldiers rallying, marching under a new flag. The born again.*

About fifteen percent were "attracted but not addicted."

Another ten percent were unaffected. They seemed immune to the language, like the subject who remains fully alert after taking a sedative.

The last page ended with heavily underlined notes.

"For the remaining five percent, near-lethal effects are documented. EXTREME CAUTION MUST BE EXERCISED."

Near lethal? The next question jolted him. *Reymann?!*

At the same time that he heard the clicks of her heels, he smelled her. Lavender and honey. Without turning, he whispered, "Reymann."

Volante slid into the chair beside him, glanced at the empty pitcher and then her wristwatch, and crossed her legs.

"Reymann," he croaked. "One of the indeterminate five percent. No immunity to it whatsoever. The language killed him."

She tipped her head. "It's clear what MCF wanted to establish: a dependent, tithing discipleship. Look at their ledgers. Their fledgling congregation of believers translated into enormous wealth. What they created worked—"

"But they didn't realize its full potential. Its power."

We always knew that the language possessed some sort of magnetizing quality, but a language that can kill? Energy buzzed through his forehead and limbs. *We must harness this for the empire! But how?*

Out of the corner of his eye, he studied her face, wondering if he would detect any sign of fear. What he saw was exultation, the glow of victory. *This is a coup of enormous value, and she knows it.*

She stood, moving toward the box and gracefully taking the lid in her hand. "I assume that you want to take these with you."

He reached out to block her hand with his own, and the heat of her skin was startling. Had he ever touched her before? *Do not move them, for now.*

"No. They stay here."

Her eyes fluttered—he thought he could observe the machinery of her mind calculating—then fixed. "Very well." In a moment, she had transferred all the documents back into the box and replaced the lid.

He stood squarely before her and looked her full in the face. "You know that this is a discovery beyond estimation. The full credit is yours, Franca. Excellent work."

Her body seemed to expand, filling the space above and between them, and her hazel eyes glittered. "Thank you, Abba."

"I know the way out."

As he strode down the front stairs into the darkness, he thought, *What sort of reward does she anticipate?*

Volante walked to the kitchen, the empty water pitcher gripped in one fist.

Like this container, she thought. *He is empty, hungry to be filled with power. With fear. He will believe that the MCF discovery cements everything. But when he failed to protect the Librah Vae-ta, he lost credibility. How long until my disciples demand more competent leadership?*

She flung the pitcher into the steel sink and watched it shatter.

CHAPTER 15

He stepped into the Officia Abba, turning over in his mind the sermon he had just delivered in the sanctuary. As the audience was graced with The Words of Reckoning, there had been a buzz in the air, a vibration just below the surface. Dark tensions swelling in the disciples, a pulsing, almost sexual heat.

Walking to the bathroom, Niccolo relieved himself, washed his hands, stepped back into the quiet room, and was approaching the bank of computers at the far wall when he heard a tap at the door.

The number who would dare spontaneous intrusion into his private chamber was extremely small.

Pulling open the door, he was faced by a slight woman. Her plain, unfitted dress swung almost to the floor. Above the plastic pearls encircling her neck, her face was pallid, accentuating eyes that seemed too large and dark to be real.

Confusion brought a deep frown to his forehead. *Her? Our business was settled long ago.*

Pressing her palms together, she looked down at her canvas shoes. "Abbah way non push tah..."

"What do you want?" He added, more softly, "Tamar, what is it?"

She trembled so violently that he thought she might collapse. Pulling in a huge breath, she whispered, "Abba, may I speak with you?"

Quickly juggling what she might want to say or the answers that she might be seeking, he swung his palm toward the conference table at the center of the room. *Whatever she wants, let's get it over with.*

He took the seat at the head of the table, and she folded herself into the chair at his right.

"We have not spoken in many years, Tamar," he said. "There has been no need for discussion. Our dealings were closed, were they not?"

Tamar dropped her head into her thin hands, then raised her eyes to meet his. He saw her lips trembling. "Yes, Abba, our dealings were closed." She paused. "Almost."

"What do you mean?"

She drew a heavy sigh. "All those years ago, I understood your need for the meh-ben. I accepted your instructions, accepted the gift of the word that you had chosen me to receive. The holy word that you spoke into my ear, your covenant with me—*me!*—that brought the wondrous spark of the meh-ben." She gulped in a breath.

Now I see where this is going. He began to craft a response.

"And I rejoiced when your word came to pass." She closed her eyes, seeming to relive beautiful memories. Her hands moved down to press against her belly. "I knew the glory of my ripening. I grew full in the glory of Highest Omega, felt the truth made flesh, swelling within me. I felt the new meh-ben in me, the presence of Omega and the holy Abba, in my own body." She leaned toward him, eyes glistening, her hands raised in supplication. "I was your chosen vessel."

He slid one hand toward her. "But why did I demand the Rite of Bhata?" *Abortion.*

Nodding, she crumbled into sobs.

This is why. He hardened his voice with a guttural tone. "Tamar, the choice for the vessel of Omega must be absolute. There could be no doubt, not a shred of uncertainty." He held her with fixed eyes. "You weren't the right one."

Omega giveth, Omega taketh away.

"You did not ask this question at the time. Why has it taken you so long to come to me for an explanation?"

"I," she gulped, "I was afraid, Abba." She wiped the back of one hand across her mouth and sat for a long minute, breathing rapidly. Eyes lowered, she whispered, "Padarah oh meh-ga."

Indeed.

He stood and took her elbow to herd her toward the door. Still sniffling, she disappeared into the hallway.

Crossing the now-empty room, he felt the impulse tiptoe upon him. Tamar's question, her melodrama, and sodden face goaded at him like a spoiled meat. He needed to cleanse his interior palate. He strode to a cabinet at the far wall, opened it, and took in the sight of hundreds of palm-size brochures: the literature that was handed to each Dosa at the beginning of training. He picked one up and gazed at its cover.

Ω

He walked back to the door and locked it.

Then, seated in the executive chair where, at the last meeting of Elders, he had stood next to her, his fingers hovering just over her creamy skin, he opened the brochure. The memory of her set up seismic tremors in his mind and body. He began to read the text in a hoarse whisper.

"Abbah way non vash ah parateh, sho day..."

Images and sensations blazed through him. Her hair, swirling like a galaxy. The smell of her hidden anger, her mouth like the barrel of a gun. He felt his chest expand, his stomach roll. Her eyes as black and heinous as the abyss, raging with the fire of destruction, the infinity of torment, her mind a pit of brimstone. His Armageddon.

His Abaddon.

He kept reading—he kept swelling. The trumpets sounded in his veins, the clouds opened into the fullness of thunder; the river flooded through his dry land, bringing the gnashing of teeth.

He saw the glowing altar where he would tie her: naked, helpless, his toy, his drug, his slave. Soon.

Padarah oh meh-ga...

His head fell against the back of the chair, his eyes squeezed tightly as need burned through him. His holy guidance was a dripping sore, a mutilated sacrifice.

The sins of the fathers!!

His sin crashed around him. In seconds, he would explode.

CHAPTER 16

"This way." Gatsby turned the key in the lock and ushered Sanderson into the lobby. He stopped to admire the Victorian furnishings and mirrors for a moment before she nudged him toward the staircase.

Once landed on the second floor, she pushed her door open. "It's not much, but it's home."

Sanderson stepped inside the flat. In her sparsely furnished living room, he turned left and right, then peeked into her office and saw the enormous mahogany desk. A smile stole over his face. "My god, you still have that monster?"

Memory sped through her: Woody helping her to haul the desk into the tiny apartment they had shared in Seattle. *Am I resurrecting ghosts that shouldn't be disturbed?* She studied his profile as the thought prickled at her, took his wool jacket, and hung it in the hall closet. "Want something? Tea? Beer?"

He shook his head. "Thanks, no. I just had lunch at the hotel. Let's get started."

She pulled a chair from the living room into the office and motioned for him to seat himself. The Baber case sat in the middle of the desk. Eyeing the digital keypad, he muttered, "The CIS must really want this thing kept off the radar."

She punched in the ten-digit sequence. The locks popped, and she pulled the book from the foam molding, sat it on the desktop, and carefully opened it to the first page.

As his eyes skittered across the writing, a frown darkened his face. "Astounding...what is it called?"

She shrugged. "I don't have an official referent, so I borrowed the last segment of the ID code and call it the Gahana." She searched his face for clues. "What do you think?"

He braced his hands atop the desk. "Gibberish or genius, that's my guess." He stared harder. "What do you know about the authors? Or about the guy who died?"

"Nothing about the writers. All the CIS agent told me is the code name and that the man was found in his home, holding this book, in a pool of his own blood."

"Code name?"

"The code name for the case." She paused, then told him. "RED-MK7."

"Wow." His eyebrows rose. "What have you determined so far?"

"I have a good start on a syllabary." She tugged a pocket folder down from her desk shelf and pulled a handful of papers from it. "Here. It's a grid of the characters along with the frequency of appearance. I've made some headway on the interrelationships. The hieroglyphic for water, equivalent to the Latin letter *n,* almost always appears at the end of a set—and what I'm thinking of as a set, or a word, is separated from the following set by a space."

He nodded, turning his lips.

"And this symbol," she pointed, "the half moon, appears only before and after sets. I think it indicates past and future tense." She paused. "I'm convinced that this is some kind of religious text."

"Why do you say that?" He turned to her with a frown.

"Because of the choice of orthographies. Modern and extinct languages number in the thousands, and yet these six systems were chosen. Latin, Aramaic, Hebrew, Arabic, and Greek—all of them are connected with the great religious texts. Aramaic was spoken during the lifetime of Jesus."

The surreal fact struck her, as if she'd just truly grasped it, that she was sitting in her office with him, fifteen years after the holocaust of their breakup, and casually discussing ancient writing systems.

Semantically yours?! Woody, how could you leave me and then stalk me under a cyber pseudonym?

She swallowed, struggling for composure, before continuing. "Th...the Christian Bible was written, rewritten, and translated into Greek and Latin. And this early version of Egyptian hieroglyphics was used only for sacred writing. It wasn't the language of the people, only of the hierophant. I think someone wants this book to look like a holy scripture but has used a language so complicated that no one else can read it."

"Except the priests," he offered, propping his elbows on his knees, chin in hand. "Institutionalized exclusivity. Allowing only the sanctified access to literature."

"*Hiero* glyphics. Sacred writing."

They nodded at each other.

"And there's this." She pointed to the symbol in the top margin of the page.

"An omega?"

"As in alpha omega, the beginning and the end. It's on every page. Singer said that he believes that the man who died was part of a cult called Omega."

Singer's voice rumbled through her mind: *Everything I tell you is absolutely confidential. It must not be discussed with anyone. Anyone.*

She felt her heart racing. *An open-and-shut case of disregard for authority, no doubt about that—but how would Singer know that I talked with Woody? Even if he finds out, is the risk worth it?* Her eyes moved up to the humming computer monitor. *If I bring the book back without any real answers, the worst I'll suffer is Singer's disappointment. But if I bring it back along with a conclusive translation that I was able to achieve with Woody's help? Approval. Commendation.*

Her heart pounded harder. *I'm violating Singer's order, but doing so might solve the case.*

She scanned Sanderson out of the corner of her eye. *And I have to know if these declarations of undying love are real or just a convenient alibi.*

Swallowing against a knot in her throat, she thought, *It's done now.*

Sanderson appeared not to have seen any sign of her internal wrangling; he was staring through his fists at the carpet. "What else did the CIS tell you about his death?"

"The guy's house alarm went off in the middle of the night. When guards arrived, they saw a trail of blood leading down a hallway, where he tripped the alarm and then fell over dead."

"Dead, just like that?"

"Dead from extreme blood loss. Hemorrhaged from his pores."

Sanderson's eyes widened. "Jesus. If only we could look at the body. Would that be possible?"

Gatsby felt her stomach tighten. "I'm not even supposed to be telling you any of this, so no."

He shook his head. "You've never had any respect for authority figures."

She turned back and forth in her chair. "Just compensating for the overly obedient, as the girl who...ah, never mind."

His forehead bunched. "No, what?"

She leaned back in her chair, and a smile pulled at her lips. "I just thought of a girl that I knew in high school." She drew out the word with great exaggeration, "My nemesis, Vic-TOR-ia."

He peered at her with a sly grin. "I never knew you had a nemesis. Do tell."

"Victoria Donahue. I was forced to sit near her because of our last names. She was a snotty rich bitch who wanted to destroy the soul of every living thing. Even her parents were terrified of her. I remember her using the phrase *just compensating for the overly obedient* anytime she got in trouble. She terrorized me endlessly over my name, my clothes, my friends, anything. Finally, I'd had enough. Just before her first class, I ambushed her in a busy hallway, covered her with whipped cream and ketchup, tore off her designer skirt, and ran."

"You hellion." He grinned.

"Yeah." The smile on her face faded. "The crazy thing was that she saved my life."

He frowned. "What happened?"

"I was jogging home after school and saw her standing near the admin wing with her coven of friends, smoking designer cigarettes. It was the dead of winter, freezing cold. I hit a puddle that had iced over, tumbled to the concrete, hit my head, and blacked out."

"Ouch." His eyebrows knitted.

"But when I came to, there's Victoria kneeling over me, saying, 'Oh my god, Gatsby, are you okay?!' She had run inside to grab the school nurse and call the paramedics. If she hadn't, I would have faced hypothermia or worse."

He steepled his fingers together. "What brought on the attack of altruism?"

"I don't know." She gazed past him. "With all the hatred between us, and my act of revenge, I would have expected her to leave me there to freeze—she had all the motivation in the world. Instead, she saved me."

He nodded, as if visualizing the scene. "What happened then?"

"We actually became good friends. The whole dynamic changed. Something had shifted in her, some deep piece of fear or anger." She sighed. "The next semester, her parents shipped her off to a Catholic school, and I never heard from her again."

"When we ever go out for burgers, remind me to remove the ketchup or whipping cream from the table, all right?"

They chuckled in unison.

Lots of stories from my past that I would have told you, Woody, if only you'd stuck around to hear them. The old hurts blanketed her like a shroud. Glancing toward the Gahana, she ran her fingers through her hair and said, "Come on, enough reminiscing. Let's take a look at this."

Wheeling his chair closer, he nodded.

"Basically, we've got morphology from seven different language systems, most of which were in use before the Common Era, each with its own sets of rules and syntax. Extracting bits and pieces from each language would destroy the semantic relationships, like trying to fit together pieces from disparate puzzles. And the authors weren't aware that—" She frowned.

He waited, then prodded, "That?"

"I just thought of something. Maybe they knew exactly what they were doing," she moved closer to the book, "and found a way to bypass the linear process of decryption. Maybe they created an orthography that isn't meant to be understood with standard analysis tools, that can only be evaluated at a more gestalt level. More right brain."

"Emotion over logic?"

She crossed her arms over her stomach. "Exactly."

He leaned back in the chair, his eyes shifting left and right. "Even if that's true, we still need to figure out exactly what this language does to the neurology." His eyebrows hitched. "It doesn't seem to affect the two of us—that I can tell, anyway."

She scooted closer. "What do you suggest?"

"Testing. We find a subject, someone who doesn't know anything about this book and can be trusted to keep quiet about it. We'd run some baseline cognition tests. In a proper lab, I'd do neural scanning, EEG, even blood work." He scratched his nose. "Obviously, it would take pulling some major strings, and you don't have the book for much longer, right?"

She nodded.

"We'd have to line up the facilities and a subject and move fast." He shook his head. "I'll call my department and invent a good reason as to why I need to spend some more time in London." His face softened. "As if seeing you again weren't enough."

"I'm sure you'll devise something." *Is it really enough?* She wondered if the skepticism showed in the tight smile. *Your talent for deception is astounding.*

Pressing his hands together, he stared into his lap. "The British Museum must have connections with labs and universities. Could you..."

"Wait a second." She spun toward him, her eyes widening with new excitement. "I've got an idea. Except...damn it, I've been told not to involve anyone else." She pictured Singer's black suit and wondered about the consequences of the idea that was already brewing. *Do I add another stick to my pyre?*

"What?"

"The friend who put me in touch with Pryce and therefore with you. Celia. She's a hypnotherapist. She might be able to help us with access to a lab."

Sanderson pulled forward. "A hypnotherapist? She would really help in analyzing the language. As I understand it, hypnosis is all about directed language."

Gatsby wheeled her chair toward the far end of the desk and reached for the phone. Her hand hovered in the air.

She stared at Sanderson for a long moment, sighed, and began pressing buttons. "I'll see if I can reach her. She never answers her phone in the evenings."

CHAPTER 17

At first glance, it reminded her of a clunky salon hairdryer from the 1950s. Attached to the cushioned seat was an apparatus that lowered over the head, completely covering the subject's face. Holes in the sides and top provided ventilation. The cables running from the headset into a wide console fed images directly to the viewing panel, fifty centimeters wide, in the adjacent monitoring room.

They paced around the long, narrow room that was lined with electronics and rolling metal tables.

Gatsby set her briefcase on the floor and dropped a three-ring binder onto a nearby table. "A seated PET scanner. I've heard about them, but I didn't know that they were available for general use."

Dropping into a wheeled chair, Celia tipped her head back to inspect the ceiling. "Well, technically, they're not."

Gatsby whirled on her. "What have you done?"

She held up her palms. "Listen, babe, I hustled to get you access to this lab and the equipment you asked for, even got you a guinea pig for your brainiac test. All I ask is that you don't probe into how I did it." She tipped her chin upward. "It's my pretty ass in a sling anyway, not yours, so what do you care?"

"Aiding and abetting, that's what I care." Gatsby groaned, shaking her head. "Who's the subject?"

Celia pulled a sheet of paper from her briefcase. "Mick Parrish. Thirty-one years old, no notable emotional blockages, raised in a secular household. He's a rock musician, his on-and-off girlfriend is an actress. He came to me for smoking cessation. My bread and butter."

"Okay, the truth, does he come to you for therapy or to get laid?"

"What do you take me for?" Celia pressed a hand to her breast, gasping in mock horror. "No, I don't cross that line. He's curious about this mad science project of yours, thinks it may make him a more creative songwriter."

Gatsby rolled a chair next to her and sat. "Sounds functional and boring."

"You didn't specify a firecracker personality, darling."

A loud knock prompted them to rise and step into the monitoring room.

Gatsby opened the door for a gangly man in faded Levi's, torn at the knees, biker boots, and a black Sex Pistols t-shirt. His eyes pawed her as he grumbled in a Guinness-and-Tareyton voice, "You're the doc, eh?"

"Yes," Gatsby said, extending her hand. "Mick Parrish? Come in."

He glanced back over his shoulder. "Hey, and you too, man?"

Sanderson eased his way around Parrish and moved forward into the room as he nodded at Celia and Gatsby. "Good, everyone's here. You must be Celia."

Celia reached out for his hand. "*This* is Definite Article?" Her eyebrows rose as she glanced at Gatsby. "I've heard all the stories about you."

"Uh oh, I'm already in trouble." Sanderson withdrew his hand and stuffed it in his pocket.

"Come on." Gatsby pushed forward to herd them into the testing room. "Let's get started."

"This isn't going to keep me from fathering sprogs, right?" Parrish chuckled.

Before Celia could toss off a retort, Gatsby said, "Of course not, it's a completely harmless process."

Sanderson turned to Parrish. "We're going to test your cognition. First, we'll ask you some simple questions. Then we'll get you set up in this imager and have you view images and listen to some recorded sounds. We'll monitor what happens in different parts of your brain, and then we're done."

"And I get my hundred quid, right?"

Gatsby shot a glare at Celia, who then glared at Parrish. "Quit joking, Mick. You get a mind-altering experience."

Parrish harrumphed, "Fair enough." Humming "Anarchy in the U.K.," he groped at the back pocket of his jeans as if hunting for a cigarette.

Sanderson moved toward the center of the room. "Mick, if you could sit over here." As Parrish dropped into a wheeled chair, Sanderson also sat, facing him, and pulled out a notebook. "Just relax and make yourself comfortable."

Parrish hooked one ankle on top of the opposite knee and glowered at Sanderson, his eyes darting.

"Great. I'm going to ask you twenty-five questions. Just say the first thing that comes to mind, and don't worry about being right or wrong. Okay?"

Parrish shrugged. "Got it."

Sanderson started reading through questions that covered simple math, language, and world history. The logic questions were constructed as stories or puzzles. The last two questions probed Parrish's knowledge of social conventions and what the majority of people would consider "immoral."

As Parrish gave his responses, he thrummed his fingers on his thigh and glanced up at the ceiling or into his lap. Gatsby jotted his answers on a notepad as well as observational notes: *Limited vocabulary but solid average intelligence. Kinesthetic descriptors.*

"Excellent," Sanderson said after the last question. "Not so tough, huh? Do you want some water or anything?"

Parrish slouched further down in the chair and shook his head.

"Gatsby, do you have the binders?"

She pulled a vinyl view binder from her briefcase and sighed. *One more act to add to my growing rap sheet.* She had carefully scanned the first eight pages of the Gahana and gathered them into the binder, which secured with a plastic slide-on clip. She tried to breathe away the flutter of anxiety in her stomach as she handed the binder to Parrish.

Sanderson said, "What you'll see on the first page is just text, and you won't recognize the language, but don't worry about that. We'd like you to just try to follow along as Gatsby reads it out loud."

Parrish sat straighter, his eyes brightening. He flipped the binder open and stared into the pages. A frown crossed his face. "Weird."

Flipping open her own binder, Gatsby started reading, referring to her notes and the guesses she'd made about the speech sounds.

"Abbah way nom watta barateh o day vashla need reh-me..."

Sanderson watched, scratching his chin, while Celia glanced between Gatsby and Parrish.

As she finished the first page, Gatsby looked up at Parrish. His pupils had dilated, moisture glistened on his forehead, and his jugular bobbed like a bandleader. She shot a glance at Sanderson, whose wide-eyed expression seemed to say, *I see it, all right,* and continued.

When she had finished the third page, Sanderson motioned for Parrish to set his binder on the counter at his left.

"Mick, are you okay?"

Parrish gripped the arms of the chair. "Just a little lightheaded."

Sanderson scribbled notes. "Let us know if you have any other unusual sensations. Okay, now we're going to run through the questions again."

Parrish nodded.

Sanderson cleared his throat and began. "What is the sum of ten and eleven?"

"Twenty-one."

"How would you say good morning to a French person?"

"Ahmm." Parrish frowned, struggling. "Guten, no. Wait, yeah, guten tag." Only minutes before, he had given the answer *bonjour* with no hesitation.

"Which period occurred earlier in history, the Middle Ages or the Bronze Age?"

"The...well, the...ahm, I guess it would be...the Middle..." Parrish slapped his palms against his thighs and snorted. "Damn."

"No problem," Sanderson said. "Let's move on. If A-B-C is equal to 1-2-3, what is D-E-F equal to?"

Scratching his head, Parrish stared into his lap. His head swayed as he chewed at his lower lip. His eyes scrunched shut, and he finally blew out a long sigh. "I can't, ahm...dunno."

When he had finished the set of questions, Sanderson said, "We're done with the baseline evaluation, so just relax for a few minutes while I make some notes."

"Right." Parrish slouched in the chair, stretching his legs out, and crossed brawny, tattooed arms over his chest.

Celia stood, silently mouthing *bathroom,* and left the room.

Gatsby reached for her notebook and the pen she'd stowed behind her ear and wrote. *After reading, cognition significantly impaired.* She handed the notebook to Sanderson, who read the words and muttered, "No kidding."

Turning to face Parrish, Sanderson said, "Okay, Mick, ready for the fun part?"

Parrish shrugged. "Let's do it."

"Okay." Sanderson pulled something from the seat of the PET scanner, which looked much like a dental chair, and motioned for Parrish to sit there. He held up something that resembled a rubber swimming cap. Attached to the cap were a dozen white nodes, and a thin wire dangled from each node. As Parrish wiggled to get comfortable in the chair, Sanderson stepped forward and began stretching the cap onto the crown of Parrish's head.

"You probably know that part of what makes the brain operate is electricity. It's an electrochemical organ. This sensor monitors the electrical impulses that your brain generates while we do the next section of text, and it sends the signals to an EEG recorder in the other room."

Parrish frowned, and his eyes darkened. "A lie detector?"

"Nope, nothing of the kind. We won't be asking you any questions, and you won't have to do anything except listen and move your eyes. You okay with that?"

Parrish shrugged, looking down. "Yeah. Sure."

"Great."

Parrish drummed his feet on the floor as Sanderson finished adjusting the cap and then checked the connections of the wires to the console behind the chair. After stepping back to Parrish's side, Sanderson opened a compartment recessed into the arm of the chair, pulled out a silver object, and pressed it down onto Parrish's index finger. "This monitors your heart rate."

Parrish looked down at his hand and flexed his fingers.

Sanderson turned toward a steel table, retrieved something from the shiny surface, and turned around holding up a syringe.

Parrish's eyes widened. "Hey!"

He jerked forward and glanced toward Celia, who was standing by the door at the other end of the room.

"Mick, it's fine." Celia stepped toward him, her hands stowed in the pockets of her long jacket. "It's standard procedure for PET scans. People have them done every day. I've had one," she grinned, "and believe me, you've done chemicals far more dangerous than this."

Parrish sat back in the chair. "What is it?"

Sanderson gazed at him while tapping a fingernail against the syringe to remove bubbles. "A radionuclide. Basically, a dye. As the chemical breaks down, it emits positrons, which create gamma rays that the scanner detects. The software in the other room analyzes the information and creates an image for us. This way we can see what's happening in your brain while we do the test."

Parrish was now grinning wickedly. "Cool."

Sanderson rubbed Parrish's forearm with an alcohol swipe, did the injection, and taped down a hunk of gauze with a smiley face Band-Aid.

"Oh man," Parrish muttered, peering at his arm and humming "Sympathy for the Devil."

Sanderson rose, reaching toward an egg-shaped apparatus behind Parrish's head. "Okay, we're getting ready for launch." He began to lower the bell over Parrish's head. "This thing is called a Syncap. It houses sensors that will create the images we'll be watching. It can also show blood flow and glucose metabolization, but we're just going to focus on your neural activity."

The Syncap dropped, making loud clicks as stabilizing pieces locked into place. Parrish blew out a deep lungful of air.

Celia looked at Gatsby and whispered, "We all should have signed waivers."

"Don't worry. None of this will hurt him in any way." *I hope.*

"Doing okay?" Sanderson said. "Don't move your head, just answer out loud."

"Fine."

"You should see a small screen right in front of your eyes. No images yet, just a black screen. Do you see it?"

"Yeah."

"Good. And this is a microphone." Sanderson took Parrish's hand, moved it up to his chin, and helped him to tap one finger against a plastic bar that curved from his ear around toward his mouth. "There are speakers on the inside of the Syncap. We'll be talking you through the whole thing."

Sanderson reached toward the counter and grabbed a lightweight blanket that lay folded there. He pulled it over Parrish's lap.

"That's it," he said in a cheery voice, "we're good to go."

"Good to go," Parrish grunted.

Gatsby, Sanderson, and Celia moved into the monitoring room. Gatsby checked the audio equipment. "Mick, can you hear me?"

"Uh huh."

"Just relax. We'll start in a minute," she said.

"Relax?" His voice crackled over the system. "Yeah, right." He started to hum "Rocket Man."

Sanderson sat before the computer keyboard and typed commands. Two rectangular images, arranged vertically, appeared on the overhead monitor: each image looked like an open book with lines of script written in Hebrew.

"Okay, Mick, look at the screen. Now you should see two images, one above the other. Can you see them?"

There was a pause. "Uh...yeah, I see it."

Sanderson launched an audio program and clicked Play. A male voice began flowing from the desktop speakers, the words corresponding to those shown in the image. Sanderson clicked Pause and glanced at Celia and Gatsby.

"Ready?"

They nodded.

He leaned toward the microphone. "Mick, are you ready?"

"Rock and roll, man."

Gatsby and Celia slid into wheeled chairs at the console. Gatsby commandeered the switches and keys that set the functions of the neural scanner and the electroencephalographic trace-recorder. She keyed a long set of commands into her own keyboard, and they all watched as a color image appeared on the monitor in a new viewing box, separate from the image of the Hebrew writing. Parrish's brain.

What would an image of my brain look like? Gatsby wondered. She remembered telling Singer that she would return the book on the "thirty-third" and shoved the memory away.

She moved the EEG trace-recorder on the counter off to her left. The device opened like a notebook PC; a thin screen flipped upward and then lit up. After the operating system launched, wavy lines began to ripple across the screen. As Sanderson had explained earlier, the lines were Parrish's brain waves being received and recorded.

"Ready," she said.

Sanderson murmured "Show time." He clicked Play.

The voice flowed from the speakers. All three turned their attention to a monitor that hung just above eye level.

Gatsby leaned toward the microphone. "Mick, let your eyes move across the words as if you were reading them. We know you don't read Hebrew—that doesn't matter, okay?"

"Got it." His voice was muffled.

Celia frowned up at the image of the writing. "What is that, the Dead Sea Scrolls?"

Gatsby turned toward her. "The Torah."

"We're recording," Sanderson said. His fingers flew over the keyboard. The images of the left and right hemispheres shifted.

"Explain these to me," Celia said, staring at the multicolored images, "what are we looking at?"

Sanderson spoke rapidly. "Different parts of the brain have adapted for specialized functions. Some areas handle language processing, some your sense of time, some monitor appetite, some regulate speech and muscle control." He pointed an index finger toward the monitor. "These are the areas that fire under emotional stress. Joy, sorrow, hate, fear, and so on."

The disembodied voice intoned:

"On the Day of Atonement, it is forbidden to eat and to drink, to wash, to anoint, to lace on shoes, and to hold sexual intercourse. A king and a bride may wash their faces..."

Celia asked, "What's going on there?"

All eyes rose to the monitor. Some yellow-colored areas in the left hemisphere had changed to dark red.

Sanderson spoke up, "Activity in Wernicke's area, in the left temporal lobe, the area that allows you to analyze and understand spoken language."

"Is anything else happening?" Gatsby asked.

They were silent for a few minutes, watching as the voice droned and the images refreshed every thirty seconds.

"No. That's it," Sanderson said. "We're at six minutes, more than enough for diagnostic purposes. All systems green on the recorders?"

Gatsby quickly checked the equipment. "Yes." She grabbed the microphone. "You doing okay, Mick?"

"Yeah," Parrish muttered.

"We're moving on to the second part of this segment. Hang on."

Within a minute, Gatsby and Sanderson had loaded the programs with the second sample: pages and readings from the Pali Canon. Again, they heard a male voice reading; this one sounded Japanese or Korean.

"What are we listening to now?" Celia asked.

Gatsby replied, "The Theravada Buddhists wrote down their scriptures in the last century BCE. The text is called the Pali Canon...Pali is the name of the language. In scholarship circles, it's thought to be one of the primary sources of Buddhist philosophy."

Celia's eyes shifted to Sanderson, who was pointing up at the screen and murmuring, "Look at this."

Over the speakers, they heard:

"What is the distinguishing characteristic of sustained thought? The distinguishing characteristic of sustained thought, your majesty, is continual examination. Give me an analogy. Just as, your majesty, when a gong is struck and continues resounding afterwards, indeed so the striking is to be understood as applied thought, and the continuance of the resounding as sustained thought..."

"I see a lot more blue and green over there," Gatsby said, pointing.

"That's the right hemisphere," Sanderson said. "Check his EEG."

Gatsby turned to the EEG recorder. Her eyes widened, and she looked back toward him. "Low theta. It looks like it's headed for delta."

Celia said, "A deep relaxation state."

"*The* deep relaxation state," Sanderson said. After checking on Parrish and looking at the timer, he said, "Okay, we're good, let's move on."

As they loaded the third sample, Sanderson whispered, "Thy kingdom come."

The recorded voice started: male, with what Gatsby had heard called a Midwest accent, the neutral, nonaccented speech that North American television anchors worked to perfect.

"What's this?" Celia asked.

"Bet you can guess," Sanderson said.

They heard:

"...and bound him a thousand years, and cast him into the bottomless pit, and shut him up, and set a seal upon him, that he should deceive the nations no more, till the thousand years should be fulfilled, and that he must be loosed a little season, and I saw thrones, and they sat upon them, and I saw the souls of them that were beheaded for the witness..."

"Mick, do you see the images?" Gatsby said into the microphone.

"Yeah, I see them." Parrish's voice carried an undertow of irritation. His hands shuffled rapidly up and down on his thighs.

"Look," Gatsby said. On the EEG recording screen, they saw a series of abrupt spikes.

"What's he doing?" Celia asked.

Sanderson's eyes moved across the neural images, watching as the sections changed at each refresh. "Increased activity, the red areas, over here in the temporal lobes, parts of the brain linked to strong emotion. They also become more active when high amounts of adrenaline or testosterone are produced."

They peered through the glass window into the testing room. Parrish was fidgeting in the chair, his fingertips carving light blue highways into the fabric of his jeans, his feet tapping arhythmically. He barked into his microphone, "Turn it up! Louder!"

"Okay, Mick, we're turning it up." Turning to Gatsby, Sanderson whispered, "Don't touch anything."

She nodded and scribbled notes: *Sample from Christian Bible, Revelation, increased physical movements, agitation.*

What had she said to Singer? *Somewhere in the bible, Revelation I think, the Christian God declared himself the alpha and the omega, the beginning and the end.*

"What's he saying?" Parrish shouted. He crossed one leg over the other, uncrossed it, then crossed it again.

"Unbelievable," Celia whispered.

"Let's load the next one," Sanderson said. His fingers flew across the keys as he started the fourth sample: pages and readings from the Koran.

The voice carried a smoky Arabic accent:

"He created the heavens and the earth with truth, and He formed you, then made goodly your forms, and to Him is the ultimate resort. He knows what is in the heavens and the earth, and He knows what you hide and what you manifest; and Allah is cognizant of what is in your hearts. Has there not come to you the story of those who disbelieved, then tasted the evil result of their conduct, and they suffered painful punishment?"

Gatsby's eyes widened as she peered up at the monitor. "Woody, what does this mean?"

They all stared: brain sectors were changing colors at a rapid rate; green to blue, yellow to red and back to yellow, orange to red, violet to solid black.

"Damn it!" Parrish shouted, his feet starting to bang against the tile.

"Are you okay?" Gatsby asked.

"It's just...God!" His voice quavered. "Feels like my head is itching, or, you know?" His fingers hammered against the armrests. "I feel like...I can't think of the right word. Hungry, no, that's...shit! Why can't I think what I wanna say?"

Sanderson and Gatsby exchanged grim glances.

Gatsby reached for the microphone. "Any physical sensations? Any pain? If you do, we'll stop right now."

"I do *not* like this," Celia whispered.

There was a pause, then Parrish's muffled voice, quieter but edged with anger, "Ahm, no, nothing like that! I just want, want to kick something over, ya know, smash something."

Sanderson pointed toward the overhead screen as he shook his head in amazement. "Look! The amygdala and temporal lobes...the limbic system."

Gatsby had wheeled her chair up to the EEG recorder. "Woody, look at these tracings."

Sanderson spun over next to her. As he stared at the screen, his eyes widened. "Off the chart!" He hustled back to the console below the overhead monitor and looked up at it. Gatsby moved up next to him.

Celia pushed forward to peer over their shoulders. "For god's sake, what's happening?"

Sanderson pointed to the images on the monitor. "Right there! See those growing red streaks and blotches? They're all in the temporal lobe, the hypothalamus, and the amygdala. There's a huge body of work that Lorenz did in the sixties on aggression, working with both animal and human subjects. Stimulation or damage to these areas causes aggressive, unpredictable, often violent behavior.

Testosterone overdose can do the same thing. He's showing all the signs."

"Cats went waltzing!" Parrish shouted.

They all frowned at each other, their lips working.

"Let's run the last test and get the hell out of here," Gatsby muttered.

"Agreed," Sanderson growled. "Loading now."

The images projected onto Parrish's miniscreen were the first four pages of the Omega text, which Gatsby had carefully scanned. She had recorded herself reading the text and then electronically modulated the recording to make the voice sound male.

Gatsby whispered, "Remember, you never saw *any* of this. You were never here."

Celia and Sanderson nodded and gazed up at the monitor as the deep voice began to roll around them.

"Abbah way nom watta barateh o day vashla need rey-meh..."

Gatsby turned to look at Parrish. His body twitched, and his head jerked back and forth, making the wires that trailed to the console behind him swing crazily.

Sanderson had popped out of his chair to move closer to the monitor. He whispered, "I don't believe this."

"Pressure monkeys! Chocolate muck the rubber stamping neon! Ahhh ssshit! Uterus rage coated blood..."

"Jesus, he's losing it!" Celia snapped.

Sanderson stared at the monitor, seemingly oblivious to Parrish's frantic word salad. "There! See these almond-shaped areas, deep in the median temporal lobes? See how they're activating?"

"I see them," Gatsby said, feeling her heart thudding. "What's going on?"

"Hoses dunk my love in the canyon! Aaagh!"

"This type of activity, in these parts of the brain, is exactly what neurochemists find in test subjects they've injected with heroin or cocaine. And that band of red, right there, indicates extreme activity in the amygdala. Ground zero for aggression! It's been shown that electrical stimulation of the amygdala brings on violent attacks, even homicide."

"What the hell are you saying?" Celia sputtered, staring at Parrish, her eyes bulging. She jumped toward the door of the testing room. "We need to end this right now and get him out of there!"

"Sleep extreme! Extreeeeme! Rat PISSING coolmoneygads allowanna..."

Parrish was crawling out of the chair, chomping, wires popping from the rubber EEG cap, his hands spread and grasping convulsively at the air as he fell to his knees.

They dashed into the testing room. Sanderson grabbed Parrish's neck and turned his head upward to check his pupils. Gatsby knelt and felt for his pulse.

"ArrrhghghOOOOO bebebebe uhhhhhh..." Parrish babbled. His legs kicked, and a glob of saliva dribbled from the corner of his mouth and splattered to the tile floor. It was thick with sangria-red blood.

"Oh shit," Gatsby whispered.

"What did you do?!" Celia shouted, pinning Parrish's legs with her own to keep him from kicking her. "What the fuck did you do to him?"

"We didn't do anything to him!" Gatsby barked. She pulled a handful of paper towels from a counter and began to mop up the red puddle, the consistency of honey, by Parrish's mouth. *Just exposed him to the words that RED-MK7 was reading when he died in a pool of blood!* Her heart slammed in her chest. She used another paper towel to clean all traces of blood off his face.

Parrish's body lurched upward, and then he collapsed onto his back. As his eyes closed, his head lolled to one side.

Gatsby croaked, "Celia, get the blanket."

Celia scrambled for the blanket that had covered Parrish's lap and pulled it over him.

"Jesus Christ," Sanderson whispered.

They maneuvered Parrish to one side of the room while keeping him covered and his head elevated. Sanderson checked his eyes again, then his pulse and breathing.

"He seems okay for now," Sanderson said, tipping back onto his heels. He scrubbed the back of his hand across his forehead and exhaled. "Heart and respiration are fine, if a bit rapid. I can't find anything that looks like real damage." He paused. "I think he's asleep."

"You bastards!" Celia snapped. "You knew that your stupid experiment was going to do *this?!*"

"We had no idea what it would do!" Gatsby slid down to sit cross-legged on the floor next to Parrish. *But you knew that someone died.* She pulled in a long breath. "Let's make sure that he's okay and get him home."

Parrish began to squirm. His eyelids fluttered.

"I think he's coming around," Sanderson said, moving up to crouch by Parrish's head.

As Parrish slowly sat up, the blanket slid into his lap. His eyes, glazed and dull, moved around the room slowly, settling on one object, then another. He combed his fingers through his spiked hair and blurted, "What a mind fuck!"

He popped to his feet, shoving his fists forward, his eyes blazing, and bellowed, "Get back where you were, now! Do it! Do it again! NOW! MOVE IT, DO IT AGAIN you mother FUCKERS!!"

Celia glanced at Gatsby, then stepped forward, her body rigid and her expression stone cold. She leaned into Parrish's burning face and said quietly, "Mick. What's your girlfriend's name?"

Chaos rippled over him; anger and confusion twisted his lips. As a deep frown rippled over his face as his body drooped and he pressed the heels of his palms against his temples. "She...Ruth. Shit, I have no right to," he stammered, "oh bloody god, I'm, uh, sorry, really *really* sorry. Stupid crap head! God, I'm so fucking shitty, I'm so stupid, just a..."

"Come on."

Celia grabbed his arm and dragged him toward the monitoring room. As he stumbled forward, he continued to mutter and curse himself.

Celia talked with him while Gatsby and Sanderson shut down the equipment and hardware. They tidied the testing room, wrapping up wires and cables, and then turned off the lights and closed the door.

Celia looked up at Gatsby. "I've called a cab." Turning to Parrish, she murmured, "How do you feel?"

He hung his head, and it swayed back and forth slowly. "Ah god, I'm so sorry. I'm really fucking..."

"Don't worry about it. You just went through a very intense experience. But tell me how you feel. Headache? Nausea? Anything like that?"

He looked up at Celia with glassy eyes. "I'm okay. Just tired." His eyes fluttered closed for a moment, then opened. With his elbows propped on his knees, he stared down at the floor. "Tired."

Celia said, "I want you to call me first thing in the morning, but right now, go home and straight to bed. Promise me."

He nodded wearily. "Don't worry, the only thing I want right now is a pillow. And a cigarette."

Sanderson moved up to his side. "Come on. I'll walk you out and wait for the cab with you."

Parrish rose and shuffled toward the exit door. As he pushed it open, he dug in the breast pocket of his shirt, found a crumpled cigarette, and stuck it between his lips. The door snicked shut behind them.

CHAPTER 18

They scooted into their seats as the waitress approached their table. Pints of beer and the Cross Keys' infamous burgers were soon on the way. With six elbows planted on the table, they formed a human triangle.

Celia pulled a napkin from the tabletop and twisted it into a knot. "Okay, wizards. What the bollocks happened back there?"

Sanderson shook his head. "We can't draw any conclusions from one trial, but there's no doubt—we all saw it—that the last three sets of readings had extreme effects on him, and the neural results are undeniable. The languages worked like a powerful stimulant, along the lines of cocaine or meth."

Gatsby tipped forward to cup her chin in her hand. "My god. A language can do that?" An old memory of the research project that her advisor had dismissed scuttled through her mind. *The pen mightier than the sword. The pen AS sword.*

"And they triggered violent behavior and chaotic thinking. There at the end, belligerence and self-loathing." Sanderson paused while a pony-tailed waitress slid plates of burgers onto the table. "As if the logic centers were shorted out by signals from the amygdala or temporal lobes."

Gatsby peered at him. "I wonder if there's something in the semantic patterns that sets up erratic brain waves. Maybe a juxtaposition of phonemes or a specific sound set that isn't used in standard English." She gnawed on a fry and then yawned. "Christ, I've been up for twenty hours. I'm exhausted."

"Me too," Sanderson said.

Her eyes half-lidded, Celia nodded.

Gatsby rose slowly. "I'll be right back." She slid away from the table and walked down a dark hallway to the restroom.

She made her way to the last stall, peed, and walked up to the sink. Peering into the mirror, she saw a woman with disheveled hair and circles under her eyes.

Ugh. A vision of beauty, aren't...

A bray of loud laughter burst from the first stall, making her gasp and whirl around. A few giggles deteriorated into what seemed to be restrained crying. Muffled, incoherent words were buried under the sobs.

"Are you all right?" She slowly stepped toward the stall, bent down, and peered under the door.

Nothing.

What the hell?

As she pushed open the door, finding only white porcelain and tile, she felt an icy finger run down her spine.

Oh boy, oh boy...I heard *someone in there, crying...*

She whirled to look in the next stall, then the next, then opened the entrance door to stare down the hallway, her heart hammering, and then stepped back to the sink. She washed her hands and dried them with a paper towel.

(Sleep extreme! Extreeeeme! Rat PISSING coolmoneygads allowanna)

Stop it! I'm exhausted, imagining things, that's all! She closed her eyes, sucked in a long breath, blew it out, and stepped into the dim hallway; where it opened to the dining room, she spied Sanderson and Celia at the table—and froze.

They were chuckling, their faces almost touching. Sanderson's lips moved and his eyebrows rose as if posing a question, and he pointed a finger toward Celia's lap. She smacked him lightly on the bicep as she purred, "Whoa, not without paperwork, baby!" Then she fell forward into him and they were drowning in each other, gasping, devouring, lips, tongues, and fingers entwined.

Inside Gatsby, a dagger ripped into a tender spot. *That bitch!!*

By the time she stood next to the table, panting, her hands cramped into fists, Sanderson and Celia were sitting back, relaxed in their chairs, and casually nibbling fries.

"What the hell was *that?!*" The words strangled in her throat.

They looked up at her with blank faces.

Sanderson frowned. "What was what?"

Gatsby reached for their beer glasses, held both up over their respective laps, and turned the glasses over.

Vehement shouts and the clatter of silverware filled the air as she dashed toward the door.

CHAPTER 19

Niccolo faced the banks of electronics in the Officia Abba, holding his white robe out in front of him, his eyes wandering over the gold-thread detailing. This one had been decorated with a large symbol: the two halves, embroidered on either side of the opening, came together as the garment was buttoned. A golden omega. Tamar's work.

He revisited Volante's campaign to rewrite the Librah Vae-ta. *Franca's sweatshop is a waste of precious time. I must have the book!* His stomach tightened. *And she must not. With the original formula documents now in her hands, might she use them for her own purposes?*

A click behind him made him whirl.

At the head of the conference table, Maia leaned against the high-backed executive chair. The black tank top accentuated the hardness of her arms; the jeans, the power of thoroughbred-taut legs. The way that her hair flowed sensuously over her shoulders made him think of whips and black candle wax.

"How did you get in here?"

She began to slide into his chair but, catching his eye, moved one chair to the right. "*Think,* Niccolo. How do I get in anywhere?"

He threaded his arms through the sleeves of the robe, sank into his chair, and glared at her while his body wormed and burned with the need to touch her.

"Talk."

Maia propped her elbows on the table. "I don't have the book, but I know who does."

A flash sizzled through him. *I will get it back!* "Who?"

"A translator. The CIS contacted her, likely betting that her linguistic background would help them to figure out what killed Reymann." Her eyes darkened. "She collected the book from the CIS, but exactly where it is now, I'm not sure."

Another obstacle. He felt his teeth grind. "She's working with the CIS? Who is she?"

"She's a translator, a linguistic consultant of some renown. An American named Donovan."

"An Ameri..."

The image rose in his mind: a folder filled with identifying documents, reports, and photographs, labeled and tucked into a tall cabinet. A file stuffed with data—the information that Volante had accumulated for nearly two decades.

More images: the Seattle university where Volante had taught. A sprawling campus, brick buildings.

The young grad student—beautiful, sexual, intelligent—who had dared to peek behind the curtain that now secreted the global empire of Omega.

Her?! Could it be? Qaz!! He struggled to breathe. "What's she doing with it?"

"Studying it." Maia leaned back in the chair. "She is working with a scientist—a psychophysiologist—and a local woman trained in hypnotherapy."

"How do you know this?"

She crossed her muscular arms over her chest. The smile played on her lips. "Have you forgotten your own teachings, Niccolo? Tangling the threads of knowledge assures protection on multiple levels. And your own orders? Never to reveal my methods or my sources, even to you."

Reeling at the bomb of realization, of old connections and their implications, he struggled to maintain a stony expression though his muscles quivered with astonishment.

"Have you talked with Volante about her?"

"Franca?" A sneer turned her lips as she puffed out a laugh. "No."

He walked to the far side of the room and a line of filing cabinets. When he had pulled out a thick file, he strode back to the conference table.

Her eyes narrowed and moved over him, as if his every emotion crawled before her. As he pushed the file at her, she tipped her chin toward him as if asking *What the hell is this?*

"Read this," he growled, "and talk to Volante. Then I want to know how the information in this file is connected to this American linguist." As he rose, the robe swished around his body. "Go."

She stood and walked out.

As soon as the door closed behind her, he tumbled back into his chair, gasping. His fingers scrabbled on the tabletop.

If it's true!! What does Franca know about this? And what has she not told me?

CHAPTER 20

She stepped from the lift into a long corridor. At the far end, below an exit sign that glowed spectral red, a philodendron hunkered against the wall. As Gatsby moved down the hallway, she read the burnished plaques on the doors.

Geoffrey Smith-Wegner, PhD
Edward Crouch, MA, MSW
Magye MacKellem, MA, CHt
Sally Bigler, PhD

She thought the building seemed oddly quiet, almost deserted. Shouldn't clients be stumbling down the hallway, their neuroses trailing behind them? When she stopped in front of the last door, her eyes moved over the name plate. Celia Devereaux, MSW, CHt.

...Celia smiling sensuously at Woody, their eyes twinkling, their lips moving against each other—*whoa, not without paperwork, baby...*

The remembered images burned, and she felt her jaw tighten. *The slag!*

She banged the door open, blurting, "What do you..."

Eyes rose to scan her. Celia sat in a wide leather armchair, prim in a burgundy silk suit and gold-rimmed glasses. The armchair facing her held a sturdy, jeans-clad woman, who glared up at Gatsby with alarm. The air in the office seemed heavy with depression.

Celia laid her hand on the woman's knee and then walked toward the doorway where Gatsby stood, shaking with anger.

"I'm in session, for chrissake," she rumbled.

"I have to talk to you. Now."

As Celia shook her head, her black hair swung against her neck. "Gats, this isn't..."

"Right *now.*"

Celia stared her down, and then turned and walked back to the woman. She whispered something to the client, who stood, frowning, her eyes moving up and down Gatsby. The woman walked past the tall bookcases that lined the paneled walls. Muttering to herself, she skirted around Celia's oak desk—an explosion of papers and jade plants. She stepped toward a door at the back end of the room and disappeared through it.

Celia sank into the larger chair and fluttered her hand for Gatsby to sit. "You've got two minutes," she growled.

"What the *hell* were you doing?" Gatsby sputtered. "Last night in The Cross Keys, snuggling up to Woody like," she was going to lose it and she knew it but blazed into it, "like the unmitigated *slut* that you are!"

Celia blinked at her. Her mouth popped open. She blinked again and burst into laughter. "Oh please!"

"I saw you! As soon as I left the table, you were wrapped around him like a fucking condom!" She wanted to smack the bitch and drag her, kicking and screaming, into the depths of hell. "The one person that I would never..."

Celia drew in a long breath and let it out as her smile disappeared. She leaned into Gatsby's face. "Okay, okay, tell me what you saw."

"You were right next to him, and you were both laughing at some private joke about paperwork," she snarled, "and then you were kissing him!" The internal images fired, her breath caught, her head throbbed angrily. "You were all over each other, a making-out-with-no-concern kiss, a lover's kiss, you bitch."

Celia gazed at her. "All right...and have you talked with him about this?"

Gatsby shook her head.

"Then *will* you?"

Gatsby frowned. "What," she started and then pulled back, her eyes shifting. "What are you saying?"

Again, Celia exhaled slowly. "Do me a favor, sweets? Talk to Woody. Ask him about last night, and find out whether his story matches mine or yours. Sweets, nothing of the sort ever happened. You got up and went to the loo. Woody and I talked about Mick wigging out during your Franken-testing. Then you came back to the table, and the next thing I know, I've peed myself with Hefeweizen. *I'm* the one who should be bent. Christ." She shook her head but held eye contact. "That's exactly what happened."

Gatsby's mind whirled. "No, you were both..."

Celia edged closer. "Talk to Woody, or to anyone who was there! They wouldn't confirm any part of what you're saying." Her hands stretched toward Gatsby. "Sweetie, why on earth would I move on him? Good lord."

She tried to remember what had happened just before seeing Sanderson and Celia, entwined, lips pressing. *In the bathroom...what was it? Laughter? No, it can't...no...*

"And of all the men in the world, the one that broke your heart into a million little pieces? And the one that I helped to run back onto your pitch?" Celia slid one hand atop Gatsby's. "Sweetie, we've known each other for a long time. Not only would I never skirt around with your bloke, I wouldn't do it with any girl's bloke. I'm an incorrigible flirt, but I'm not *mad,* for chrissake."

Gatsby whirled on her, her voice edged with fury. "But I saw you. I saw it! Don't make me think..." *I saw them!!*

Celia pressed an index finger to her chin. "Wait, wait, wait. Mick." Her eyes widened. "Remember what happened to him? He went frigging sideways during that test, completely delusional. Maybe the testing affected you as well."

Wrestling inwardly, ready to burst into tears or smash something, Gatsby silently chewed her lower lip.

Celia moved closer, slipped her hands into Gatsby's, and squeezed, her face soft, her fingers warm.

Gatsby closed her eyes. "Oh my god." She leaned back, her hair pressing against the leather, and sighed.

...aggressive, unpredictable, and often violent behavior...rat PISSING coolmoneygads allowanna...

"Could it?" Her heart drummed in her ears. "God, Celia...but I can't believe..." She smashed her palms over her eyes. "I'm sorry."

No, I know what I saw!

Celia gave her a stern frown and then cracked a smile. "Good. Not as sorry as you're going to be if I don't finish my session." She glanced toward the room where the woman was waiting. "Are you okay now?"

"I...listen, whether I saw something that only I was experiencing, I don't have an answer for that. Yet." Gatsby rose, her thigh muscles contracting slowly, knee joints grinding. "I'll talk to you tomorrow."

As they stood at the door, Celia hugged her. "I'm your friend, babe, not the other woman. Call me if you need to talk."

Gatsby stumbled down the hallway and toward the lift. Her brain zigzagged: left, right, logic, emotion. Truth? Deception? A headache pounded mercilessly at her brain.

I have to know what it will take to stop feeling this feeling.

CHAPTER 21

Gatsby tossed the carcass of a microwave dinner box into the trash bin under the sink. She peered at the clock on the oven that was used only for storing pizza trays: 7:26.

The encounter that morning with Celia, images of Woody's face, and snippets of scriptural edicts ping-ponged in her head.

What is that, the Dead Sea Scrolls?

Talk to anyone who was there, they wouldn't confirm any part of what you're...

Allah is cognizant of what is in the abba way non vass ah parateh show day to vahla meed pressure monkeys!

Her eyes squeezed shut against the onslaught. *I gotta get out of here.* She pulled on a denim jacket and grabbed her shoulderbag.

From her building, she wandered down King's Road. At night, it was a circus of multicolored shop lights that twinkled like calliopes, restaurants and clubs catering to the sleep-deprived. Some neon, some music, and some pedestrians scuffling, meandering, in sufficient numbers for her to feel safe there after sunset.

She went to The Foxfire, the only pub in London that she'd visited a handful of times. It was a decent place to have a drink without being accosted by ear-bleeding music or drunken Gen-X mutants.

As she wandered toward a booth at the back of the room, her head spun, a Wizard of Oz tornado of sounds, faces, voices.

I was no good for you, Kama.

Chaotic spikes on the EEG, the sliver of blood swaying from Parrish's lip.

Exactly what neurochemists find in the test subjects they've just injected with heroin or cocaine...

A Gen-X waiter took her request for India Pale Ale and shuffled away.

In all that questing, there was only one thing, one answer, that I knew without a doubt. That I would always love you, Gatsby.

Her chin dropped. Salt stung at the corners of her eyes.

"Are you all right?"

She jumped. Turning toward the voice, she looked up to see a man beside the table, frowning down at her.

She saw salt-and-pepper hair that was short and wavy on top and long in back, pulled into a ponytail that draped over his shoulder. A posh business jacket topped the distressed Levi's. No jewelry except a wide silver band around his left thumb. She wondered if he was a work-a-day businessman or a secret billionaire, a Sir Richard Branson anonymously slumming it in a middle-class bar.

"You look out of place," she murmured.

"So do you." He tipped his head, his expression soft, as if practicing his bedside manner. "You seemed upset. Being the gallant gent that I am, I thought I might offer a sympathetic ear."

She looked into her lap. "Thanks, but I don't..."

...metah push tah ah me-gah rubber stamping neon! Shit! Arrrhghgh OOOOO bebebebe uh hhhhh...

She scrubbed the back of her hand across her eyes and sighed. "Yes, I do." She nodded toward the opposite side of the booth. "Join me?"

A smile warmed his face. "Thanks." He slid into the booth, arranging his jacket around him and setting his glass of porter on the table.

"What's your name?"

He gazed down for a moment as if mulling. "Judas."

Yeah, right. Odd choice for a fake name. Well, if that's the game we're going to play...

"And you?"

She studied him before settling on a response. "Eve."

Exchanging chary smiles, like chess masters sizing each other up as they took the board, they sipped from their glasses and muddled through questions about livelihood, background, and family. She noticed that he spoke with a subtle lisp; occasionally an *s* came out as a *th*, and his mouth worked as if the muscles were weak or perhaps the motions of speaking were painful.

With a buzz creeping over her, the adrenaline shocks of the last twenty-four hours melting, Gatsby thought she sensed a considerate quality in him, an openness. Running one fingertip around the edge of a round coaster, she murmured, "Isn't it odd how people sometimes speak more freely with strangers than with old friends?"

The jacket rustled as he shrugged. "I'm convinced that more therapy is done in pubs than behind shingled doors. The great sodium pentothal is alcohol, you know. Pour it in, and people pith out their life stories."

She searched his face. He wasn't quite handsome but far from repellant. His look and demeanor gave a mixed vibe: kind, perhaps likeable, but secreted. Walled off.

"Are you trying to get me to piss out my life story?"

"Are you?" He eyed her with a trace of a smile. "I'm just offering a congenial ear. A few minutes ago, you were wet-eyed over thomething." Head cocked, he waited.

She weighed the responses. "Some very bizarre things are happening right now." She took a deep breath, steeling herself for what she dreaded she was about to say, "Some of it, well, it goes back a long way. Years ago. A very," her voice caught, "traumatic event."

As soon as I got into grad school, everything turned traumatic. She crossed her arms, feeling her heartbeat throbbing in her ears.

His eyes danced across her, seeming to pick out unspoken signals. He frowned. "Well." He reached for his glass and took a long draw. "I'm a member of that miserable club."

She had expected some sort of maudlin consolation, not personal disclosure. Emboldened, she managed to maintain a casual tone as she asked, "Oh? How so?"

He glanced toward the taps at the bar, then his eyes followed the servers as they moved around the room, delivering trays of alcohol. "My own PTSD." He looked her in the eye and said, his voice flat, "I was raped."

She stopped, caught, jolted.

"Someone that I trusted completely. It was emotional at first, then physical."

Gatsby swallowed. "God. I..."

"You don't usually hear men's stories," he swirled the murky liquid in his glass. "Women's, yes, but not as often men's."

She wondered how much to press. How much to divulge? A million responses raced through her—some too patronizing, some horrifically trite. Some far too revealing for a casual chat with a stranger in a bar.

The images flashed through her mind: altar, pews, black robe. The smell of burning candles. Cold air creeping across her naked skin.

...and God's pure love will wash away all fear, all confusion...

While a droplet slid down his glass and tumbled over his fingers, she searched for a reply that would reflect the appropriate level of sympathy. Looking into his face, she saw deep lines and wondered if they were the artifacts of years of suffering. Finally, she cleared her throat and whispered, "How did you cope with the pain? The hate?"

His face hardened to iron. "I killed him."

She scanned for any hint of sarcasm, found none, and felt her stomach clench.

He whispered, his voice gritty, "Would you do the same?"

A knee-jerk answer—*I'd kill the fucker*—almost spilled out, but she stopped it. *If I said that I'd never considered it, I'd be lying, but even if that's the truth, this guy is a total stranger! You can't just...*

He pushed his porter to the side of the table and leaned toward her. "Your traumatic event. I think we're both talking about the same thing, aren't we? And somewhere, deep in the back of your mind, you have thought about it, haven't you?"

She shifted against the seat while planning how to ease out of an encounter with a man who called himself Judas and wanted to casually discuss homicide. Finally, she said, "We all think about things that we know we will never act on. Impulse control is the foundation of a civilized culture."

"A civilized culture. Indeed. As is a jury of one's peers. Like the jury that acquitted me. I presented the facts, and the evidence was incontrovertible. It was thelf-defense." He looked into her face, "And it was. Don't think I'm some axe-wielding psychopath. It would have been one of us, the sadistic prick or me. It was him." He took a deep breath. "But he deserved it. He'd been doing it for years, to lots of boys."

She sighed. "Every time I hear a story of...violation..." She shook her head with such force that the beer in her glass splashed onto the wood.

His head swung slowly. "If it hadn't gone as it did, I think I would have killed him anyway."

Gatsby stared into the man's eyes, scrambling for clues. *Who IS he? What does he really want? Is he fabricating this story just to gain my sympathy? Is he setting me up for something? Working for someone?* One last sentence, and she would leave "Judas" to his own creepy company.

"It is the ultimate morality question, isn't it? Payback. Is it justified?" She leveled a hard stare at him.

He sat back, his jaw muscles clenching, and regarded her with reptile-cool eyes. "The lex talionis? Quid pro quo? We always have the choice, do we not? Perpetuate a chain of violence or break it. Turn the other cheek or take an eye for an eye." He reached for his glass, then his fingers thrummed against it. "They're both biblical."

"Yes, we have the choice."

"I used a handgun. What would you use?"

She swallowed. *That's it, Judas. I'm getting OUT of here.*

The question ghosted through her mind again: *I killed him. Would you do the same?*

"Silence? Doesn't work quite as well. It's all part of what they teach us as babes in catechism or thynagogue. Obey the ten commandments. Thou shalt not kill." He sighed. "Love thy buggering neighbor as thyself."

She sipped from her glass, staring down into its amber depths, feeling his eyes creeping over her, wanting to run but still needing to know more of his story, especially whether or not it was pure fiction.

"Noble prescriptions from a merciful God, for whom millions of innocent people have died." His laugh sounded bitter. "Who is the lord of heaven, the supreme being, the higher power, the good shepherd. The alpha. The omega."

Oh god.

"You know about Omega, don't you?" he whispered, nodding as if he knew long ago that the question was rhetorical.

Her breath quickened. "I have no idea what..."

"I think you do. And Omega knows about you," he leaned closer, "and I think I know *why* you know about it."

"What the hell are you talking about?" Now panting with fear, she reached toward her shoulderbag. *My only connection to this Omega group is the Gahana, but how the hell would HE know that? Who IS he?!* She suddenly felt that her every move was as naked as a prisoner, stripped and trembling in a spotlight.

As he leaned forward, the shock of his ponytail tumbled toward the tabletop. His eyes were ice-hot blue. "Listen to me. I *know* about Omega, more than I ever wanted to know, and if one of them approaches you, run, run like hell," his face inched closer to hers, "or you're risking everything, including your life."

Singer's face and deep voice rose in her mind: *Something changed dramatically. Exactly what set him off we don't know. At that point, he got involved with a new organization...*

"What happened to you, the man who hurt you," the words tumbled out before she could stop them, "was it Omega?"

His eyes darted rapidly. "I can't tell you that."

She felt her stomach grip like she'd been punched.

"But I can show you thith."

Leaning toward her, he stuck his tongue out and moved one hand upward to press one finger against the lower edge of it. Repelled, she looked closer. About three centimeters from his fingernail, she saw something raised, like a welt would look on the back or the leg, but it was a recognizable symbol: Ω

Hideous realization struck her.

"Thith wathn't voluntary," he hissed.

She bolted.

CHAPTER 22

She signed in and was told to sit. In a few minutes, Singer arrived, escorted her down the stark hallways to his office, and offered her the same bitter coffee.

"Thanks, no," Gatsby said, settling into the chair that faced his desk.

He leaned forward into his computer monitor, eyes scanning as he muttered something, clicked the mouse, and turned to face her.

"I want to bring you up to date on what we've learned about this group, Omega. We have someone working undercover who we think has reached some of the key players. Our agent went to them seeking conversion, I guess you'd call it." He paused as if he were about to voice an opinion and then decided against it. "This group has roots far deeper than we could have ever imagined. That's all I can say about it, the rest is classified."

"What's its allure?" Gatsby asked.

He propped his elbow on the desk. "The things that always draw people into groups of this nature. Power, a higher purpose, the need to belong. Sometimes the structure or discipline that they can't manage on their own." He pulled a manila folder from a side drawer of his desk and opened it to read from a stack of print-outs. "The group is abstemious, demanding strict obedience. Denial of the individual, denial of pleasure. Sexual activity is permitted only when allowed or demanded by the patriarchal leader, known as an Abba. The group requires constant devotion and aggressively pushes recruiting. Its propaganda promises admittance to Omega," he drew the folder closer to his face and carefully articulated each word, "a plane far higher and purer than the Judeo-Christian heaven or the Islamic paradise. Members are told that, quote, heaven is a dirty prison but Omega is pure knowledge and pure truth."

She took a deep breath. "Makes me think of Charles Manson and Jonestown. Koresh, Heaven's Gate." She heard Woody's voice: *I took acid and had visions of my death and* *resurrection...I saw Reiki masters and gurus who walked on burning coals...*The question shot through her, *While Woody tried every pseudoreligion under the sun, did* he *ever wander into Omega?*

"There are similarities. The main difference between the cults that you mention and Omega is the numbers." He sat the folder on the desk. "RED-MK7 alerted us to an organization that has been growing in vast numbers for years but has managed to keep so quiet that investigative agencies had no idea that it existed."

"It always seems that groups like this flourish for a while until something sets one of them off. The leader dies, or the followers kill themselves." She frowned. "Is there any indication that this group is operating illegally? Abusing its members?"

I can show you thith. She shuddered.

A cloud passed over Singer's face. "Not yet, but it's probably only a matter of time. The icon that seems to hold the organization together is the book." He leaned toward her. "It's now the tenth, Dr. Donovan. Are you going to beg for more time?"

She ran her hands through her hair. "I'm just now making some sense of the deeper constructs of the language. Yes, I need more time. Otherwise, my efforts are probably going to be wasted. You said that your crypto division had no luck with it, right?"

Singer stared past her for a moment, as if weighing options. "That's right."

"One more week. Can you do that?"

"I'll have to check with the director of the EU." He picked up a pencil and tapped it on the desktop. "What have you learned about it?"

On the way there, she'd wrangled with herself over how to discuss the work without mentioning Woody or Celia. *Use only first person, and don't screw up!* "I've completed, or mostly completed, a syllabary. A map of all the symbols and how often they appear. There's little or no punctuation, so it's tough to figure out where one word or sound ends and the next begins. I have the feeling that some of the symbols might be used in the same way as a rebus."

"Meaning?"

"Meaning that an obvious symbol, such as a drawing of a human eye, is probably used to mean the word *I,* and if you put an *m* before it, you have *my.*"

Singer frowned. "Sounds like something for children, primary schoolers. Why would an established group like Omega use such a simplistic method of writing?"

"Maybe because it is simple. Making it simple would enable more people to learn the language in a shorter time. Then again, this may be only one version of the language, one specifically created for beginners."

He nodded. "I see."

"And w..." She clamped her lips together against the word *we.* "I think I've identified something that indicates future and past tenses."

"Good. Keep up your work." Singer leaned back in his chair. "At this point, do you have any thoughts about the book's significance to this group?"

"I do think that it's been created as a religious text, a holy scripture. I kept wondering why someone, or a group of people, would choose, out of thousands of languages, these six to design a new system." She combed her hands through her hair again. "It must be the psychological draw of the orthographies. Latin, Greek, Aramaic, Arabic, Hebrew— they're all tied to the great world religious texts."

"Can you actually read any of it yet?"

"I've made some educated guesses. I think I've figured out which symbols indicate nouns and verbs and which are articles." She sighed deeply and closed her eyes for a second; the long nights, the emotional roller coasters, and the nights of erratic sleep and bloody dreams were draining her reserves. "But we haven't made any truly definitive translations."

Singer's eyes narrowed. "*We?*"

Her brain spun. "*I* haven't made any truly def..."

Singer's eyes zipped over her like airport search wands. He pressed toward her. "Have you told someone about this?

I was explicitly clear that all information about this case must be kept absolutely confidential."

She stared at him as the options whirled in her head, knowing that the long silence was itself an answer, and finally too tired to devise or sustain a lie, she said, "Yes," and braced herself for the outburst.

He drummed his fingers on the desktop. "Who?"

Still tensed for a reaction, she told him the story: Celia helping her to find Sanderson, their meeting, and the formation of a research triad that was now working on the Gahana.

"This complicates things. This is a serious breach." He closed the folder.

She felt her palms sweating, her face burning. "But I couldn't do it alone! It was the only way to understand how this language affects the physiology, how it may have been the key to RED-MK7."

His eyes blazed. "New protocol measures must be taken, and I must speak with my supervisor about this."

I've done it now!

She wished that he would break the torturous stare that he'd fixed on her and fiddle with his tie, or berate her, or throw the folder at her, anything but the dead silence.

Forget WE...I am in deep shit.

CHAPTER 23

Gatsby opened her door to see Sanderson slouched in the hallway, his Lancaster raincoat thrown over one arm.

"Hi." Nothing in his smile said *Glad to see you.*

She ushered him into the living room. The rain had subsided, and sunlight poured in through the window, illuminating dust motes. Smells of coffee, raspberry jam, and French toast still hung in the air. They settled on the couch and fidgeted.

She pulled in a breath, unsure if any reasonable explanation was possible. *Who's the guilty party, me or him? Or something else?*

"At The Cross Keys," she looked down at her bare toes, then into his face, "I saw something, but I have to find out whether I really saw it."

He anchored his elbows on his knees. "Well, *something* caused you to freak out. I called you four times yesterday."

"Celia." Her hands twisted against each other, and the words spilled out in a gush. "When I came back from the loo, the two of you...I saw her wrapped around you, saw her kissing you madly, saw you kissing her back, like wild lovers!"

He recoiled. "What?!"

"But then when I went to her office yesterday to confront her, she said that it never happened."

"It didn't! My god, how the hell could you think that I'd..." His face flushing, he started to rise but then flopped back onto the couch. "This is why you baptized me with beer? You thought I was making out with her?"

"I didn't *think* it, Woody, I *saw* it. God. It would be bad enough if it were true..."

He turned away as if unwilling or unable to look at her.

"But there may be another explanation that's closer to the truth. The delusions that we saw with Parrish, when he was raving, belligerent, nonsensical?" She drew in a deep breath. "What if the language somehow affected me in the same way? What if it skewed my own perception of reality?

Made me *think* I experienced something? If the language did that, Woody, we need to be careful. And very skeptical of what we think we perceive."

His lips twisted. "Jesus. You actually saw that?"

"It was as real as you sitting here right now...with a stunned look on your face."

He scrubbed his palms over his cheeks. "If you're right, if the language doesn't just alter emotions and consciousness but can bring on hallucinations, we do need to be very careful." He met her eyes. "We need to establish measures for monitoring each other, checks and balances, so that we know we aren't driving under the influence, so to speak."

"Yes. Good idea." She sighed. "I knew that it couldn't be true, but..." Her voice caught.

He slid closer to her. "Kama..."

A loud knock made them both jump. It became more insistent.

She hustled toward the door and opened it. "Come in."

Celia stepped into the entryway, unfurling out of her soft wool cape. Gatsby herded her into the living room, and all three stood appraising each other as if waiting for a first move. Finally, Celia turned to Gatsby and asked, "Well? The dangerous liaison that never was? Have you solved the crime and beheaded the guilty?"

Gatsby shook her head. "The only question I'm concerned about is how this language, this book, is able to grossly tweak someone's reality."

"So we're sorted. Grand." Celia glanced at Sanderson, then Gatsby. "And just for the record, I'm not bumping uglies with either one of you." She planted her hands on her hips. "That position is filled, sweets."

"I have no doubt," Gatsby muttered. "Come on, this way."

They filed into Gatsby's office and approached the Gahana, which Gatsby had taken out of the Baber case and set out on her desk.

"So that's the bugger," Celia whispered as her eyes moved across it. She tilted her head. "Oh, I talked with Mick yesterday."

"And?" Sanderson said.

She toyed with a strand of dark hair. "Well, he hasn't sprouted horns. Except for a headache, he seems to have recovered without damage."

Gatsby went to a shelf above the desk that held a wild collection of books, folders, dictionaries, pens, and wax paper wrappers that had once held white chocolate truffles. She pulled out the three-ring binder that she'd had with her at the lab and dropped into her computer chair.

Sanderson dragged in two more chairs from the living room.

As they settled, Gatsby said, "Listen, both of you. I'm already in trouble with the CIS for telling you about any of this. Don't discuss it with anyone else." She hoped that her glare transferred the tension gnawing at her. "I'm very serious. The book, the language, the test we did on Mick, all of it...you can't tell a soul. Promise me."

Celia turned back and forth in the chair. "I'll go one step further. Once we're done here, I'll trigger an amnesia process. Poof, details gone!"

Gatsby frowned. "You can do that? Even on yourself?"

Celia's lips curled into a smile. "Babe, you'd be amazed at what I can do even on myself."

She shook her head. "That, I don't even want to know. What about Mick? Can he be trusted to keep all this quiet?"

Celia crossed her legs. "Don't worry. I'll deal with him."

Gatsby turned toward Sanderson. "Woody?"

His mouth worked and eyes darted as if he were shuffling conflicting thoughts. "If this language does what we think it does, you know that it has to be properly studied. You're going to need experts, a lot of them. A whole slew of linguists, historians, medical..."

"I know that, Sand—" She stopped, assessing the message that using his last name might send. "I know, and you can be assured that I'd make that happen, but not now. The last thing I need is to risk being blacklisted by the British government or any other government." She looked at the Gahana, then back at him. "I want your word, Woody."

He glanced at the book and sighed. "All right."

"Good." She went into the kitchen to make a fresh pot of coffee.

They set up camp, a buzzing triumvirate hovering over the Gahana.

Seated at Sanderson's right, Celia used one red fingernail to flick at the cover. "This is what pitched Mick off his trolley? Un-bloody-believable. Have you made anything of it?"

Gatsby took a pocket folder down from the shelf and pulled a wad of papers from it. "I've identified the six systems: Egyptian hieroglyphics, Greek, Aramaic, Hebrew, Arabic, and Latin. I have a good start on a grid of all the characters along with the frequency of appearance, and I've made some headway on the interrelationships. The water symbol, which is equivalent to the Latin letter n, almost always appears at the end of a set."

Celia peered at her over the tops of her gold-rimmed glasses, then took them off and began polishing them with a corner of her sweater.

"What I'm thinking of as a set, or a word, is separated from the next set by a space." She pointed to a symbol that resembled a crescent moon. "And this appears only before or after discrete sets, so I think that it indicates past and future tense. I'm guessing that some of the symbols work in the same way as a rebus."

Sanderson cleared his throat. "What about the semantics? The overall construction?"

"I think I'm making headway there. Writing systems can be classified as alphabetic, syllabic, or ideographic. English is obviously alphabetic, as is Greek. Hebrew and Arabic are syllabic and consonantal—no vowels—so to indicate the syllable *kol*, you'd write KL. Egyptian hieroglyphics are a complicated mix of pictographic symbols, mostly consonants that can be monoliteral, bilateral, or trilateral, and some can represent both the sound and the meaning."

Celia clucked her tongue. "Mono, bi, tri? Sounds like the party I hosted last spring. What's that all about?"

Gatsby leaned over the desk, picked up a pen, and began drawing on a blank sheet of paper. "Okay, to write *cat*, you would draw four symbols. The owl image represents the sound *m,* the reed is an *i* sound, and the quail chick stands for the *w* sound. Together, you have the morpheme *mir.* Then you have to add the determinative, the picture of a cat, to indicate the category."

She leaned back. "That's just the tip of the iceberg. Working through the entire text would take a long time—depending on the mandate of the CIS, time that we probably don't have."

Celia propped her glasses back on her nose. "For godssake, Gats, are you ignoring the bigger question here? Why pursue this monstrosity? You've got a book that even the CIS can't crack, and someone's already died because of it, and Mick practically flipped an embolism just listening to you read from it." She stretched her hand toward the Gahana, and Gatsby instinctively inched forward, readying to stop her from touching it. "What's the worst that would happen if you returned this bastard to the CIS and ever-so-graciously bowed out?"

Sanderson scratched under his chin. As he looked toward Gatsby, he said, "I know what you'll say."

Gatsby dropped into her chair. "I've asked myself that a hundred times, but the same answer keeps coming up. This is a language that someone, or a large group of people, took a hell of a lot of effort to devise, perhaps knowing the danger they were playing with, perhaps not."

She reminded herself, *I haven't told Celia anything about the Omega group, and Woody knows only vague details. Better keep it that way.*

"But given the chance to figure it out," she sighed, "I can't *not* do it. This is what I do. It's what I am! Turning mystery into meaning is a type of alchemy, it's the closest thing we have to..."

Sanderson was smiling, shaking his head.

Power and purpose surged through her. "Demons, angels, miracles? They don't exist, but there are wonders." She looked toward the Gahana, her fingers skimming the edges of the pages, barely touching them. "This is a wonder. You couldn't send a deep-sea diver into the ocean, give him the coordinates to something like the Titanic, and expect him to *not* haul it to the surface."

Celia rolled her eyes in Sanderson's direction. "I've seen her give up every human comfort in the name of the almighty alphabet, but this may finally do her in. Will you help me keep an eye on her?"

He chuckled. "I'll keep her away from whipping cream and ketchup."

Celia's quizzical look seemed to retort *Huh?*

"Inside joke."

"Are you done?" Gatsby growled. "Jesus, pay attention. Look, while I was examining the book, I found this."

She bent toward the Gahana and moved all the pages to the verso side, keeping her movements slow and steady so that they jostled as little as possible. The leather binding only partially covered the backing, leaving a thin space between it and the cardboard. A piece of paper had been tucked into the space. Gripping it between two fingers, Gatsby slid it out and set it on the desktop for them to view.

"It's a short section that was ridiculously easy to translate. Someone put little effort into obscuring the meaning of the passage. Maybe they were just learning the language and needed some writing practice, or maybe they were forced to write this and deliberately did a sloppy job." She shrugged. "It's Greek and English. Here." She pulled from the pocket folder the page on which she had written her translation, then placed the second sheet next to the original from the Gahana.

Sanderson and Celia leaned forward to read:

```
"When you fold your hands together, you feel
the fire of Omega. Through prayer and sacrifice
shall the firm disciple find the way to Omega,
for his faith is his salvation. He shall give
up his red robes, and his warm house, and his
wife, and his children unto the Path of Truth.
He shall submit as the newborn babe, so that he
becomes holy. He looks deeper, deeper, even
deeper into the depths of his dark heart. He
prepares for his rising into the Truth by his
chastity and his tithing. Daughters and sons,
bring your heart to the heart of Omega.
```

```
Minister the Word to all along the road, all
that you see by the sea, professing to them the
steps of redemption. You will give testimony to
the power of Omega and to the terrible
damnation of Omega. See how the back of the
disbeliever will break these commandments and
you will suffer. To suffer shall be. The
disbelievers will bow in trembling; they see
the sea of blood that will take them. Do they
not wonder whether they can find their way in
Omega? If they have turned their eyes and ears
from Omega, they send their souls and the souls
of the children to the black and eternal fire."
```

Sanderson rubbed his chin. "That could have come straight from the Bible or the Koran."

Celia sat straighter. "Whoever wrote this knew a hell of a lot about subconscious languaging. Not only the surface-level techniques of hypnosis but some of the much more subtle Ericksonian techniques." She pointed to the phrases as she called them out. "Here, these are modal operators of necessity. That's phonological ambiguity. This is ambiguous punctuation. And here? Repetition and alliteration. The writer knew how the patterns work and how effective they are. Pleasurable persuasion." She turned toward Gatsby. "Seamless, effortless, invisible access to the subconscious. It's the type of language that delivers suggestions in a way that meets with little resistance. Greases the wheels, in other words."

"My god." Gatsby shook her head. "Could you implant something that brings on a specific state? Deliberately induce an emotion like obeisance? Or hostility?"

"Not sure. In the eighties, a hypnotherapist named Rosenberg published his claims that certain emotions could be induced based on the subject's state at the time of a hypnotic induction. He called the technique directed empathics. Rosenberg claimed that in a relaxed state, feelings of vulnerability and obedience could be implanted, whereas if inducting when the subject was angry, hostility or even murderous impulses could be implanted." She slid her fingertips against her opposite hand. "His theories were never tested under scientific methods, and he was dismissed as a crank."

"But it has been considered, and if one person published about it, you can bet that there are dozens more trying to answer the same question. How hypnosis can produce a specific emotional state—not what the client wants but what the practitioner wants." Seeing the frown on Sanderson's face and the rapid movements of his eyes, she said, "Woody, what are you thinking?"

He laced his hands behind his head. "I'm thinking about the neural activity triggered by this language. The man who died. He was found with this book, right?"

"Yes."

"So it's likely that he was exposed to the language by reading the book—parts of it, if not the entire text."

"That's likely."

"And if he was reading it just before he died, whether aloud or silently, he experienced the sounds of the words. You can't hear a word in a familiar language and not imagine what it means, and you can't read something and not experience the sounds of the words, because thoughts are just subvocalized speech."

Gatsby and Celia nodded.

"Think about the planes-trains-automobiles process of hearing. Your ear funnels sound waves into the ear canal, and the waves travel along this passage until they hit your eardrum and cause it to vibrate. This causes the ossicles to start moving, and they pass on the vibrations to a layer of tissue at the entrance of the inner ear called the oval window."

He leaned forward while circling his hands around his ears. "The movement of the window sets up wave-like motions in the fluid inside the cochlea and stimulates sensory hair cells in the cochlea, generating a nerve impulse that travels along the cochlear nerve to your brain. Specifically, to the temporal lobe."

Celia goggled at him. "But what does all that have to do with the bloody book?"

"The temporal lobe." Sanderson smacked a fist against his palm. "It's the key. For healthy people, the nerve impulses traveling to their temporal lobes are processed in an orderly way. The activity is smooth and regular. But for RED-MK7..."

"Red who?" Celia broke in.

"The guy who died," Gatsby muttered.

Sanderson continued. "Maybe the sound waves generated by reading the text caused erratic nerve impulses and electrical discharges that hit his temporal lobe and then spread throughout his brain. It's what causes epileptic seizures. The brain's electrical signals misfire, causing a person's actions and consciousness to be altered."

Gatsby asked, "Could a severe reaction happen the very first time that someone was exposed to the language?"

"It did with Parrish. Maybe RED-MK7 had already been exposed to the language but not for any duration, or he'd had minor exposures in the past, and the neurological impact occurred over time, bit by bit." He glanced at the book.

"So the more familiar he became with the language, the more it damaged him?"

"It makes sense. Repeated exposure to the language may have eroded the area of the brain that was trying to process the abnormal electrical impulses, eventually destroying that section or entire regions." He shook his head. "You'd see psychopathology and then full-blown attack. The shutdown of the vital systems, lungs, heart, brain."

They all stared at each other silently.

Celia nodded toward the kitchen and stood. "I need a break."

Gatsby followed her, then Sanderson.

When all three had caravanned back to the living room with cups of fresh coffee in their hands, Celia nestled in the armchair and wrapped her cape around her shoulders.

Gatsby sank into the couch. "We're going to have to do what we can, as fast as we can. Singer told me not to copy the damn thing, and..."

"But you did make a copy," Sanderson said.

"Only the first few pages—I didn't dare copy any more. And Singer wants the book back in the next few days."

Celia sipped. Sanderson stood to pace the room, stuffing his hands into the pockets of his jeans and then pulling them out to gesture.

"Well, before you take it back, my god, think about the import, the big picture of all this." His breath came in rapid bursts. "What we're dealing with is every variety of religious fanaticism. Parrish flipped out when we read from the Gahana, but he also had intense physical and emotional reactions to the Koran and Christian Bible. Think about it: why do religious extremists think and behave with such fervor? In large part, because of the scriptures they read. The language of their holy texts works on them like a drug. They are ingesting a drug, being slipped a drug—and the language is the carrier! Like you said, Celia, this languaging is seamless, it's invisible. It sinks into the subconscious like an odorless gas seeps into the body. It's psychic DMSO!" His face flushed deeper as the speed and volume of his voice rose. "The religious go to their churches, get their weekly fix, get just as high as they would on heroin or cocaine or meth. *The* opium of the people. God!!"

He dropped onto the couch and then catapulted up again. Gatsby's head pivoted, Wimbledon-like, as he crisscrossed the room, and the ghosts howled through her mind:

...and God's pure love will wash away all fear, all confusion...

"Or an anesthetic," she murmured, "all fears and doubts, all anxiety, all pain washed away."

Celia folded her legs under her. "Well, sure, as well as identity and self-determination. And in plenty of cases, all self-esteem."

Sanderson started back across the room. "Then Christians and Muslims, maybe countless other sects, have been under the influence of these language drugs for millennia, and because their beliefs have become so ingrained in world culture and are so socially sanctioned, even glorified, the addicts have no idea how addicted and delusional they are!"

Gatsby looked toward the Gahana. "Drug addicts glorify their substance abuse...in this case, they call the addiction piety."

"Piety, devotion, worship, faith! Salvation!" Sanderson pinned his arms across his chest. "All those masters that I read, all the gurus that I bowed before..." He trailed off, hanging his head.

Celia sipped her coffee and sat the mug on an end table. "People living empty lives volunteer for all kinds of slavery at the drop of a hat. It's apotheosis. I see it on a regular basis in my office. At some point, anything that can be turned into an addiction will be."

Gatsby tugged her t-shirt from her jeans. The room felt hot and pendant; sweat had darkened the cotton fabric under her armpits. "But would the same stimulus affect people differently? Some worshippers might be exposed to a book, or language, or lifestyle, and move on without a second thought, while others are instant converts." She frowned. "You see people with extreme religious addictions, some with only minor symptoms, and some who seem completely immune."

Sanderson nodded. "Just like substance users. There are people who get hammered just thinking about alcohol and then those who can ingest the most toxic chemical and show no effects whatsoever."

Gatsby stood and walked to the large window at the far side of the room. She stared down at King's Road; streetlights were beginning to glow to life as the sun set over the treetops.

"The longer that we work with this language, the more closely we'll have to monitor each other. We have to watch what we say and do and what we *think* is real. We are dealing with mechanisms that affect the mind and body in the extreme. They may be able to induce killing behavior or actually kill."

As she turned back to face Sanderson and Celia, her vision shifted. Their faces seemed almost painfully distinct, every hair and pore and vein brilliantly defined. "Remember what we learned on the playground as kids? Sticks and stones may break my bones, but words will never hurt me?"

CHAPTER 24

While Sanderson huddled in her office with the book, Celia herded Gatsby down the hallway and into the bedroom.

"Sweetie, being with him—how it hurt you so badly, and now dredging it all back up to the surface," her eyes radiated concern, "are you coping?"

"Except for hallucinations of sexual misconduct, yeah, I suppose I'm holding up." Gatsby shrugged and tried to laugh but only managed a raspy string of exhalations.

"If you need an ear to pour some desperation into, I'm here, babe."

They turned to walk down the hallway together.

Sanderson looked up from the book. "There you two are." He glanced at his wristwatch. "It's late. I should get back to the hotel. Expecting a fractious call from the department."

After Gatsby pulled his raincoat from the front closet, they stopped at the door, and stood, staring, gesturing fitfully. Finally, he dipped toward her and quickly kissed her on the cheek. "I'll call you tomorrow."

Watching him disappear down the hallway, she tried to remember the last time he'd kissed her. *That* night, in the apartment. Watts and Plato and Leary strewn across the ginger-colored carpet, the air sodden with incense and Jack Daniels.

I was in the agonizing place where liberation was in conflict with kama. The latter had to be...

Sacrificed.

Her lips ground against her teeth, tasting something like ash.

Celia wandered to the armchair in the living room, scooped up her cape, and turned to face her. "What do you think?"

"Of the book?" She leaned against the arm of the couch, limp, groggy, aware of the distant howl of a headache.

"Of him." Celia tilted her head. "Is he what you thought he'd be?"

All that email from Definite Article...

Each breath seemed to stab at her temples. "Are any of us what we thought we'd be?"

Celia threaded her arms through the sleeves of the cape. "Just remember what I said. If you ever needed a friend, I think you need one now. Call me if you want to talk." She wrapped her arms around Gatsby, turned, and headed for the staircase.

Gatsby closed the door and went back to her office.

She slid down into her chair and peered at the Gahana—eyelids fluttering—symbols floated around and through her field of vision, moving forward and back like clumsy dance partners, taunting her in six ancient tongues.

☾☥S𐤉𐤉O𐤌⊠✗

Are any of us what we thought we'd be?

The rush of cars on King's Road and the dull hum of the computer were soothing in their monotony, but the canvas of darkness provided by her closed lids filled with images...voices...

(Semantically yours, D)

(Semantically yours, B)

The only way that I could reach out to you was through an admittedly slippery back door.

It was slippery all right. A midnight escape, an "I have no choice" message, and fifteen frigging years of silence. The covert online attempt to reach out to me. What was the real reason for his anonymity? What was he really hiding from?

...and God's pure love will wash away all fear, all confusion...

The fever flickered, smoldered.

The thought struck her with chilling force: *What if he knew about the rape? Somehow learned about it from the police or* Religious Affairs?

She swallowed hard. *If he did, would THAT explain why he was so secretive about contacting me? But if he knew, what did he know, and why would he deny the knowledge? When we met at his hotel, he pointedly asked why I had never told him about it, but...*

As she opened her eyes and let them travel over the angles and swirls of the letters, the symbols started to swim, melting together and breaking apart—tiny continents drifting and then shattering, making crackling sounds as they shifted—filtered through the throbbing buzz in her head. Then, as if commanded by a magus, the symbols returned to their places.

She smelled dust and onions and bergamot.

CHAPTER 25

Deep shadows fell across the distressed maple floorboards. Beyond the ceiling-high windows, stars shimmered in the sky.

The fragrance of lavender tiptoed through the room.

Niccolo's eyes moved over folding tables that overflowed with writing implements, a dozen varieties of paper, pens, and notepads.

Twin notebook computers sat at one end of one table. He noticed a dark shape beside one of them and strode toward it. A stack of papers.

As he fingered through the pages, Volante emerged from the shadowed corner of the main room and moved toward him. She still wore her business attire: a marble-grey Burberry suit with matching heels and silk stockings. Moonlight reflected as tiny gleams in her pearl earrings. The way that her hair was pulled back into a tight bun accentuated her cheekbones. She silently approached Niccolo.

"The MCF documents," he said. "I want two complete copies. Have them made and delivered to my office. Tonight." *In case something should happen to you.*

Volante nodded. "Immediately." She added, her voice flat, "There is a...problem within the *hewat*."

He frowned. "What do you mean?"

She walked to the opposite side of the table and faced him. "Isma'il was making excellent progress. He was well into transcribing five of the thirteen books even before we found the MCF formula." She nodded toward the stack of paper that Niccolo had been examining. "The discovery of the original notes brought direction and complication at the same time, because the hewat now has eight different interpretations of the process." Her lips pursed. "They are blocked and haggling like jackals over a bone."

"There's no time for haggling," Niccolo growled. "Do you know how vital this is? What's at stake?" He slammed his fist on the table, making the pens scatter. "The longer that the Librah Vae-ta is out of our grasp, the greater the danger to the empire!" He whirled on her, pumping hot, angry breath into her face. "Put a stop to their infantile shit. You're not a fucking babysitter. I want a restored book, not excuses." He fixed a stare on her. "You must command the hewat. Loosen your controls or tighten them, whatever gets results. Do you understand me?"

Volante raised her chin as her eyes narrowed to slits. "An executive decision. Yes, I understand."

He retreated a half-step, eyeing her. "What are you thinking?"

She pushed her hands into the pockets of her suit jacket. "One member is agitating the others. Blocking our progress. If this member is removed from the hewat, we will see infinitely more rapid results."

Niccolo appraised Volante up and down, trying to track what might be circling through the woman's eternally busy mind. "Who?"

"Maia."

The word hit him like a slap. "Explain yourself."

Volante seemed to grow taller as she slid closer to him; her eyes burned like coals. "We've both seen situations where a great ability, in this case her great fluency with the language, is attached to a great sense of ownership. She thinks that she has the answers to all the questions that the group presents. She won't listen to them, or to me." Her eyebrows rose. "She's an obstruction. The sooner that she's gone, the faster the re-creation of the book will be complete."

Is this merely Franca's method of sabotage? Manipulating the players? Niccolo spun to face the far wall as his thoughts raced. *Maia's orders are to retrieve the Librah Vae-ta and eliminate the outside parties. Why would she block the hewat from restoring the book?* He pressed a fist against clenched thigh muscles.

Volante watched him, her eyes darting like scattering birds.

Conflict of interest. Yes. If the hewat succeeds at a restoration, there is no need to retrieve the original...therefore no motivation and no reward. He turned back to face her. "If she is blocking the hewat, remove her," he muttered.

"And if she also presents a threat to the Dama?"

She's dropping tactical breadcrumbs! In one driving step, he was at Volante's face. His voice was a gritty growl. "Do *not* play these games, Franca. If you have something to say, disclose it now."

Volante licked her lips. In steady voice, she said, "I believe that her loyalty has been compromised and that she is at the point of desertion." She pressed forward while looking directly into Niccolo's eyes. "And I believe that if she deserts Omega, she will single-handedly bring down the empire."

He stared at her, aghast, feeling his pulse throbbing at his neck.

"You know what she is capable of. Her talents. If she is not loyal to Omega, then she is an enemy of the empire and a powerful one. A red-level threat to all in key positions." Her eyes flashed, and he saw the fusion of logic, self-service, and ambition. "Including myself. Including you."

Niccolo felt all his muscles tighten, his mouth suddenly rough and dry as concrete.

What prompts her to bring me a slanderous rumor about a fellow Elder? What does she crave more, the vitality of the empire or her own advancement? His voice was the cold edge of a blade. "How do you know this? What's your evidence?

"I could tell you that now, or I could reveal it later." She stared, cool and inquisitive. "Which do you prefer?"

Do I take her at her word and affirm my trust in her? Or challenge her? Force her to prove this allegation, a clear signal that I question her loyalty? He watched her staring at him, waiting in infinite patience. *Once seeds of distrust are sewn, they are almost impossible to destroy.*

He could smell her, the honey-lavender fragrance, but now he imagined that smell in combination with the smell of Maia's hot skin—how her sweat would smell as he circled a fingertip through it, the sweet scent of her hair as it tumbled across his neck—and the need for her was more painful than ever.

An image blazed into his mind: he saw a wide sea, himself in a boat holding two braided tethers. At the end of one: Maia. At the end of the other: Volante and the empire. There was not enough room in the boat for both. Only one could be pulled toward him. Only one could survive.

He stepped forward, his face now a hand's width from hers. For the first time, he noticed marks on her cheeks, tiny indentations that looked as if they had healed over long ago. Her eyes, a dusty hazel green like scorched grass, the lines etched at the corners. The fine edge of her nose. Her face reflected a deadly drive toward perfection but also something hidden much deeper at her core.

Unflinching, she stared back.

His tone was as hollow as the barrel of a gun. "Bring me your evidence. Specific, documented evidence."

The gauntlet. Now the consequences—for both of them. He quoted from The Words of Reckoning. "If they find that devotion to Omega has been lost, the faithful shall not suffer an apostate to live."

Volante withdrew her hands from her jacket pockets and raised them upward in a gesture of prayer. "Padarah oh mehga."

Does the play of her lips betray terror or glee?

He left her standing in the shadows.

CHAPTER 26

Two hundred pounds and no more, girl!

Celia tried to bully herself into thrift as she descended into the high drama of Ormonde Jayne: enormous glass cases, shelves, and displays of steel and gleaming black, accented with sunflower gold tapestries and fresh-cut gardenia arrangements. Cedar, mimosa, patchouli, rosewood, and vanilla swirled together in an olfactory tango. She saw, scattered across the counters, sniffing bowls filled with raw coffee beans.

A nice afternoon of hooky and self-indulgence—long overdue, she thought, meandering down the main aisle with intense attention on proximity: if she turned abruptly and her handbag toppled a display, one broken bottle of perfume would become a puddle of several month's rent.

As she walked by the testing counter, she caught the eye of an attendant. The young woman acknowledged her with a nod and stepped toward her. "May I help you find something?"

"Opium Orchidee. Yves Saint..."

"Laurent, yes, I know it well. A dangerous floral." Smiling, she held out a hand. "Please come with me." The woman hustled her to a tall display at the far left side of the shop, and once Celia was entrenched in crystal, she floated away.

As Celia knelt to study the items on the bottom row, a pair of kitten-grey heels crept into her peripheral vision. A voice floated down. "Do you know the origin of it?"

She turned toward the voice, frowning. *Who's this gauche tart? You don't chat up other patrons in a place like this.* She rose to face a woman: petite and lofty in high heels, wrapped in a black-and-white Lacroix suit. Her hair was pulled back into a bun so tight that it seemed to rein the skin on her cheeks. In one hand, she held a bottle of lavender oil; in the other, a bottle of Opium Orchidee.

Moving one finger toward one of the less-expensive bottles—only seventy pounds—Celia said, "I know that it was developed in Nice for the French king's mistress."

"That's right." The woman turned a half-lidded look on Celia that, under much different circumstances, might have been taken as flirtation. "But there's far more to the story of Opium Orchidee. The artisans stumbled across a blend that they believed possessed a secret power, the power to enslave any person who breathed it. They became addicted to it."

"Fanciful story." Celia felt the woman's eyes moving up and down her as if sifting options.

The woman murmured, "There's a good deal about sensual attraction—yes, well, human behavior in general—that we have yet to understand. For instance, what instills in humans a sense of purpose."

A tight smile tugged at Celia's lips, one that she hoped sent the message *Thanks ever so much! Now get out of my face, weirdo.* "Can't say that I see what connects perfume with a sense of purpose," she muttered, edging toward the next display.

The woman slid toward her. Intention seemed to burn in her hazel eyes. "Everything we do is connected with purpose." She glanced down at the slate floor, chuckled softly, and then looked up at Celia. "I'm sorry, you must be thinking I'm some sort of lunatic, babbling philosophic questions in the middle of a perfumery." Her face softened.

At least she realizes it. Celia laughed, relaxing a bit. "Yes, I am, and I'm not gay, if that's what you're thinking."

The woman broke into laughter, and she pressed her handbag against her abdomen. "Oh my god, I've given you entirely the wrong impression. I'm so sorry to have bothered you. Forgive me." Her voice dropped to a lower tone. "I'm just nervous, I suppose, about the talk that I'm giving tonight."

"A talk on what?"

The woman tipped her head. "The ideas that I made a terrible muddle of a moment ago. What some say are the greatest of all questions. How to find the meaning of all our struggles. Finding our deepest purpose."

What is she, one of these evangelistic self-help gurus? Celia clucked her tongue against the roof of her mouth. "Are you a therapist?"

"Of a sort. I help people to realize their full potential, to move toward the next level."

Irritation and curiosity clawing inside her, Celia wondered, *Next level of what? How not to pick up chicks in shops?*

The woman retreated a step, slid her hand into her bag, pulled out a trifold flyer, and held it out. The text on the cover read, *Whether you believe that you live forever—or you don't—you're right.*

"There's a new take on an old axiom," Celia muttered, taking the flyer.

"Yes, and you see, that's what my talk is about. What we believe we are capable of or how we keep ourselves stuck in despair, unknowing and unsatisfied."

Celia flipped the flyer over and scanned the lines on the back. "What did you say your name was?" She took a longer look at the woman. Against the backdrop of the shop's architecture, post-modern with abrupt angles, she suddenly looked jarringly out of place. Too incandescent for Mayfair's cutting-edge *haute couture.*

"I didn't." The woman maneuvered closer. "Sylvia Volante." She extended her hand.

Celia frowned. "Unknowing and unsatisfied? What made you want to speak on such a depressing topic?" *What is she really addressing? Self-concept? Worth? Inadequacy? All issues that my clients deal with.*

"Nothing depressing about it at all when you offer people something better."

"And what would that be?" *What sad flavor of redemption is she espousing?*

Again, the woman dipped her hand into her bag to withdraw a card, which she handed to Celia. "If you'd like to attend the lecture tonight and find out, you're welcome to come. Eight o'clock at the Strathmore Center." Eyebrows raised, she smiled. "I'd be honored to have you there as my guest, miss..."

"Devereaux," Celia said. *Probably a gathering of New Age change workers, the old camp in updated window dressing. I'd love to find out how they've packaged whatever snake oil they're selling.*

"Devereaux. Wonderful. If you don't have a prior commitment, please come. Nothing to lose. Think it over." The woman cleared her throat. "It was a pleasure to meet you, Ms. Devereaux." She raised an index finger toward the gleaming, black bottles of Opium Orchidee. "And be careful with that stuff. It's quite dangerous."

The woman turned on her heels, strutted down the main aisle, heels clicking on the marble, and left through the glass entrance door.

Celia shoved the card into the basement of her handbag. *Some of us handle danger better than others, sweets.*

CHAPTER 27

Volante stepped onto the stage.

Hungry faces, aged early twenties to thirties, stared up at her. She saw a pierced nose, ragged jeans, leather boots, and a denim jacket with a button reading "Hate Is Not a Family Value" on the pocket. Sitting cross-legged or in A-frame shapes on the hardwood floor, they shifted uncomfortably as they waited.

The pantsuit of ivory silk caressed her skin. She slid her hands into the pockets of the tunic and gazed out across them, her body relaxed and alert.

Start your engines.

She pulled her shoulders back, closed her eyes, and began with the Prayer of Devotion. "Abbah way non vash ah parateh, sho day too vashla meed neh-vee von besh garah, mem vahla padarah oh meh-ga."

Seated at the back of the room, a lithe woman with short black hair murmured, "Nah-maen."

Volante sent an approving smile toward the woman, then thought, *Start with assumption.* She said softly, "You are wondering."

Attention pulled forward. A gum bubble popped.

She walked to the other side of the stage, silently assessing.

A cough. Their heads moved as one turned toward another. Whispering, nervous murmurs. A bracelet rattled.

Gliding back to the center of the stage, she faced them and said in a deeper, stronger tone, "What you believe in, and why what you believe in matters."

Heads nodded in rhythm.

She shifted her weight to the other heel. "And you are wondering...how what I have to say to you tonight will make a difference in your life. Your life today, your life tomorrow," she added deliberate emphasis, "and your life eternal."

As if waking from comas, their eyes began to widen.

"Am I right?"

Heads bobbed as murmured assent rose.

"Because there isn't anything in this world that moves you, buoys you, raises you out of the sludge and the pain of modern life and gives you a deeper sense of nobility. Am I right?"

"Yeah!"

Volante's eyes turned to the owner of the voice, the girl's spiked hair, streaked with red and purple, her nose ring, and her jack boots, painted with red swastikas.

"You've been to private schools. You sat in mass, took communion, you were baptized or bar mitzvahed. You read your holy book. You confessed your sins. You fasted for Ramadan. You ate the body and drank the blood. And *still!*" She stomped her heel against the parquet. "Still you are hungry for the truth, the real truth, the highest truth. Right?"

"Right on!" a man in torn jeans shouted.

She meandered to the other side of the stage. "Today you are ralea, the heretic. You are submerged in the black shadow of falsehood. You have never been exposed to the path that leaves all others in the dust."

Haughty grins began to emerge.

Like teens bragging about losing their virginity. Even the anticipation of power is a sweet seduction. The image of the glass pitcher shattering in her sink flashed through her mind.

"And before you leave today, you will be faced with an important choice. Continue as dirty ralea or ascend to washed-clean Dosa. If you take this step, you will be welcomed to Omega with open arms. You will have taken that first step on the path toward ultimate truth."

Murmuring excitedly, eyes lambent, their bodies swayed as if to unheard music.

She continued. "With further teaching in the foundations of the faith, and by offering before witnesses your vow to uphold the precepts, you will ascend to the level of Shoto. Then your Ordering begins. The stripping away of illusion, the extinction of attachment to a meaningless world, the pash-lo, that offers only the empty shadows of truth."

Truth? A useful commodity. Well-oiled wheels turned in her mind. She turned to pace the stage again. "You will have many weeks of training. You will learn a new language. You will read a new book, one you've never read before, never even knew of before. Then and only then may you apply for admittance to the Dama."

A chubby woman with dreadlocks raised her hand. "What's that?"

"The Dama is the inner discipleship, the select members who may attend the Damaii service. As Habareh, I lead the Damaii and serve on the Council of Elders," she paused, "the body that serves the Abba, push tah non ah meh-gah."

Rustling, breathing.

"I now offer you that choice. Those who wish to leave may do so, but those who wish to initiate their membership into the Dosa should stay to talk with me individually." She steepled her hands in front of her, offering the audience a soft gaze. "I thank you all for coming. Dajva."

As they uncurled and rose, shoes scuffled on the floor, trinkets and chains rattled, and the white noise of conversation droned through the room. Volante watched as a handful of people headed toward the exit sign. Those who remained, close to fifty, glanced at her and at each other and then trundled into a queue.

Not bad, she thought.

The first person in the line was a wide man in dusty jeans and a denim jacket, perhaps having come directly from a construction site. As he approached her, his blue eyes fluttered; she saw the shadow of skepticism. She smiled warmly and moved toward him. He stepped into her space, and she tilted her head forward, her lips close to his ear as she whispered. A light filled his eyes.

Beaming, he straightened and walked slowly toward the door. The line shuffled forward.

The next person was the trim woman with short black hair. She stepped toward Volante. Smiling but wide-eyed, she seemed caught between smugness and caution.

Volante bent and whispered to her, "A wise choice, Celia, I commend you. Stay after the others have gone. I have an important question for you."

CHAPTER 28

She turned the key in the lock, pushed open the door, tossed her raincoat onto a coat rack, and entered the loft apartment. In the cavernous silence, each click of her heels on the hardwood floor echoed. Recruiting assemblies were well-scripted performances, usually requiring little effort, but this one had drained her. After dismissing the new initiates, she'd talked with Devereaux for almost two hours. Her shoulder muscles ached.

"It won't work, Franca." The voice was fossil dry.

Volante whirled, her gut clutching.

The hulking form at the front door floated toward her: pants of brushed cotton, a black tank top. A menacing expression and dark eyes that burned.

Volante swallowed to release her vocal cords. "You? Christ. Get out of my house. You're trespassing. I'll call the..."

"Police?" Maia laughed. "Can you really be that thick?" She inched closer. Her body suggested the power of a bulldozer, but she moved with fluid, silent grace.

"What do you want?" Volante said flatly.

"I know all about your smear campaign," Maia growled. "Oh, you think you are the only one with informants?" Her eyes narrowed. "Trying to discredit and eliminate me. Niccolo won't fall for that."

Volante smiled. *He already has.*

"Even if he speaks to the opposite," Maia said. "He might say something like 'remove her from the hewat, from the Dama, and if she shows any signs of desertion, take the appropriate action.'"

Volante felt her mouth go dry. While fighting to hide any sign of inward battle, she felt a bead of sweat run down the middle of her back.

Maia stepped forward, her body moving like a tank that was never heard. A vein in her neck throbbed with metronomic steadiness. "What I have in mind for *Niccolo*," she spat the name, "he has no concept of. His battles weaken him, blind him. They will destroy him." She paused. "You will be wise to reverse course."

Volante locked eyes with her. "And if I do not?"

What will you do, whore? Turn his lust against him, then turn him against me? He needs my means and ends far more than he needs an assassin that he can screw.

Maia began a slow circle around her, her hands on her hips, her eyes moving over Volante's body as if assessing height and weight. Volante watched, hyperaware of the hiss of her own ragged breathing and Maia's utter silence.

Face to face again, Maia said, "When you look far enough down the road, Franca, you can see that we both want the same thing."

"You have no idea what I want," Volante muttered and winced, regretting saying it aloud.

"That is where, as in a few other issues, some you are not even aware of, you are dead wrong."

At the word *dead,* Volante felt her lips turn cold.

"Among those issues is that of experience." The edges of her lips quivered as if a bitter smile were imminent. "We both know of the discrepancy between your track record and mine."

Her body trembling with anger, Volante thought, *The line in the desert sand!*

"Make your executive decision, Franca, but know that what you're planning will cost you."

Not as much as it will cost you. She started to bellow, *Get out, you bitch!!* Instead, she said, her tone cold, "Get out, Maia."

Keeping her eyes fixed on Volante, Maia slowly stepped backward toward the door, then turned and slid into the darkness.

Her heart pounding, Volante leaned back against her sofa, working to slow her breath. In a moment, she straightened and walked to her kitchen. She kicked her high heels into the corner and pulled a mug from the cupboard.

A few minutes later, she was in the upper-level office, booting up her Internet connection. The cup of Darjeeling Dragon sat on the desktop, the tendrils of steam spiraling toward the ceiling like exorcised demons.

An executive decision.

Illuminated only by the blue glow of the monitor, Volante's fingers danced over the keyboard.

CHAPTER 29

Gatsby felt the lift quake as it rumbled to life and the buttons light up: G - 2 - 3...

With a *ding,* the doors opened.

She stepped into the chaos of the mall that had taken over Covent Garden: three levels of shops and restaurants, overpriced gewgaws of every kind, the flurry of a traveling circus including a central plaza where undertalented teen acts tap-danced or sang Broadway tunes.

Ambling down the crowded aisle, she felt her head swim. Images, faces, sounds, and memories poured through her like a carbonated liquid of the psyche, popping and fizzing through her neurons.

How can the Gahana do what it does? What is its hidden secret? What are the keys? Will we be able to crack the language before it's too late?

She remembered Parrish's face, the muscles contracting under the fabric of his jeans, the thread of bloody saliva that spiraled from his lip. *What if the journey costs us far more than we imagined?*

Thith wasn't voluntary...

She shuddered and jogged forward, passing display cases packed with the sirens of the material world. Hip-hugging jeans. Cornsilk facial scrub. iPods and HDTV, duvets and camcorders and Godiva gift baskets wrapped in crinkly red cellophane. Black and orange window displays that blared cautionary warnings about Friday the thirteenth.

An image of her desk calendar rose in her mind. *Friday the thirteenth? So it is.*

Stopping at a chocolatier, she bought a bag of caramel turtles, ate one, and stuffed the rest into her shoulderbag. Glancing at her watch, she did a slow about-face and headed down the aisle toward the bank of lifts at the far end. When the doors opened, she stepped into the car and slid toward one side as a woman moved in to stand next to her. The doors closed.

She felt a quiet curiosity drift over her; there was something intriguing about the woman. Without turning her head, she picked out details: loose, soft-fabric pants, a black tank top, silky, black hair that swirled around her muscular shoulders. It struck her as odd that the woman would wear a sleeveless tee-shirt in mid-October. The temperature had dropped into the low fifties. More than the clothes, Gatsby noted the woman's commanding body. *A body-building competition winner?*

As the woman stared at the operation panel on the front wall, she gave off a clear *Don't fuck with me* signal.

The woman pulled something from the pocket of her pants, reached toward the panel, and inserted a silver key. Her finger hovered over the red STOP button and then pushed it.

The car jolted violently. Cables sizzled and brakes screamed as the car shuddered to a stop.

"What the hell are you doing?!" Gatsby shouted.

The woman turned to her with cold eyes. "Saving your life."

Gatsby felt herself gasp. Her mind spiraled crazily in a million directions, trying to assess what was happening and what the woman might want.

The emergency telephone and alarm bell on the wall?

The woman was planted, rooted as a truck, between her and the panel.

The fear rose as anger. "Listen, you crazy bit..."

"Shut up." Clipped, cold.

Gatsby blinked. *Who is she?!*

The woman hissed, "There's no time to explain! I'm going to say this once, and then you'll never see me again. I am doing this to save your life. Are you listening?"

Eyes wide, Gatsby nodded. The smell of sweat floated over her.

"They know what you're doing. You, the man, and the woman. They want the Librah Vae-ta. They're poised to retrieve it, and they don't care who dies."

Gatsby swallowed back a scream.

"Return it to them."

"Who?" she whispered.

The woman's expression soured. "You can't be that stupid."

I know about Omega, more than I ever wanted to know, and if one of them approaches you, run, run like hell, or you're risking everything, including your life...

Spikes of panic shot through her. "Omega."

The woman folded one hand into a gun shape. With each word, she jabbed an index finger toward Gatsby's face. "They—don't—care—who—dies." She seemed to stifle a shudder. "The great eternal truth awaits them in the afterlife. Not for me."

Gatsby scrambled to think while her muscles cramped with fear. "They rejected you?"

"No, they pulled me in with thousands of arms and gave me...a post. Today I am resigning my position. I have been ordered to kill for the last time."

Her mind whirled to the face of the man in the bar, the omega branded onto his tongue. She felt herself trembling violently. Hypothermia of the soul.

"Do whatever it takes to protect yourself. Run, disappear, whatever it takes. You're in the crosshairs, and they won't give up until they have what they want."

"What do they want?" Gatsby whispered.

"The book, but ultimately, they want what they can never truly have. Their path to salvation is fear. Terrorism, bloodshed. But they are blind to their own brutality, and that is what makes them so deadly."

In the beat of silence, they watched each other, breathing hard.

The woman stretched her hand out, fit the key into the operation panel, and turned it. The car wheezed and jolted into motion. At the second level, it stopped.

She slid toward Gatsby, close enough that their shoulders almost touched, and whispered, "Ride to the ground level and go straight to the Tube. Don't get off at your usual stop. Take aberrant routes for the next few days. Don't go to any usual places. Stay with crowds."

The doors slid open with a *whhhsssh* sound.

As the woman turned to Gatsby, her body seemed to go rigid, then pliant, as if emotions warred within. Finally, she whispered, "You need to know this. Your file is substantial, and I have read all of it. He didn't want to hurt you, but what he wants from you now is something far..."

As if panicked by an assailant, she bolted out of the lift and ran, her meaty arms pumping by her sides.

Gatsby leaped forward as the lift doors closed behind her. "Wait!"

He didn't want to hurt you? Who? Chaos rampaged through her. *Oh my god—Woody?!* The second bomb exploded: *WHAT file?! Who has a substantial file on me?!?*

She doubled over, arms pressed against her stomach, her universe detonating.

CHAPTER 30

"They're her's."

Volante's voice seemed to reverberate in the Officia Abba and ghost through the empty building. She pushed a sheet of card stock across the conference table and peered at Niccolo.

He bent toward it to examine the four fingerprints that were aligned horizontally across the card. Below each, notes scrawled in black ink detailed the categories of the matching nodes.

"These could have been lifted off a drinking glass. A phone, anything."

"They could have." Volante rose like a silk-tailored phantom and walked to the far side of the room. As she approached the acrylic case that housed his collection of knives, her hand moved toward its steel edge. "But they weren't. They were found on this."

He felt his breath catch.

"And on that case." She pointed to the open door of the vault that was tucked inside a false cabinet—the custom-designed vault with steel walls and coded locks that his experts had crafted to protect the Librah Vae-ta.

A sinking feeling of shock pushed Niccolo into the tallest chair at the head of the table. He watched Volante with narrowed eyes as she returned to the table and took a seat at his left.

"Fingerprints prove nothing," he growled.

"But they don't work in her behalf." She leaned down toward the briefcase that she had stowed under the table, pulled out a manila folder, and fanned it open in front of him.

He scanned the pages. The text was sprinkled with coded gibberish and symbols: ampersands, pound signs, brackets, exclamation marks. "What is this?"

"She used an ingenious technique. Hide information inside the system of those who must not see it—then encrypt it. These were found on your network." She turned toward the bank of computers at the back of the room.

What would she hide from me? And why?! He felt his teeth grinding. "Encrypted? On my network?"

She nodded.

"How did you discover them?"

"Kuznetsov, our electronic bug zapper. He found a virus, that led to another virus, that led to a system crash. In rebuilding everything, he found a cache of .xte files that didn't belong anywhere. When he realized that they were text files, he found a backdoor method to download them."

"But you said they were encrypted."

"Even more clever. Her fluency with the Omega language is only one level of her aptitude. She was able to devise a mutated version of it, one that would seem familiar and therefore go unnoticed, at least for a while, but one that only she could understand." She sat back in the chair. "Maia has been one step ahead of us for a long time."

He drew in a long breath, palms sweating, emotions tearing through him like a machine gun, and swallowed hard. "Have you decrypted it?"

She pulled one of the pages from his hand. "Ivan and I worked all night. We were able to isolate two letters, A and B. From that, we could identify the references to *Abba.*" She fixed cold eyes on him. "Many hours after that, we could read everything."

He rubbed his forehead hard enough to chafe the skin. "What do they say?"

She pulled her hands onto the table slowly, as if bracing herself. "I will give you a complete report when we've worked through the entirety of it, but the crux is this." She licked her lips. "She has not only left the discipleship, but she has selected her target. Not the target that you ordered her to find and eliminate." She paused. "The target is *you.*"

A blade of fear sliced through him. He found himself gulping for air, almost choking.

No! Not her, the one that I would...

She watched him for a moment, then held up a text-sprinkled page. "She details how she has you right where she wants you. Bound by conflicting emotions, distracted, muddled, your defenses down. She says that you won't see it coming, especially if she waits for a short period. But as soon as you relax your defenses, she plans to strike."

He held a breath, pressed his slippery palms together, and blew it out. "Are they private, some sort of diary? Or messages that she's sending to someone else?"

She shook her head. "It could be either. We can't tell."

Interrogate Kuznetsov, get some confirmation! If ANY of this is true! He felt blood rushing to his face, blasts of anger, the desire to throttle, to beat into submission, and at the same time, all the sensations of her—her face, her hair, her skin, black eyes, the lips that would taste of salt and fire—pumped through his body. He wanted her dead. He wanted his desire for her to kill him.

How could I not see this?!

Finally, he croaked, "Bring her to me."

Volante shifted in her chair. "She's disappeared."

He froze. "What are you saying?"

She pushed her chair back. "I've had disciples search every quadrant of the city, but we both know that her greatest talent is being invisible." She tilted her head. "She will be very, very difficult to find."

Panic propelled him out of his chair. He strode to the far side of the room, turned away from Volante, dug his cell phone from his pocket, and dialed. He felt, in his memory, her fingers grazing his as she had taught him what to do if he wished to reach her privately: not a number but an alpha-symbolic code that connected his phone, and his only, to her custom-made phone, and hers only.

Each unanswered ring screamed into the pit of his soul.

He snapped the phone shut. Shoving the phone back into his pocket, he stepped to a desk in the far corner, opened a shallow drawer, and peered inside. The metal case, about the size of a deck of playing cards, was undisturbed. He pushed against the locks and lifted the lid.

Her tracking device lay in its silicon container.

If she needed to be found, she would have taken it.

Immediate and mandatory decisions pummeled him.

Volante's voice, a serpentine hiss in his ear, made him jump. "I knew that it was my duty to tell you."

I must confirm everything! This evidence is strong, but...

The agony that whipped at him began to flutter downward into his depths, where all was cold and black.

Volante warned me. The empire's most successful assassin is now the enemy of the empire—and of me. He waited for the stab of sorrow but felt it drift away, like dust clouds on a deserted city street. *And if she does not want to be found, I will never see her again.*

He stilled himself by walking back to his executive chair, standing behind it, and gripping its back. It was heavy, moveable, but solid, like the empire that he would command—with or without Maia. With or without the pain of her, the addiction that he craved with every fiber. He stared at the folder on the table.

"Find out where she is. What she's doing. If she has shifted her loyalties elsewhere, find out who she now serves."

Volante drummed her fingertips together.

"Meet me, here. Monday morning."

She gathered the papers into the folder, which she then slipped into her briefcase. Rising, she moved closer to Niccolo; her fragrant smell drifted over him.

"I will dedicate every available resource to gathering the information. You have my word." Her hands rose, as if she might slide her palm against his forearm, but then moved back to her sides. "I can do this, Niccolo."

He watched her walk from the room, thinking, *She has not earned the right to call me by my name!*

Or has she?

Click click click click click...

From the Officia Abba, Volante strode down the dark hallway toward the front door of the building. The sound of her heels tapping on the wood punctuated her thoughts like needle pricks. When certain that Niccolo would not see her, she allowed the smile.

He bought it!! All of it, every fake document, every lie!

Her smile widened. *Oh poor Abba. And poor Maia. Missing? Oh no, Niccolo. I know exactly where she is.*

CHAPTER 31

Tube passengers bustled past her as she slid from the crowd to stand alone by the tile wall. When the cell phone vibrated in the pocket of her blazer, she pulled it out and flipped it open. She pressed the phone against her ear; the back of her pearl earring stabbed into her neck, making her wince.

As a voice began to flow from the phone, she turned to face the wall. Her eyes darted left and right.

A moment later, she said, "When?"

She raised her left arm and peered at her watch. Her voice dropped to a whisper.

"The s-weight?"

She ran her tongue over painted lips.

"Colindale Farms. A kilometer of orchard, then the Harrows Bridge. Wait for one hour."

She snapped the phone shut and stowed it in her pocket.

The lines of Niccolo's drawn face appeared in her mind; she heard his gravelly voice and the Words of Reckoning: *The faithful shall not suffer an apostate to live.*

And now the wheels spin freely, Volante thought. She moved forward and disappeared into the jostling crowd.

Crimson clouds bled from the black fabric toward the surface of the water. Strands of long, dark hair swirled into fractal coils, then slowly unwound as the body sank, bubbling, silent.

CHAPTER 32

As Niccolo pulled his car behind the main building and parked, he thought, *Actions and consequences. We must get to business, quickly.* He headed for the Officia Abba.

The executive chairs still huddled around the table like pawns around a king. In less than a minute, as he stood before his desk, Volante walked into the room. The lines of her face seemed more pronounced, her perfect hair subtly tousled.

Something is costing her sleep?

She slid into the same chair that she'd occupied two evenings before and looked up at him, the glow of expectation in her eyes.

He moved to the far wall, his back to her, staring at the case and the spray of knives. His eyes crept across the razor-sharp edges and the handles carved with stars, arrows, fangs.

I have held each one of them in my hand and so often thought of their inventive uses. Especially the gishtal. His chest filled, then released both oxygen and hope. *But that is not to be.*

Heat exploded through his body, so intense that his face flushed and lights sparkled in his vision. An image rose in his mind: long dark strands, like the trails of a dying star, floating, slowly submerging, drowning, sinking into an abyss black as death. Going...

Gone.

The waters rippled, erasing all trace, and flowed away into a sea of amnesia. A leaden heaviness seeped through his muscles. He shuffled back to the table and sat next to Volante with a sigh.

"There are advisors with whom you have not yet spoken. You will meet them tomorrow. More importantly, you now have an assignment." The chaos of lust and loss burned in his body, and his eyes dropped to the seams in the floor. "The one at which she failed."

"The Librah Vae-ta."

"Yes. With every second, the danger of its destruction increases," his lips curled, "or its decryption, and I do not have to explain what either circumstance means to the empire."

"You do not."

"All officers must be reinterviewed. Separately. Each one must be verified, from the senior Elder to the freshest Dosa. Even your personal zasha."

A muscle under Volante's eye twitched. "I have replaced my zasha."

He frowned. *What's she planning?* "Why?"

"I have recruited someone that I believe will better serve the needs of Omega." She looked away for a moment. "Tracking Donovan has proved extremely difficult. The phone taps were unsuccessful—disrupted and then joy-phreaked by the CIS, Kuznetsov thinks. But my new zasha will take us directly to Donovan and the Librah Vae-ta. It's the hypnotherapist. Devereaux."

Niccolo fell back in his chair, his mouth popping open. "Qaz!! How did you maneuver that?"

"Never reveal my methods or my sources, even to you. Remember? As you told me, tangling the threads of knowledge assures protection on multiple levels." She fixed a steely stare on him. "I committed to your instruction as soon as it was spoken."

He drew in a long pull of air. As his eyes swept over her, he wanted to smile at her efficiency but could not. "I knew my intuition about you would prove correct."

Efficient...but sly. I must watch her very carefully.

He nodded toward the banks of computer equipment. "Devereaux. Start a file on her."

Her hazel eyes flared. "It's already done."

CHAPTER 33

From the lift at the mall, Gatsby emerged into the ground level of a parking structure, glancing right and left, listening for footsteps. She checked her watch: 4:16. Now low in the sky, the sun blanketed London with shadows.

Take aberrant routes for the next few days. Don't go to any usual places. Stay with crowds.

She started down the sidewalk, hyperaware of her heart pounding. Rounding a corner, the covered entrance to the Tube opened before her. She descended into the belly of the subway and boarded the Blue line rather than the Red line that, on a typical commute, took her directly to King's Road. All around her, the faces of passengers were masks, each hiding a ruthless secret. Each bag or briefcase could contain a gun, a knife, a bomb.

At Leicester Square, she changed to the Red line. Tottenham Court Road, then Piccadilly Circus.

She leapt from the train and onto the platform, then sprinted up the stairs until she reached the sidewalk. Many stores were still open, and their light spilled from their windows. At each corner, she furtively glanced left and right.

Crossing the street at the intersection of Royale and Burlington, she jumped at a brusque shout, "Hey!" Whirling, she saw a man closing the door of his building and trotting toward a waiting taxi. Her lungs filled with air.

Every tree hid a sniper.

The sun dipped behind an invisible cloud, shrouding the air, seeming to draw an oily cast over the street busy with cabs, buses, and people. She swallowed and walked faster.

The store fronts seemed to be moving by her rather than her by them as she slid down the street. Garish displays filled with mannequins, boots, CDs, flowers, coats, clocks—she sped past them, licking her lips and registering a faint ammonia taste.

A building front, boarded over with plywood, fluttered with adverts. One huge poster, awash with loud primary colors, advertised the upcoming Josh Damien concert at the

Hammersmith Apollo, and below the singer's pensive stare and wavy locks, she saw:

$$\text{☾☥S⑂⑂O⋔⟐✗}$$

"Oh god...no..."

Elbows and briefcases brushed her as people moved around her on the sidewalk. She turned abruptly and collided with a fifty-ish gentleman in a grey mackintosh.

"Sorry!"

As the man's eyes narrowed, he spat, "Deh-resu metah shah no!"

He shoved past her, leaving her standing slack-jawed. A foul taste began to seep into her mouth.

No...no...no...no...

Was she speaking aloud or thinking the words? Did it matter?

Thoughts are just subvocalized speech.

A high buzz started up in her head, like a sprite-demon trepanning her skull with a drill.

Out of nowhere, music began to float toward her, high voices like those of castrati, their songs swirling against the stones of an ancient cathedral and up toward eternity: *Kyrie eleison, Christe eleison, Kyrie abbah way non push tah non ah meh-gah...*

Gatsby dashed down the sidewalk, leaping over the bag or dog or child that obstructed her, sprinting down Piccadilly and through the pigeon-infested plaza at Wellington Arch, racing down Grosvenor Place until she was at King's Road.

Running from the shadowy figures that galloped behind her, howling her name and then funerary dirges in Latin, monotone Hebraic chanting overlaid with garage-acid-metal sung in Arabic...she ran and ran, harder, her lungs heaving, her heart about to burst from her chest, her brain a war zone, and she ran harder, feeling fear like a tsunami swelling over her—

She crashed against the door of her building, choking for air and digging in her shoulderbag for the key, then pushed through the doorway and into the carpeted hall. She was instantly engulfed in the smells of guttered ash and candle wax.

The foyer spun.

Gasping, she slid down on the first stair. Her shoulderbag landed by her feet with a thud as she dropped her head into shaking hands, whispering, "I'd kill the fucker, I'd kill him sho ri-deh-resu through prayer and sacrifice shall the firm disciple find the way, professing to them the way of redemption, you give testimony to the power and to the terrible damnation of the disbelievers will bow in trembling, they see the sea of blood that will take them..."

She clamped both hands over her mouth, but the words gushed, unstoppable lamentations of power, destruction, insanity.

The power and the terrible damnation and they see the sea of blood that will take them...

What he took from me! He violated me!!

...and God's pure love will wash away all fear, all confusion...

...see the sea of blood that will take them...

Tears tumbled over her clenched fists.

He abandoned me! And for what? God?!

Terror melted over her body; fury glistened on its black surface.

I have to know, I have to know, I have to know...

The words spun in her head—relentless, the maddening itch that she would sell her soul to scratch, the cancer that killed one cell at a time.

I have to know what it will take to stop feeling this feeling.

With a glass of Glenlivet tinkling in her hand, she burrowed into her living room couch and called Sanderson. After six rings, and just as she turned to hang up, the line connected.

"Hello?"

The fear she had reined in for hours burst to the surface. "Woody, they know! They're coming for us!"

She heard him pull in a breath.

"Woody!"

"I'm here, what's happened? Slow down, start from the beginning."

She told him. Covent Garden. The elevator, the woman, the look on her face when she said, *They are blind to their own brutality, and that is what makes them so deadly.*

She choked back a cry, pressing one hot palm over her eyes.

A hard swallow. "If anything happened to you. Gatsby, I love you, Kama, I've always loved you."

You left me!!

"But you're okay? She didn't hurt you, did she?"

She sighed wearily, her eyes still closed. "No, but we are being watched, Woody."

"I know we are."

The question flared: *Just how do you know?* A frown bunched her forehead.

"Stay where you are. I'm coming over," he said.

"No!"

She didn't want to see him, suddenly didn't want to be talking to him. Wanted only to know what he was hiding from her. Why he was concealing the *real* reason that he had just happened to come to London for a conference at the same time that a book worth killing for—and that perhaps had killed—had surfaced, why the man with a history so rich in religious study was conveniently available, and willing, to help her analyze a book of religious doctrine.

She heard a voice whispering, the obscura epitaph of an eternity of punishment—

(but the fearful, and unbelieving, and the abominable, and murderers, and whoremongers, and sorcerers, and idolaters, and all liars, shall have their part in the lake which burneth with fire and brimstone—which is the second death—I am Alpha and Omega, the beginning and the end)

—and did not realize that the voice was her own.

"Gatsby? Wait, what are you saying?! You're not making any..."

She slammed the phone down, breathing hard. Stared at the room. The corners were all wrong. The air smelled of sand and rotting flesh, the carpet was yellow, then black marble, then salt.

She tipped over into the cushions.

CHAPTER 34

"What did you expect me to do?" Sanderson pushed past her and into the hallway. He threw his overcoat into the love seat in the living room. "You call me, tell me that a woman trapped you in an elevator and told you that your life is in danger, and you think, what, I'd go clubbing?!"

She wriggled into the cushions of the couch. *What did I want him to do?* She only vaguely remembered making the call.

He sat next to her and took her hand. "You were babbling on the phone, I couldn't understand any of it." He peered into her eyes. "Are you okay?"

She nodded. "Woody, I never imagined that getting involved with this book would..." She stared down at the carpet. "I just want to know."

I have to know what it will take to stop feeling this feeling.

Fear turned in her organs. She shook herself. "I want to know how this language works. How in the hell it..."

(is dissolving my sanity)

"...does what we think it does."

He watched her for a moment, his eyes dark. "As long as you're *sure* that you're all right." He exhaled slowly. "Jesus. Should we report it to the police?"

"The CIS hardly knows anything about these people, so what would the police be able to do?"

"Talk to this woman, question her!"

She sighed. "No. She did me a favor. I'm not getting the police involved."

He pulled back, seeming to evaluate whether or not it was worth it to try to get her to change her mind, and finally muttered, "Fine. Okay, one thing at a time. Let's go over what we know so far."

He stood and shuffled slowly across the room, raising a finger with each point. "All right. Celia discovered that the language includes embedded hypnotic commands. When we tested Parrish, he became increasingly agitated as we progressed from the Torah, the Pali Canon, the Christian Bible, and the Koran to the Gahana, which had the most damaging effects. The last three caused dangerous psychological changes, the first two didn't."

She frowned. "Actually, the reading from the Pali Canon took him toward delta. Deep relaxation."

He nodded. "True. The Pali Canon. What's the language?"

She shrugged helplessly. "Pali, but I don't really know anything about it, just that it's a derivation...

(sho ri-deh-resu through prayer and sacrifice shall the firm disciple)

...of Sanskrit."

"It's the only script of the five that wouldn't be categorized as Western or Middle Eastern."

"And that predates all the languages in the Gahana."

He gave a snort. "Interesting. How many Sanskrit-speaking terrorists or suicide bombers do you read about?" Shaking his head, he continued. "But what we still don't know is what makes these specific combinations of sounds work on the neurology in the same way as a drug."

"Right."

He recrossed the room. "And without diagnostic technology, the creators would be able to test the language only through trial and error, slowly but eventually finding the exact combination that produced physiological triggers."

"And we don't have slow and eventual." She pressed her thumbs against her temples. "The CIS wants the Gahana back. I'm on borrowed time."

Borrowed sanity?

He frowned. "Wait. What if a complete decryption isn't the real objective?"

"What?"

"Maybe we shouldn't focus on what makes this language work but on what makes it *not* work. What if we can find a way to scramble it? Restructure it so that it's as benign as any other piece of literature?"

She rubbed her chin. "What do you mean? Rewire it?"

He nodded.

Her eyes darted. "I suppose...you could keep the overarching structure and infiltrate it with another system. Start with minute changes in the easy words and increase the level of change in the more sophisticated vocabulary—what do you think?"

"You're the linguist." He dropped onto the couch. "But say for argument's sake that method works. What should we do with the revised language?"

She pressed her lips together. "We could write a message in the new system and plant it in the Gahana. Then suggest that the CIS offer to return the book on the condition that the owners first read the planted notes."

"Hm." He pondered. "Sounds workable. But if the new system is a mutation of the original, what guarantee is there that the authors will be able to read it?"

"They won't, at least not right away, but the people that wrote this book clearly understand the structures of language systems. They'd be desperate to figure out how someone has meddled with their clever word drug."

He popped up from the couch, his face glowing with energy. "Come on."

In her office, they wheeled chairs up to her desk. With several books retrieved from the shelves, her syllabary and notes in hand, and her favorite search engine open on the computer monitor, they huddled together in invention.

"This one, the moon symbol," she murmured, pointing to the syllabary, "appears only at the beginning or end of a symbol set. I'm convinced that it indicates future or past tense. Changing everything to future tense would create a sense of looking forward, a presupposition of the future. A linguistic connection between present actions and later consequences."

His eyes warmed on her. "That's good."

She leaned forward into the notes scattered across the desk. "And some languages that have no punctuation, such as the early Semitic systems. Nothing to indicate a stressed word, no exclamation points."

"What would that do?"

"Soften the language. Democratization. All statements become equal. It forces the listeners to apply their own emphasis to the writing and doesn't direct them toward any predetermined emotion."

"Brilliant," he said.

She scribbled notes while he looked on. Cocking his head to one side, he said, "What about taxonomy? I remember reading about how languages specify certain characteristics of an object through, what are they, suffixes?"

She nodded. "Some languages use prefixes, suffixes, or other morphemes that reveal the classification of the word. Whether it belongs to the class of inanimate objects, animals, people, concepts, and so on." She frowned, then toyed with an ink pen. "We could apply to each noun a suffix that indicates human being. You hear that people who injure or kill others don't see them as human, only as objects. This change would create the presupposition that all parts of speech relate to human beings. Give it a strong humanitarian quality."

Sanderson tipped back in his chair as he rubbed his neck. "The big question is how we would know if the revised language worked."

"I guess we'd have to do more testing—like Parrish, only on a wider scale. We'd have to find subjects who were willing to be exposed to the," she stopped, "there's got to be a referent for it. We need a name."

"Well, the original language brought on states of intense submission and addiction. We could call that one Logos-Servitus."

"Words of slavery?" She nodded. "And for the restructured language. How about Logos-Pax?"

"Why do I feel like we're picking out the names of our children?" He elbowed her, grinning.

Instantly, she felt her face flush. *Thanks for the reminder, Woody. We did once talk about the names of kids.* Her gaze dropped to the floor. The tiny apartment that they'd shared. The cracked bathtub that he would fill with bubble bath for her. Watching midnight monster movies on a dilapidated TV. *He derails me with a single sentence. Damn it!*

"I, uh, I'll be right back." She stood and walked down the hallway. Phantoms of their past flitted along beside her as she stepped into the bathroom and closed the door.

All that we had wanted together, all that we shared. Or would have...

She lowered the lid of the toilet and sat on it, dropping her chin to rest in her cupped hands, feeling the engine of anger growling in her gut.

Kama, I did what I had to do, though I know you won't see it that way. I had no choice.

You had a bloody choice. Her stomach was rolling now, her hands clenched into white fists.

All the parts of speech related to human beings, a distinctly humanitarian quality—what if they were stripped out? What if the taxonomies and prefixes and tenses and punctuation were changed—drastically—and the effect went beyond what we saw with Parrish? Even beyond what the originators of the language knew, or feared, it was capable of? What if it could...

As the word burned through her, her teeth closed on her lower lip, making her wince.

Destroy?

Logos-Pax, Woody? More like Logos-Thanatos.

Still chewing on the ideas, like a bitter weed of the mind, she made her way back down the hall and into the living room.

Sanderson followed her. Once he had found a comfortable spot on her couch, he asked, "Are you okay?"

"Fine." She ran a shaking hand through her hair. "I'm just trying to figure out how anyone could have created this language. We lucked into the use of that PET scanner and EEG, but unless the designers had that kind of technology, how could they have engineered the process?"

"They'd have to test the patterns on human subjects and see how they were affected."

She nodded. "And if your only method is trial and error, it would have taken an interminable time to perfect the language. Not decades but centuries!"

He frowned up at her. "Well, the system is made up of known languages like Greek and Latin. How long have those languages been around?"

It was her turn to pace the living room. "Hieroglyphics developed about 3100 BCE. Greek came into use later on, around 1100 BCE." She spun and walked back. "Aramaic was then developed about 1000 BCE and Hebrew close to the same period. The first Latin writing is estimated at 700 BCE. Arabic came into use around 500 CE while English was originating in Northern Europe."

He pursed his lips. "I'm impressed."

She spun and paced again, one finger pressed against the side of her cheek. "Let's say that the language of the Gahana is modern. Created in this century. The engineers would have to have the deepest possible level of knowledge of *all* of those languages and probably even the related offshoots. And not only the current uses and meanings but the entire evolution and lifecycle of each language as it changed over time." Her hands shot into the air. "They'd have to be superlinguists!"

"Perhaps they were so fanatical about this project that they devoted every minute of their lives to it."

She whirled to face him with a stunned expression. "Wait." She lurched forward. "What if the engineering *isn't* modern?" Her eyes widened. "What if it has been going on from the very beginning?"

Deep wrinkles creased his forehead. "The beginning of what?"

"Of *language.*"

Realization exploded through her:

Some of the most compelling revolutions of human history have arguably originated in politico-religious regimes. From the Code of Hammurabi onward, the most destructive empires have spread as their writings have proliferated, especially those with so-called holy scriptures: the Muhammadic Koran, the Christian Bible, and to a certain extent, the Jewish Torah. Could the authors of these texts have had any idea of the widespread and enduring power that their words held, their capacity to ignite both ecstasy and global crusades? Or were they fully aware of the influence that the writing wielded?

She sank onto the couch next to him, shaking her head as if warding off the knowledge of certain death. "Oh my god."

"What?" Frowning furiously, he whispered, "What? Tell me."

"You might not remember this. Back at Blake. I started a thesis on the history of religious texts, focusing on those that have notable connections with violence."

"Yes?"

She whirled toward him. "The minute that I took it to my advisor, she rejected it and pointedly refused to tell me why."

"Who was your advisor?" he prodded.

"Volante. Professor Volante." Alarm stabbed at her. *Could* she *have had some connection with the people who designed this book? Fifteen years ago? On another continent?*

Fear and frustration were bearing down on her—she pulled in a shuddering breath as she tipped toward him. Warmth emanated from his body, bringing with it the sweet, earthy smell of his skin that she had once described as the scent of creation. It tugged her nearer, and her head flopped onto his shoulder. "Good god."

Sanderson tentatively reached up to stroke her hair. "You okay?"

"Exhausted." Her eyes closed for a moment. "I'm...yeah, I'm exhausted." She sat up, turning half-lidded eyes toward the carpet. "I think it's time for bed."

"Me too. It's late." He started to rise.

She met his eyes and thought she saw them filled with fifteen years of unspoken questions. "Do you..."

Oh, don't do the dumbest *thing of your entire life.*

"Do you want to stay here tonight?" *Just here on the couch. Doesn't constitute betrothal.* She patted the cushion.

He stared for a moment, his eyes moving over her face. "Give up a Posturepedic in a posh hotel for this lumpy green thing?" He smiled. "Sure."

CHAPTER 35

Rubbing her eyes, she tossed the comforter back, tugged on a flannel shirt and pair of sweatpants, and stumbled toward the hall. A light was on in the kitchen.

She smelled fresh-ground coffee and heard Sanderson's voice, morning-rough and groggy but still bubbling with enthusiasm. "Cream and sugar?"

He stepped from around the corner to hand her a steaming mug.

"Thanks." She nodded at the mound of blankets on the couch. "Did you sleep okay?"

"Worst night's sleep ever. I tossed like a netted trout."

Smiling, she sipped the coffee. "Sorry."

He looked back at her with a playful look. "You never know, maybe sleep deprivation will bring on a bolt of genius. Why don't we..."

The phone rang.

"Callers at eight in the morning?" he muttered.

Mug in hand, she walked toward her office and reached for the phone. *I think I know who it is.* "Hello?"

"Dr. Donovan? It's Singer. I hope I haven't called too early."

She switched the phone to the other hand. "No, I was just getting up."

"Very good. I spoke yesterday with the deputy of the EU."

She sighed. "He wants the book, right?"

"He granted the request to keep it until the eighteenth, but it must be returned..."

She broke in, "But I'm just at the brink of breaking the system. I'm just starting to understand the cohesion of it!"

"I'm sorry. I can't stall him any longer. The book must be at the EU in forty-eight hours."

Forty-eight hours!

"Dr. Donovan? Did you hear me?"

"Yes." Chewing her lower lip, she muttered, "I'll bring it in."

She hung up, frowning at Sanderson, who stood at the doorway of the office.

"Bad news?"

She sighed. "Singer. He wants the book back by Thursday."

He stepped toward her. "Then let's see what we can do in two days."

They sat their mugs on a curio table at the entrance to the office. The Gahana lay where they had left it the night before, in the middle of the mahogany desk. She moved it to the work table on the opposite side of the room and began to load the desktop with folders and notes.

He sniffed the air. "Wow, something smells good in here. What is it?"

"Penelope sent me this." She reached to a shelf over the desk that held an assortment of pencil holders and reference books, picked up a squat, amber-colored bottle with a stopper lid, and held it toward him. "For my birthday. It's oil scented with myrrh." She shrugged as he sniffed at it and then sat the bottle at the far end of the desk. "Not anything that I'd buy for myself, but it makes the place smell nice."

"Almost as nice as you smell," he said, grinning at her. He started toward her, as if he might wrap his arms around her. The back of his hand connected with the bottle, sending it skittering across the surface of the desk, and oil flooded over the wood.

"Shit, sorry! Where are your paper towels?"

"I'll get it," she said, dashing to the kitchen. She returned with a wad of paper towels and moved toward the desk, where drops of oil were trickling off the edge.

"Do you want me to do that?"

"It's okay." She sopped up the fragrant oil. Though the bulk of the liquid was absorbed into the towels, a glistening smear remained on the surface.

"I got most of it. Great, now this desk permanently smells like myrrh." She dropped the towels into the waste basket. "Now, where were we?"

As they reviewed her notes and discussed the construction of the language, Gatsby stood before the desk while Sanderson leaned back against it, then paced, then stood watching her.

Staring at the assorted pages of notes, in which she'd copied passages of the text, the symbols seemed to swirl, moving, fading in and out like miscreant particles. Her thoughts skittered back to the conversation she'd had with herself the night before.

Even beyond what the originators of the language knew, or feared, it was capable of? What if it could destroy?

"...a section that I wanted to ask you about."

With a jolt, she snapped back, trying to fill in whatever it was that she'd missed.

"Where the format changes, and it's hard to tell whether the symbols are read right to left or left to right. Do you know the section that I'm talking about?"

"I'm not sure." She cleared her throat. "Where does it appear?" She leaned forward to plant her elbows on the desktop and peer at the notes, her face hovering over the pages.

"Toward the middle. You wrote down something about it, somewhere...here?" He moved up to stand behind her and to her left. His body edged closer; his shirtsleeve brushed her arm. Stretching both hands out, he bent forward to brace himself on the desktop. He didn't notice that his left hand had landed in the oil smear, and as he shifted his full weight onto his palms, his hand skidded off the edge of the desk.

He tumbled with a surprised grunt, his body collapsing onto her, knocking her facedown onto the desk. Her chin connected with solid mahogany, and she howled in pain and the...

(heavy body pumping, hot, panting, grunting, moving against her back)

(candle wax and guttered ash smell)

(naked skin, prickling with gooseflesh)

The images sizzled through her mind. An avalanche of memories flooded her, each one bringing back the SCREAM, the buried scream that wanted to throttle up through her organs and into her throat and explode from her mouth.

"No!!"

She tumbled to the carpet, bringing Sanderson with her.

He rolled onto his side, panting, massaging the elbow that had smacked against the desk during the fall, and grinned up at her as she scrambled to her feet.

She leaned back against the desk and looked down at him, her blood thudding in her ears.

"Are you o..."

"It was *YOU.*"

His forehead furrowed. "What?"

Her hands flew up to smash against her temples. "Shit!! How could I have..." She inched away from him. "That night, the Interfaith Center," her eyes misted, "it was you, oh my motherfucking god, it was you!"

He slowly rose, brushing at the knees of his pants, his face a kaleidoscope of bewilderment. "What the hell are you talking about?"

She began to edge toward him, fueled with an intensity that radiated in waves. "Why were you slipping away from me? So distracted by your God quest," her voice quivered, "so caught up in finding yourself, in saving yourself..."

...and God's pure love will wash away all fear, all confusion...

He swallowed. "I have no idea wh..."

"So concerned with redemption," she barreled into it head on, "with the verdict for your eternal fucking soul!!"

His hands rose to his chest as his throat worked. "What is this? What are you talking about?"

"And then you took off with your heavenly whore, your invisible deified friend, walked away and abandoned me because you couldn't stand it anymore! Couldn't live with yourself, couldn't look at me anymore, couldn't look into the face of your guilt!"

No wonder you drank and ran from everything, allegedly went on a crusade to find God or forget yourself!!

He shook his head wordlessly, eyes wide, as she advanced on him.

She pulled a chair toward her—the wheels squealed— and dug her fingernails deep into the fabric. "And *then* you thought you could redeem yourself by contacting me, anonymously, through the Web? Definite Article? Still hiding from me, from the world? From your own sins?"

"Why?" His voice cracked. "Why are you doing this?"

Her eyes narrowed. "I'm not hearing denial."

He stiffened as though flailing through innumerable conflicting impulses and then spoke slowly, his voice low, "When you told me about that night, you said you knew the guy. Now you're saying that it *wasn't* him, that it was me?! Think, Gatsby! Remember what we talked about with Celia? After testing Parrish? The effect that this book has on anyone who reads it? On us? Remember *that* conversation?" He inched backward. "It's doing that. The Gahana...it's tweaking you like it did Parrish!"

"Get out."

He blinked.

"I don't want to look at your face." She closed her eyes, cringing, then stared hard at him. "I mean it. Get out, now." She took a step toward the living room.

He turned with her. "Please, Gatsby, listen! How can you possibly..."

She whirled. "Last time I'm going to say it. Get the— fuck—out."

His face began to crumble. "Kama..."

The words barreled through her body and exploded from her mouth: "Petash e-fama ra no mahji!!"

He gasped and pinwheeled to the carpet, as if body-slammed by a heavyweight wrestler, landing hard with a thud. A wail burst from his lips, and he cupped two bruised palms together, panting. As he stared down into hands, he saw a glistening red blob on his upturned palm.

"Oh my god..."

He trailed a finger through the blob and then swiped the back of his hand under his nose. Blood smeared his knuckles.

"Go!!"

She grabbed his shirt, hauled him to his feet, and shoved him toward the front door.

Blood struggled down his chin; a fat drop broke and splattered into the carpet. He stumbled through the doorway, shouting, "It's the fucking book!"

When she slammed the door as hard as she could—BAM!—the wall shuddered.

She huddled on the couch, hugging her knees, rocking. Dead-fish eyes, blank, bloodless. Staring at the wall but not seeing it.

How could he?!

She knew that she should be hysterical, slipping into shock. She rocked and stared. Her pulse pounded steadily, dully.

It was him. It was always him.

...and God's pure love will wash away all fear, all confusion...

A glitch blipped in the deepest shadows of her mind, then receded.

What's it going to be, Woody? The love of the great truth, your eternal pseudo-father figure? The big fucking cosmic clock-maker? Or me? Which is it?

Her body felt like an icon becoming wax, a figurine melting as fire within raged, turning bone and sinew into a toxic river.

A sound seemed to float down from the ceiling. She turned her face up toward it. Soft, somber, monophonic melody, lyrical voices reverberating against the stones of an ancient cathedral...*Kyrie eleison, Christe abbah way non push tah non ah meh-gah...*

The motes in the air congealed into terrible forms, the faces of monsters, demons howling and flitting around her, images of mutilated bodies, all the murderers of the innocent mutating into one, hideous laughter scalding her brain like battery acid.

She rocked and swallowed against the ammonia taste in her mouth.

Too much...too much...it hurts too much...

Then she saw the face of the woman in the elevator, heard the edge of terror in her voice: *Do whatever it takes to save yourself.*

Then: *I have no choice.*

Whose voice was it? Woody's? The woman's? Her own? Or that of some terrible power?

She found herself in her office, sitting at her desk amid the piles of notes and scattered notebooks. The smell of myrrh mixed with ammonia made her stomach lurch. Pen in hand, she wrote:

– Change all tenses to present (no consideration for the future or consequences for actions)

– Chop sentences (every sentence less than five words)

– Delete all "human" endings, so that all words relate to it/thing, inanimate, not to sentient creatures

She jerked backward, making a chaotic, blue ink scrawl across the paper.

Jesus! Stop! A voice, hers but now not hers, shouted as she drummed one heel against the carpet, hard enough to set her teeth clattering. *Psychic assassination? If this worked, I'd have a technology that every back-alley killer—every corrupt government—would want! But what would they do to get the information?*

Her lungs filled and emptied like bellows.

And how would I know if it actually worked? It would have to be something animate, but not a dog or a rat, the language programs aren't there, it would have to be...

The saliva that she gulped tasted of bile.

CHAPTER 36

She found herself in the lobby, staring at the door.

How did I get here?

Her last memory was sitting in her office, huddled over the Gahana. An invisible, magnetic force tugged at her body and dragged her forward into the street.

Sounds sprinkled around her, undulating waves of chaos. Living rainbows streamed through her vision.

Gatsby walked without knowing where or why. Cool air rushed over her face, fluttering her hair against her neck.

The sounds of metropolis—car horns, laughter, shouts, a dog barking, the pings and dings of traffic signals—melted into white noise, monotonous in the depths of her neurons.

A branch scratched against her cheek and jerked her to awareness. Gasping, she glanced around, her head swiveling left and right. Basswood. Alder trees. Tables, wrought-iron benches. A patch of the great lake, The Serpentine. The gurgle of a nearby fountain. Birds floating in a steel-grey sky.

Hyde Park.

Mechanically, the information registered.

Words blared in her head, swirling like leaves in a rushing river, pulsing against each other as hip-hop downbeats and syncopation, as the sounds of Babel slammed across her synapses: *Push tah tus me pnévma msh ha-adam Abbah way bene nsw 'alehem et iure liberi iw metaksí nascuntur non ah meh...*

Jerked forward by the force, she moved across a long lawn and toward an L-shaped thicket of hawthorn. As she stepped around one corner, she noticed a heap on the ground and realized that it was a human being—lying on its side, ratted hair sticking out in clumps, tennis shoes worn to the brink of destruction, layered in blankets and newspapers. The face was shrouded, tucked down into the chest.

Push tah tus msh ha-adam liberi iw non ah meh me pnévma Abbah way bene...

A blip of recognition. She catalogued the data, then turned away and started toward the fountain.

Something slapped hard against her face.

Dirt-caked fingers ground against her teeth and furrowed into her cheeks. As her breath surged into her lungs and mouth, the voice growled in her ear, "Not a sound."

Struggling against the body pressed to her back, she felt a whip-lean frame and hard muscles; taller than her but not by much. The voice was androgynous.

Scream!! Fight! Part of her brain shouted, but another part had taken control, guiding her neurology. The mind of the samurai who discounts his own death. No time for panic. No use for fear.

The attacker dragged her backward and behind the thicket to isolate them from witnessing eyes and ears.

"Your time has come, Donovan," the voice hissed, sending foul breath swirling into her nostrils.

He knows my name!!

At the same time that she felt the gritty fingers encircling her throat and something sharp poking against her lower back, and as the rank smell of the body rolled into a ball of acid in her stomach, and as every muscle contracted, and as the power blasted through her lungs and across her lips, the words exploded from her.

"Petash e-fama ra no mahji! Nima runapa!"

Red and blue and black, flames, swirling, the smell of rotting flesh. She was lost in the holocaust as it spewed into the air like psychic vomit, and she spun in it, hearing so vaguely, so far away, the syllables...

"Pa-tah sho DAY PUSH!"

...and the screams as the grimy attacker crumpled to the ground, kicking, his face a rictus of agony, eyes bulging, tongue writhing against his lips and smearing the blood that flowed from his nostrils and ears and mouth.

Blades of grass tickled her forearm.

She glanced down, realizing that she was now sitting cross-legged next to the man, whose howls were a dreary black-and-white program with the sound turned off. She plucked a blade of grass and held it up toward the sun, fascinated by the glistening red drops.

She turned toward the body that was now inert on the ground. A black-red puddle had collected in the grass under his open, frozen, blood-splattered lips.

Push tah tus me pnévma msh ha-adam Abbah way bene nsw 'alehem et iure liberi iw metaksí nascuntur non ah meh...

The words rolled through her head, in the sing-songy voices of children: *Sticks and stones may break my bones, but words will never hurt me.*

Sleep extreme! Extreeeeme! Rat PISSING coolmoneygads allowanna

Where did I hear that craziness? Who is speaking?

Within her mind, the words were clear as a Tibetan chime tinkling at sunrise, rustled by a soft breeze.

Logos-Thanatos kills.

The invisible force lifted her to her feet and nudged her forward. She balled her hands tightly enough to sink the fingernails into the skin of her palms, drawing tiny crescent moons of blood.

Then she stood at the door of her flat.

The world faded in like mist dissipating from the surface of a mountain lake. The taupe carpet. Entertainment center, DVD player, the black, blank face of the television. Coffee table, lettuce-colored love seat.

She blinked. Her lungs hitched, then began pumping bursts of air that accelerated, faster and faster.

No consideration for the future or consequences for actions...

What would they do to extract the information?

Flames of panic blazed and then engulfed her mind.

CHAPTER 37

Staring at the stack of pamphlets on his dining room table, he felt fury swell over him.

The book is still in the hands of an infidel! Volante and her litter of idiots, all fucking incompetents! Imbeciles!

Niccolo smashed his arm through the stack, sending hundreds of carefully folded pamphlets to the floor in an explosion of multicolored paper.

He dropped into a padded chair and turned toward the darkened windows that flanked the dining room. As his gaze turned down toward the piles scattered around his feet, the thought rose before he could squelch it. *She alone has been of any real value.*

The pain that shuddered through him was followed by the thought: *I must take care of the insurgents myself.* He drummed his fingers on the top of the table. *Without Franca.*

He thought of Volante's promise: *My new zasha will take us directly to Donovan and the Librah Vae-ta.*

Devereaux. The outsider who is now an insider. Loyalties on both sides, perhaps, but like all fresh converts, one who can be easily swayed.

Fueled with energy, he rushed to his upstairs room and toward the desk in the corner. There they were: the MCF documents. Volante had made sure that two copies were packed in a sturdy cardboard box.

He sat and logged onto his computer, quickly pulling up a database. In less than a minute, he was looking at the file that Volante had created on Celia Devereaux. Full name, age, place of birth, current and past addresses, email, phone number, and much more.

A smile moved over his lined face. He strolled from the room and down the stairs, back to the dining room. Picking up his cell phone from the walnut table, he dialed.

The line connected. "Hello?"

He gave his voice a peaceful, fatherly timbre. "Ms. Devereaux?"

"Yes?"

CHAPTER 38

He held the door open for her to enter the Officia Abba. As he moved toward the conference table at the center of the room, he watched her eyes moving over the computer peripherals, bookcases, chairs, and filing cabinets. "Please, have a seat."

Celia slid into the nearest chair.

Volante usually prepares the ground admirably with new Dosa, but I must test this one.

He took a seat to the left of the executive chair, bowed his head, and murmured the Prayer of Devotion. "Abbah way non vash ah parateh, sho day too vashla meed neh-vee von besh garah, mem vahla padarah oh meh-ga. Nah-maen." Looking up, he smiled at her.

Celia shrugged. "Is this your office?"

"Oh no. This is the office of the Abba, push tah non ah meh-gah, but he has allowed me to meet here with you. I am a wisdom elder. I serve on a hewat...a committee...as one of the language experts." Folding his hands in his lap, he studied her face and immediately saw the changes. A subtle relaxation of the eyes and deep, diaphragmatic breathing.

"I see."

"I understand that you have not only joined us as a Dosa but have been invited by the Habareh to train for the role of zasha."

A smile tugged at her lips. "Yes, I have. It is a great honor, Lee," she paused, "I'm sorry, what was your name again?"

"Liat."

She nodded. "Yes, that's right, Liat. And acting as her personal zasha...what does that mean?"

"It's an important position. You will be asked to help her with her duties, assist at the Damaii gatherings, and oversee the collection of the honorum mati."

"Ms. Volante mentioned these responsibilities."

She gave her real name?! He bristled while filing the data for later action.

"And how did you meet?"

"We were buying the same perfume at a shop in Mayfair, and we struck up a conversation. She said that she was giving a lecture that night and invited me to attend."

"And she has described to you our order's structure and purpose?"

Her face brightened. "Yes. I'm fascinated. I see so much violence in the world, and in this group, I see glimmers of hope, a way of living that pushes past the emptiness of illusion and toward real truth. I want to know everything!"

The gushing enthusiasm of the born again. He gave his voice a gentle tone. "And we are happy to guide you, but there is one question I must ask you."

"What?"

Carefully, he thought. "Did Ms. Volante tell you about our scripture?"

He thought he saw a shadow flutter over her face. "Well, she talked about a lost book."

Setting his face with a calm expression, he said, "Yes. Our holy scripture. The Abba, push tah non ah meh-gah, asked me to speak with you about it. You see, the most important principles of our order are contained in it." He did not say Librah Vae-ta. *Not yet.* "It is a wondrous testament to the glory of Omega. It holds the keys to all the questions with which humankind has wrestled. To eternity."

She leaned forward. "How?"

He chuckled. "The answer is complex, but let me ask you another question. I am told by the Habareh that you know where the book is. That, in fact, you are helping some friends to discover its messages." Monitoring his breathing to keep it slow and steady, he let his eyes relax. "Is this true?"

She frowned. "How do you know that?"

He leaned forward in his chair, a smile playing on his lips. As if revealing a deep secret, he whispered, "Believe me, Volante knows a lot. She's very resourceful."

Resourceful enough to bring you to me!

"Wellll." Her frown deepened. "What does the group intend to do about the book?"

"Simply use it to help bring newcomers into the fold." He pressed his palms together. "The Abba, push tah non ah meh-gah, has personally asked me to help them, and you, to fully understand the message of the book. I wish to speak with your friends, and I will be happy to explain to them everything about how the language works."

Her eyes widened. "The group will surely want the book returned, won't it?"

Turning up the warmth in his smile, he chuckled. "The book itself is not what's really important. The message of enlightenment that it holds is all that truly matters." He exhaled slowly. "We are glad to talk with your friends, to welcome them into the truth of Great Omega, to reveal all the intricacies of its language and the wisdom that it offers. It is a wondrous opportunity. You do see this, of course."

Watching the sedation seep into her eyes and through her body, he thought, *She's almost there.*

She nodded slowly and whispered, "Yes. I see."

He leaned forward to prop his elbows on his knees, lowering his head so that she gazed downward into his face. He deepened his voice. "Are you now...ready to bring your friends to the truth of Omega?"

In her face and breathing patterns, he saw the energy spreading, her nerve endings firing in chorus.

"Yes." Her voice was breathy, as if postcoital.

He sighed and murmured, "Padarah oh meh-ga."

"Nah-maen," she whispered.

Beautiful. She now feels that she has broken through a personal barrier. Dosa are so easily led.

He allowed his gaze to move over her lithe body, touching gently on points of interest, especially her silky, pitch-black hair.

Pushing away the memory-urge that began to swell, he said, "This is a joyous occasion. And now I want to meet your friends! Both of them. Please, invite them here!" He spread his arms wide. "The Abba, push tah non ah meh-gah, has given me permission to meet with them in this office."

Her eyes darted. "I *think* that they will speak with you, but it must be very soon. Otherwise, I suspect..."

What are they planning? "Yes, yes, then right away. Why don't you call them now?"

She dug into her purse and pulled out a metallic blue cell phone. Before opening it, she hesitated, eyeing him.

He rose and made a curt bow. "Ah, you wish to speak in private. I will step out into the hall."

As she flipped the phone open, he pulled the door closed behind him.

CHAPTER 39

When the line connected, Celia blurted, "Gats, it's me."

"Oh Celia, something horrible has happened!" Gatsby's voice crackled like severed power lines. "I think I've...oh my god, the book, there's more to it than w—"

"That's what I'm calling you about, the book. Do you want to know everything about how it was written and why?"

"Of course, but..."

"Then listen. I met with someone who wants to speak with you right now. I think he's one of the people who helped to write it."

"What?" A pause. "It's ten o'clock, Celia. What is this, a joke?"

"No joke. Bring Sanderson, too. I'm in the man's office, and he wants to talk to both of you."

"You won't be seeing Woody again." Her voice trembled. "And neither will I. Ever."

"What? Why?"

"Because the bastard's been lying to me from day one! I can't give all the details right now, Celia, I have to tell you..."

"This is too important. Rouse him and get down here."

"No, wait, you don't understand! There's something..."

"Listen, do you want to unravel this bloody mystery or not?" On the verge of shouting, she crushed the phone against her cheek. "I've got all your answers right here. It's show time. He insists that both of you come. Now are you going to grab this opportunity before it walks away and disappears forever?"

After a full minute of labored breathing, Gatsby said, "All right. Jesus. Who the hell is this guy?"

"I'll explain it when you get here. Quite a story." She rattled off the street address.

"Okay, I'll call Woody. You're on your cell?"

"Uh huh."

"Keep it on. I'll take my car. We'll be there in thirty minutes."

Snapping the phone shut, Celia stuffed it into her pants pocket and strode toward the far side of the table. She glanced around the room again, seeing cabinets, bookcases, and half a dozen blinking, humming computers.

When her eyes swept over an acrylic display case, full of glittering knives, on the wall, she gasped.

The largest knife caught her attention. The top and bottom edges curved in wave-like shapes. Sharp peaks, resembling fangs, protruded in both directions from the handle.

A pain suddenly shot across her abdomen, making her press her hand to her belly. *Yow! What was that?*

Frowning, she walked slowly to the door and pulled it open.

Liat turned, smiled, and moved toward her.

"They're on their way."

"Ah, wonderful." His voice trembled slightly. As he strolled toward the conference table, he said, "Would you like some tea while we wait?"

Groaning, Celia pressed her hands against her abdomen again and then her forehead. She dropped into a chair. "No, I'm not feeling well. My stomach." Wincing, she prodded her side and swallowed several times. "Aaughh, God, it feels like food poisoning. Where's the bathroom?"

He laid a hand on her forearm, gazing at her with a frown. "My, you do look pale. There's a restroom right here." He crossed the room and pointed at the door of the bathroom.

"Thank you."

She stepped into the small room, flicked on the light, and closed the door. Hearing the snick of the latch, she whirled toward the wash basin and dropped her face into it, waiting for something vile to hit her throat. She closed her eyes, feeling her blood pounding in her head and the jagged edges of a headache, and choked on a mouthful of saliva. After spitting twice into the basin, she straightened and looked around.

What have I eaten?!

Dropping her pants, she sat on the toilet and urinated. The nausea abated for a moment.

She pulled her pants back up and pressed her hands to her face. Her cheeks had flushed bright red, and she felt beads of sweat trickling down the side of her neck.

Jesus, this may be a trip to an urgent care, but I can't leave now, Gatsby and Woody will be here any minute!

She glanced over her shoulder toward a tall cabinet that straddled the toilet: the top shelf held assorted soaps, and the lower shelf was stuffed with hand towels, some stacked atop each other, a few pushed roughly into the space between the stack and the cabinet wall. She grabbed a white cloth from the space and tugged it free. As it popped out and fluttered to the floor, she stifled a scream.

On the cloth, a shape was clearly outlined. It swooped gently at the top and bottom edges, and toward the bottom of the shape, fang-like points protruded on either side. The negative space in the white fabric was outlined with mud-brown spatters, flecks, blotches.

It's blood! Whose blood? Her stomach lurched. *And it's the shape of that knife on the wall!*

With shaking hands, she pulled her phone from her pocket and punched in Gatsby's number. The blue screen pulsed the message NO SIGNAL.

Shit! I just called her! She snapped the phone shut, panting. *And no one else knows I'm here!*

A singing pain had pounded through her head since she began talking with Liat, and as she closed her eyes and took several deep breaths, she felt it begin to subside.

I'll tell him I must go to the hospital. She pushed the bloodied cloth back into the space it had fallen from, ran water into the sink, dried her hands with a paper towel, and tossed the wad into the toilet. Trying to breathe evenly, she slowly pushed open the door.

Liat rose from his chair and stepped toward her. "I hope you are feeling better?"

She barely managed to keep her voice level. "Much worse. It's bad. I have to go an urgent care right now."

Out of the corner of her eye, she glanced at the case of knives on the wall, noting the lock on the side. The lid was now slightly ajar.

Oh god—get the hell out of here!!

He stepped toward her. "My dear, you're in no condition to drive yourself. I'll call for an ambulance." He crept closer. "Until it arrives," he was so close that she felt his breath flowing over her face, saw his eyes dancing as his body slid another inch toward hers, "won't it be delightful to chat, just the two of us, for a few more minutes?"

Electrified with terror, she shouted, "I have to go now!"

As she spun away from him and bolted out the door, she heard him shout, "Your friends? They have the address?"

Plunging down the dark hallway and toward the lobby, she held her stomach and fought swells of nausea. She pushed open the front door, stumbled down the front stairs of the building, dashed for her car, dove behind the wheel, slammed the door shut, and locked it. Snatching up her cell phone, panting, she tried Gatsby's number again.

This time she got a signal. The line rang three, four, then five times.

A message appeared on the screen: RECEIVER'S DEVICE IS OUT OF THE SERVICE AREA. PRESS 7 TO LEAVE A MESSAGE.

"Shit!!"

At the long beep, she bellowed, "For godssake, don't come! I think it's a fucking trap!"

A cramp hit with such intensity that she doubled over, groaning, and collapsed into the leather seat. Dots sparkled, and everything went black.

CHAPTER 40

Niccolo strolled through the Officia facility, peering into rooms and turning off overhead lights. He continued until he knew that the building was empty.

He made his way to the lobby to see a dark figure struggling with a raincoat.

Who...ah yes, she cleans the offices at night.

The woman looked up as he approached, then lowered her eyes and murmured, "Abbah way non push tah non ah meh-gah."

"Ah meh-gah sho met yah. Good evening, Emily."

She stared back with the twitchiness of a rat.

"A woman with dark hair came through here just now. Did you see her?"

Emily's eyes moved up and then back and forth several times. She shook her head.

Good.

"That's fine. Now I'm expecting some visitors in a few minutes—a man and a woman—and I want to speak with them in the lower offices. When they arrive, please show them to the lift and then go home. Don't worry about locking up, I will do that. Do you understand?"

She bowed her head. "Yes. Padarah oh meh-ga."

As he slid down the dark hallway, he thought, *Devereaux can go, she doesn't matter. She was just bait and can be reinitiated if I need her. Only the others concern me, the psychophysiologist and the American linguist—qaz, could it really be Donovan?!*

Back inside the Officia Abba, he went to the display case on the wall and pulled its lid open. He wrapped his fingers around the *gishtal*, The Wrath of Omega, that swooped gently at the top edge and curved at the bottom. Moving his robe to one side, he slid the knife into the sheath strapped to his thigh. He walked back to the door, turned off the light, and stepped into the hallway.

"Please, will you please *say* something?" Sanderson's voice broke the silence as the Volvo sped down the thoroughfare.

Her hands gripping the wheel like vises, Gatsby glanced at him and then back at the road.

"Gatsby!"

She stared ahead as if he didn't exist. The feelings she'd once had for him belonged to someone else, some other woman, long dead, far away.

Street signs loomed and disappeared; the Doppler-effect of a car horn blared at them and then died away.

He shook his head, then crossed his arms over his chest. "At least tell me where we're going, for chrissake. She didn't tell you anything about this mystery person?" His voice rose to a petulant tone. "How she met him, or what he knows about the Gahana?"

She stared at the windshield. "She said that he was willing to meet with us, now, and would tell us everything about the creation of the book and the language. I think it's worth the investment of my time, and Celia's not going to lead me on a wild goose chase." She stole a sideways glance at him. "Her, I can trust."

He dropped his head against the headrest, groaning.

The streetlights loomed over the dark London streets like glowing, spindly aliens.

Niccolo strode toward the end of the hall and spied the button that called the lift. He heard feet shuffling behind him, then a stage whisper, "Abbah way non push tah non ah meh-gah."

He spun toward the voice. *But I checked every room!*

A wiry figure moved toward him. As the young man stepped closer, Niccolo recognized him. Guy Corwin.

Volante's former zasha?!

"Abba, dal shavha," Corwin whispered as he approached. "As instructed." He held a briefcase forward.

"What the hell are you doing here?!" Niccolo hissed.

Corwin's eyes widened as his body froze. "As I was instructed by Disciple Burke, delivering the honorum mati."

Does Volante know about this? Did she stage *it? Is it a ploy? A distraction?*

"The idiot has misinformed you!" Niccolo grabbed the case out of Corwin's hand and snarled, "The honorum is never kept on these premises. Now get out!"

Sounds floated toward them from the lobby: Emily's bird voice, then other voices, too soft to make out.

Niccolo turned back to Corwin. "I said get out, now!"

Corwin whirled and sprinted toward the exit at the rear of the building.

Niccolo stepped to the button on the wall and pushed it. The doors of the lift whispered open. Stepping into the car, his heart pounding, he waited until the doors were fully closed before pushing against the clasps of the briefcase. The lid popped opened, and as he rifled through the bundles of envelopes, he pulled in a long breath.

Just over a million pounds! Franca did not exaggerate.

The car lurched and began its descent.

Emily raised a hand toward the hallway. "I am happy to welcome you. Please come with me."

Glancing at each other, Gatsby and Sanderson followed her down a dim hallway.

"What is this, some kind of community center?" Gatsby asked.

The woman mumbled something and kept walking.

Sanderson and Gatsby frowned at each other as if to ask, *What the hell?*

Emily pointed toward the door of the lift. "Level three. He is waiting for you there." She turned and shuffled back toward the lobby.

"I don't like any of this," Sanderson growled. He pushed the call button on the wall, and the doors opened.

Out of the corner of her eye, Gatsby saw the woman pull on a raincoat, lean against the front door, and disappear into the night.

"I don't either." She frowned as they stepped into the car. "She said level three? I don't think this building has three floors."

"It doesn't." As the car jerked and began to move, he sputtered, "Wait a second...feel that? We're going *down*, not up."

He frantically thumbed the buttons, but the car continued to descend.

"Oh god." She looked at the faux paneling of the car but vividly visualized Covent Garden—the dark-haired woman in the elevator.

You're in the crosshairs, and they won't give up until they have what they want.

"I think we're in trouble," she whispered.

The car grunted to a stop.

He reached out and took her hand.

The doors slid opened.

They saw only darkness—then a flash.

The robed figure flew at them, and the knife sailed down, ripping into Sanderson's side. He screamed as a spray of blood arced through the air, splattering bright red streaks across his shirt and pants, across Gatsby's sweatshirt, across the attacker's robe.

She dove for the man, but he clouted her across the face hard enough to send her spinning to the floor, keening in pain.

Sanderson had collapsed onto the concrete floor. Niccolo jerked the knife out, and Sanderson shrieked, his hands smashed against the wound, trying to hold back the blood that flowed through his fingers.

Niccolo drew the knife upward.

"I'll slit his throat." His voice carried the chill of the killer who has nothing to lose.

Tears running down her cheeks, gulping for air, she howled, "Who are you?!"

Her eyes flashed to angular shapes at the side of the room: a table, an open briefcase containing thick envelopes.

She glanced back at Woody, who was panting hard, gripping his side, staring up at her with terrified eyes.

He'll die if we don't get out of here, fast!

"That bitch Devereaux brought you right to me," Niccolo muttered.

Realization exploded in her. *Celia!!*

"You think that you can unravel our book? You cannot, and you will not. You're about to enter whatever heaven or hell you subscribe to. Him first." He poked Sanderson with the toe of his boot. The hand holding the blade inched toward Sanderson's throat.

Terror barreled through her. "You fucking prick!!"

Niccolo's eyebrows rose. "Oh?" He chuckled. "Perhaps there's more fire in you than I had imagined. And you're absolutely as beautiful now as you were then."

His eyes narrowed as an array of alternate plans began to cascade through him. *He's disposable, but her? Volante's file confirms the depth of her knowledge. Better to exploit her talents, yes, but how? Threat? Bribery? Seduction?*

A blood bubble popped on Sanderson's lip.

"You would be immensely valuable to the empire." He lowered the knife.

"Think again, asshole!" Her body heaving, blood-splattered strings of hair strewn across her face, she hissed, "What do you want?"

"You. I was set to kill you, and you could become a statistic, right now—or you could become a very powerful leader. A general to the millions of disciples for whom I am the fast track to salvation. I know every word in that dossier, Donovan, the one that Volante has kept on you since you attended that dreary university in Seattle."

Impossible!

"I know of your unquenchable thirst for knowledge. I know how you revel in achievement." He glanced at the table and the briefcase bulging with envelopes. "And do you see that? There's more of it than you can possibly imagine. Think of the possibilities that would unfold by joining me, Gatsby Donovan. Immeasurable wealth. Sweet cash for the soul. But more than that, you'd have solace. Nothing to fear, ever again."

...and God's pure love will wash away all fear, all confusion...

Her brain spun, the hurricane crashed.

(candle wax and guttered ash smell)

(naked skin, prickling with gooseflesh)

The images ran backward:

Inside she silently SCREAMS IN RAGE.

He shuffles away and then out of the dark room, leaving the door ajar behind him.

He licks his lips, panting, and straightens his clothing.

His hot breath flows over her back, her bare skin rippling with gooseflesh.

He explodes, gasping thanks to the Great Divinity that gave him guidance and permission; his hot breath flows over her back, her bare skin rippling with gooseflesh.

His fingers roughly explore and probe, while he fondles cotton and lace, while the tissues tear, while he pumps into her.

Rigid, pliable, mute, helpless—

She can't move, can't make a sound—

Every muscle locks, deaf and dumb to the emergency alarm shrilling through her nervous system, impenetrable, cut off from the voice shrieking inside her—

He whispers a single word, one that she does not remember later or—

Connection and horror blasted through her.

"Hurry!" Sanderson croaked, his eyes fluttering, seeming to beg her. A tear of blood zigzagged down his chin.

As she staggered to her feet and crept toward Niccolo, she watched his eyes widen, and when her nose was only inches from his, she stopped, panting waves of hatred into his face.

In the abyss of his eyes, she saw only cruelty.

She reached down into the black hell of her pain, and the barricades exploded, and she knew it. The word, the single word that she had blocked for fifteen years.

She grasped the hissing creature of three syllables and whispered it.

"Abaddon."

Instantly, Niccolo's pupils shrunk to pinholes. Joints, muscles, nerves, tendons: his entire body froze as if injected with a paralytic.

"No!" he hissed.

Sanderson gurgled; a fresh rivulet of blood trickled through his fingers.

Jesus! Did it work?

No time for questions. She slammed her fist into Niccolo's stomach as hard as she could. He bellowed in pain, his eyes squeezing tight, but didn't move. To her astonishment, he broke into laughter.

"Is *that* the best you can do? Let's go! Come on, come on!!" His arms and legs rigid as marble, he hollered, taunting her like an inmate raging in a straightjacket, "You pathetic cooze! I should have slit you from mouth to cunt when I had the chance! And I *had* the chance! That room in the Interfaith Center? How did you like it, sweet Gatsby? Your defilement? Getting fucked by a servant of heaven?!"

She was frozen, lost in a maelstrom of rage.

"Did you get off on it?" he snarled.

Something glittered: a silver chain hanging around his neck. Her hand flew to it, and she crushed it in her fist, twisting it hard, again and again, digging the links deeper and tighter into his neck.

I will KILL you!!!

He howled, coughing, his eyes squeezing against the pain, a litany of obscenities gushing from his mouth.

She heard the lisping voice of Judas: *I used a handgun. What would you use?*

I'd kill the fucker...

She wanted to shriek, but the words were a ragged whisper, "You don't deserve to live."

She shoved him hard.

He smacked against the wall, then slid to the floor, his arms lifeless at his sides, his legs locked and straight out in front of him. A putty mannequin in a cleric's robe, splattered with blood and death and sin.

What if he knows another trigger word?

She jerked off her sweatshirt, wrapped it around his face, stuffing a ball of fabric into his mouth, and then knotted the sleeves tightly at the back of his head.

"Mgghghhrhrhg!!"

"You don't deserve..."

Pain blasted through her with an intensity that rocked her. The end of everything. All the grief that had been buried so deep, for so long. The tears coursed down her cheeks.

Sanderson's eyes rolled underneath drooping lids. "Hrrrhhh..."

She dropped to his side and, cradling his head in her hands, leaned down toward his face. "Woody, can you hear me?"

His mouth worked, and his eyelids fluttered. Another blood bubble popped on his lip as he tried to croak an answer. His eyes clouded, stilled, and then closed as his head toppled to one side. His mouth gaped open. No air flowed from it.

"Woody!" She grasped his shoulders to shake him. His head jiggled like a marionette; his hair and shirt flopped.

"Woody, no! Don't leave me!" She tumbled onto his chest, straining to hear a heartbeat or the pull of breath.

The muscles around his eyes began to go slack.

I loved you then, Kama. I always will. I never considered going through life without you.

It took all that traveling to realize that where I had to be was right where I had begun.

She lifted her head from his blood-splattered chest and turned to face Niccolo. Their eyes blazed into each other.

Change all tenses to present!

Chop the sentences!

Delete all human endings!!

Tears dripped off her chin and fell onto Niccolo's frozen hand as she hissed, "Petash e-fama ra no mahji!! Nima runapa pa-tah shod..."

Niccolo screamed. His body began to convulse, muscles jerking and shuddering, the heels of his shoes drumming on the concrete. His eyes raced back and forth as his teeth champed against the sweatshirt. Saliva gushed down his chin and flowed to his chest as blood began to seep from his nose and ears.

"You don't deserve to..."

The images exploded through her mind:

The faces of her mother and father, Clive Gruedin's sideways grin, Woody's sable-brown eyes, Celia's filigree tattoo, Victoria Donahue, hunched over her—*Are you okay?*

The edges of the world blurred as she tipped forward. The heel of her hand slapped against Niccolo's sternum, and her fingers connected with the silver chain. With a scream, she swung her fist toward the ceiling, pulling on the chain until it broke—*snap!*—and spun crazily around her fist.

She stared at it, panting, lowered her hand, and let it drop it into her pocket.

The words were wrenched from her. They were the cries of all the souls of all who had died under the sword, the knife, the hooks, the flames, the rope, the bullet. They were the summation of all evil perpetrated in the name of a merciful god, perpetrated in fear and hatred.

Apply to each noun a suffix that indicates a human being. People who kill or injure others don't see them as human, only as objects.

"Runapai pa-tahi sho dayi too vashla mehi no sho ri-dehi-resu..." She choked back a cry. "Metah shme tah noni..."

Niccolo's body went limp. He closed his eyes, panting hard, his head swaying from side to side. A gooey stain of blood and saliva glistened on his chest. An inch at a time, he raised one hand to his mouth, tugged away the sweatshirt, and whispered, "You should have killed me."

His body lurched, making her jump back with a gasp. The bloody knife had skittered a few feet away. He flung one arm toward it and snatched it up in his fist, looking up at her with round, wet eyes.

"Plea...please...oh god, oh god, p-please forgive me ...forgive meee, I wasn't...I don't deserve..." His whining barreled into hiccupping sobs. "Ohhhhh dear god, I, I...I...I d-don't deserve to live!"

His arm swung upward, the tip of the knife directed at the flesh below his ear.

She sprang forward and landed hard, the sole of her shoe connecting with his wrist and smashing it to the concrete. The knife rattled to the floor.

Yowling, he glared up at her with burning eyes.

"Wh...Why?"

(Why?)

As it swept over her, she almost felt it physically—like a breeze, or a finger brushing her cheek, or was it a voice, an infinite voice that floated on the waves of the universe, a voice that shifted the galaxies as the words formed: *They may be lost in their addiction—their insanity—but no matter what they pray to, no matter what they believe in, no one should die for it.*

She swiped one hand across her face, and it came away streaked with blood.

She wanted to scream into his face but only managed to pant, "This...thing, this power that you believe in...is it worth killing for?"

His eyes softened with fresh tears.

There had to be something: rope, wire, tape, something. There—a tall cabinet. She clambered across the room, tested the cabinet's weight, and tipped it over. It fell to the floor with a thunderous crash and tornados of dust. She tugged on one end of it, and, using her full body weight and all her strength, was able to drag it across the floor to Niccolo's side. With a huge grunt, she lifted the edge and then let it slide onto his body, pinning him.

"You're not going anywhere, bastard," she muttered.

Sanderson groaned.

Scuttling toward him, she crouched by his side and pressed her fingers to his neck. His pulse was slow but steady, his breath coming in hitches.

"Oh my god...Woody?"

His eyes fluttered. His mouth closed, then opened, and she leaned closer to hear what he was whispering.

"Kama."

As she kissed his forehead, she whispered, "Hold on, Woody." She dug her cell phone from her pocket and dialed 999.

CHAPTER 41

The two-toned howl of the police siren woke Celia. Her eyes opened slowly, and she wrestled up from where she'd been cramped across the seat and gear console.

Where am I? What happened? As her gaze slid to the dark Officia, her thoughts tumbled: flying out the front door, the nausea lurching through her stomach, the bloody towel in the bathroom, the knives on the wall, calling Gatsby to urge a meeting with Liat, bringing Sanderson with her.

"Oh god, no..."

Just as she opened the driver's door, the squad car roared into the lot and stopped next to her car.

Two officers popped their doors open and stepped toward her. "Hey! Identify yourself! What are you doing here?" A tall officer slid forward. "Someone placed a 999 call from this location. You?"

Her eyes darted over his face as realization hit her. "They're already here!"

"Who?" he barked.

"My friends. They must be inside the building!" She swallowed. "They must have made the emergency call, and I think they're in terrible danger...there's someone inside, a man...I saw a case full of knives, and a towel covered in blood. Hurry!"

Two more squad cars rolled up; the officers tumbled out and moved into a circle around her.

"Why don't you start from the beginning?"

"You've got to get inside that building and find them, now!"

Police were surrounding the Officia. While Celia gave the story to the officer, explaining how Liat had convinced her to call Gatsby, the other officers thumbed the catches on their guns and began to move toward the entrance of the building. The front door was ajar.

"I must have left it open when I ran out!" Celia shouted as she made a dash toward it.

"Hey, hey, hey! You're staying right here," the officer snarled, grabbing her arm and jerking her back.

"Go, for god's sake! He was in the office, at the end of the main hall!"

A group of five officers nudged the front door open and stepped inside. They crept down the hallway to the Officia Abba but found it empty.

"No one here." The sergeant pulled out his walkie-talkie to relay information to the officers waiting outside when they heard muffled sounds—voices crying *Help!*—from below them.

"Basement," he murmured.

The group moved from the room and crept down the hallway. Just past the lift, they saw a flight of stairs and tiptoed down it.

When they stood at the base of the stairs, huddled before a heavy door, the sergeant whispered to the group, "Five-ten procedure. Wait for my signal. Three, two..."

They crashed through the door and into the dark room, weapons raised.

Sanderson lay prone and shivering on the concrete floor.

Huddled by his side, Gatsby looked up. "He's hurt! Get him to a hospital, now!"

As the sergeant approached her, she looked toward Niccolo, who cowered under the cabinet, and muttered, "He tried to kill us." She nodded at the table at the far side of the room. "And there's a lot of money over there."

A cluster of paramedics flowed into the room, hauling a wheeled stretcher. One took information from Gatsby, recording it all on a clipboard, while the others lifted Sanderson onto the stretcher. When he was covered with a blanket and secured with nylon straps, they maneuvered him up the stairway.

The officers hefted the cabinet off Niccolo and dragged him to his feet. As they handcuffed him, they read him his rights.

"Do you understand these rights?" The sergeant stared into his eyes.

He nodded, sniffling.

"Out loud."

"Yes," he muttered, grimacing. Underneath his jeans, at the point where the corner of the cabinet had crushed his right thigh, the knot had swollen to the size of a grapefruit. When his knees buckled and he dropped to the concrete with a grunt, they hauled him up again.

"Are you carrying any sharp objects on your person?"

"No."

They frisked him and dragged him out of the building to the squad car. He sobbed without stopping.

CHAPTER 42

As the paramedics secured Sanderson into the bay of the ambulance, Celia stepped toward Gatsby, shaking her head.

"I called you again, I tried to warn you!" She fell into Gatsby's arms and hugged her tightly; flecks of blood spotted her white blouse. "Oh Jesus, I didn't know, and it was so real, I was so positive that I could trust..." A cry caught in her throat. "Whatever their language did to Mick, and to you? It did it to me." She whirled toward the building, her eyes burning. "This whole temple of deceit, it's one big fucking lie, a con, a trap!" She spun back into Gatsby's arms.

Gatsby held her quietly, then stepped back, took a long breath, and blew it out slowly. *But no more. The chain is broken.*

Gazing at Celia, an exhausted smile began to move across her face. Her body felt light, translucent. The edges of the building, the lights of the squad cars—all slid into focus with almost painful clarity.

"Celia, it's okay now." She remembered sitting in a dark bar with Judas, a man branded by senseless brutality. *Quid pro quo? We always have the choice, do we not? Perpetuate a chain of violence or break it. Turn the other cheek or take an eye for an eye.*

Celia sniffed, frowning. "What do you mean?"

Gatsby slid her hand down into her pocket and withdrew the silver chain that she'd torn from Niccolo's neck.

Holding it up before Celia's tear-filled eyes, she murmured, "It *is* okay now. I'm okay."

CHAPTER 43

Both officers moved in to push Niccolo into the back seat of the Vauxhall Vetra squad car. He stole a glance at their name tags—the taller, stockier one was Cheyefski, Robertson was lean and bearded.

"In the car," Robertson grunted.

After slamming the door shut, they walked to opposite sides of the car. While Robertson slid into the driver's seat, Cheyefski took the passenger side. He used a pen to scribble on the plastic bag that held the bloody knife, then dropped the bag into an evidence container by his feet. As Cheyefski lowered the keyboard of the on-board computer and typed, Robertson gunned the engine.

The car began to move down the dark street. Cheyefski glanced back over his shoulder, scrutinizing his prisoner through the security glass.

Niccolo hung his head lower as his body pumped with noiseless sobs. The denim covering his thighs was splattered with blood and tears. A thread of saliva swung like a pendulum from his lower lip.

All gone, all ruined, and for what? What have I gained? His entire being throbbed with the agony of regret.

The occasional streetlights became the glare of shop fronts as the squad car picked up speed. Robertson turned onto Greville, a street that cut through the Wakefield district.

Niccolo stared down into his lap, his head swimming. Every cell screamed in pain, but the voices in his mind—the damned, the reviled, the deceived, the dead—screamed much louder.

We obey the precepts, we pray for guidance, we deliver our minds and bodies to the Abba, truth in his words, we follow the path that leads to the Kingdom of Truth...

He wanted to shake his head *no* but did not have the strength. His lips moved as he whispered, "There is only one path to Omega."

Cheyefski's head swiveled toward him. "What?"

Niccolo saw the images swirling, floating toward him, ghostly faces. Kuznetsov, Enright, Fitch. The curves of Anne Jillette's face. The bedraggled Tamar. The blood flushing Donovan's cheeks as she screamed into his face.

He saw Franca Volante's concrete stare, her ice-chip eyes. Heard the power straining in her voice, as if it were something that could be bound and tortured, when she had murmured, *If she is not loyal to Omega, she is an enemy, and a powerful one—I could tell you that now or I could reveal it later—which do you prefer?*

Every muscle shuddered uncontrollably. He heard the words rolling from his mouth and was incapable of stopping them. "Vash an parate oh me-gah falaji atab raaloh..."

The officers frowned at each other.

"What's that?" Robertson said.

"Mem vahla padarah oh meh-ga." The words flowed, unbidden and hated. He choked back a cry, swallowed saliva that tasted like rotted meat. "Travi ash ahta rom chahava ri-ana el-faj..."

"What the hell is he saying?" Robertson barked.

Cheyefski cocked his head, then shrugged and turned back to Robertson. "Sounds like some kind of prayer or something."

Robertson snorted. "Bastard can pray all he wants. He's still headed straight for Belmarsh."

Niccolo squeezed his eyes shut. *So much has been lost, so many innocents raped of their possessions, their livelihood, their loved ones! Their souls!! So many years of cultivating fear. So much that I pillaged from them and from myself.* The pangs ripped through him like the knives in his own case. He doubled forward, pressing his fists to his cheeks as sobs possessed him.

Cheyefski glanced back at him with a deep frown. "God almighty," he nodded toward Robertson, "ever seen a bloke work this hard for sympathy?"

"It's all a game," Robertson growled. "Sympathy my ass. Under all the waterworks, they're just planning their next move."

The squad car sped down a wide boulevard. Commercial buildings were interspersed with Indian groceries, late-night petrol stations, and middle-class neighborhoods.

The words exploded from Niccolo's mouth. "Pay lashi deh-raz oh nera!"

"Hey! Pipe down!" Robertson snarled.

There was no stopping it. The Prayer of Devotion gushed from his lips. "Abbah way non vash ah parateh, sho day too vashla meed neh-vee von besh garah, mem vahla padarah oh meh-ga."

Cheyefski's lips parted and then twitched. He pulled in a gasp of air and whispered on the exhale, "Mem vahla padarah oh meh-ga..."

Robertson's body stiffened as if a sedative pumped through his veins. His breath caught. The blood drained from his cheeks as he intoned, "Mem vahla padarah oh meh-ga..."

They wanted wisdom! Niccolo felt his mind spiraling toward lunacy. *I brought ruin! And most of all...*

He leaned against the door, barely aware of the electric jolts sizzling up his leg. *Most of all, I wanted her!*

The last verse of the Words of Reckoning flowed from him as a long howl.

"Da-chala ah salesh mana nyaja goppa nen hunamaaa..."

On the final day, at the last proclamation of Truth, the damned shall take their final breath...

Both officers gasped.

Niccolo's head popped up; he stared toward them.

Cheyefski's hands were poised just over the keyboard; the ball of Robertson's left hand rested against the steering wheel while his right hand hovered by the digital CCTV system. Their eyes darted back and forth, but both men seemed to have solidified, rigid as mannequins.

The Vetra barreled down the road at ninety kilometers per hour.

Niccolo watched the steering wheel begin to turn.

The car drifted toward the left edge of the road. A hard bump and THUD shook them, and he looked out the window to see that the car had jumped a curb and was careening into a parking lot.

The car sped across the asphalt. Both ends of the lot were flanked by shops, but the trajectory of the car would send it toward a section of fencing that ran between the lot and a row of houses.

His eyes bulging, Niccolo tried to scream. "N...!!"

The car crashed through the fence, sending posts and splinters flying. It careened across a yard and, with a roar of grating steel, rubber, and wood, crashed into the back of a two-story bungalow.

When the airbags exploded open, the officers simultaneously sank into the cushion of blue nylon.

Niccolo felt himself flying toward the security glass— the sound of his temple cracking against a steel bar was like a baseball bat connecting with a ball. One shoulder smacked against the reinforced backs of the seats, bringing an excruciating pop in his elbow. At the same moment, glass shattered, raining shards across him and the officers.

Panting, he slowly raised his head to see that the car had lodged in a utility room; a clothes washer was accordioned around the front fender. He glanced at the officers. Both remained face down in the airbags, inert as crash dummies.

Lights inside the house winked on.

Grunting against the pain in his swollen thigh and the blasts of pain from the fractured left elbow, he pulled himself across the back seat toward the shattered window. At the impact, the handcuffs had crashed against steel, crushing the lock just enough that he could wrestle his bruised hands free. Groaning, he wriggled through the opening and tumbled to the dirt. Electric jolts exploded at wounds from his crown to heels, and he ground his teeth together to keep from screaming.

More lights popped on in neighboring houses. He heard high, panicked shouts.

The vision of Maia floated into his head, the inferno in her eyes, the secret cauldron of her emotions, which he had never fully grasped—hate? fear? desire? revulsion? *What did she feel when she gazed into the eyes of a man who wanted her so badly that he would...*

Then: *She wouldn't crawl before me. She had the courage that I lacked.*

He crawled across scattered splinters of glass and the manicured lawn toward the protective darkness of a thicket.

CHAPTER 44

He limped down the side of the apartment building and into the tiny yard. A sliding glass door flanked a concrete patio: he remembered locking all the doors, including that one, that morning. He moved toward the window to the left of the door and tested it. It slid open with a squeal.

Niccolo struggled through the opening, floundered onto a wooden kitchen table, and dropped to the floor.

Quick!

His leg screaming, he hobbled up the stairs to the bedroom, tugged a suitcase from the closet, and stuffed it with pants, shirts, and socks. His gaze traveled to the desk at the far side of the room.

The cardboard boxes. The MCF documents.

He felt a sigh move him as the pieces of his life shifted into place. All the terrible disappointments over the years. All the empty promises from schools, from so-called friends, and from the holy teachers who sold him their privileged, members-only paths to knowledge. To truth.

His chest rose and fell, like the deathbed wheezing of the emphysema patient.

He edged toward the table and opened the first box. Fingering the sheaves of paper, he shuddered, seeing Volante's face, hearing the exultance in her voice: *These are the originals, the lost Omega scrolls.*

But they didn't realize its full potential, its power.

The forbidden vision floated into his mind's eye: her arms, Herculean, the black abyss of her eyes, the heat of her tawny skin, and the sheen of her black hair, swirling into the jaws of eternity, drowning in the hell that was his soul.

"No." The sound of his voice, croaking the word, startled him. "Belief should illuminate, not destroy. The old way is dead. I must start a new path."

Staring dully at the papers in the box, he replaced the lid.

Should I take them? Burn them? He shook his head. *No. Let her do what she pleases with them. I have no more use for the ruin they bring.*

He grabbed the set of keys from the top drawer.

Each movement sent cascades of pain through his thigh as he limped down the stairs and through the front door to stumble toward his car, which was parked by the curb.

As he stepped toward the driver's-side door, he glanced up. His building was dark, as were most of the flats on the street. No faces, no neighbors, no one on their evening walk. One solitary streetlight buzzed on the corner.

He opened the door and slid into the seat. As his hand moved toward the ignition, he thought, *No, the police surely will know my vehicle, address...*

He heard a rustle from the back seat and was flooded by the smells: lavender and rosewood and honey.

Something lurching forward, a blur, a flash of something metallic, and then a whip of pain around his windpipe.

"Push tah non ah meh-gah."

The whisper slithered into his ear, the voice icy as the basement of the sea. "Struggle one millimeter, Niccolo, and your blood flows until none remains." Her laughter was a hiss. "Just like Reymann."

Franca!!

He steeled himself not to move, to swallow, to breathe. He knew the mechanism that she had around his throat, the garrote, and how easily it would slice through his flesh.

"There is not...enough...treasure in the empire...to deter you," his Adam's apple worked with each word, pain ripped through the skin, "is there, Franca?" He felt sweat gushing into the collar of his shirt, his bladder about to open.

Her lips nuzzled against his ear. "The empire *is* the treasure, you fool, and it's mine now, with or without the Librah Vae-ta. Every church needs its martyr, doesn't it?" She sighed as if drawing out the moment brought on sexual ecstasy. "The death of the great spiritual leader births a legend, and the legend strengthens the faith of the disciples. The disciples bring in more converts, more worker slaves. More *wealth.* And the rich get richer off their addiction."

He squeezed his eyes shut against the salty sting of tears. "What have I created?"

As she tightened the wire, she whispered, "A deathbed conversion? How *droll*. You created exactly what you set out to create: the expression of yourself, mirrored in a thousand faces. The pathetic Dosa end their prayers by contemplating how they are made in God's image. We who understand how religion truly works know that all gods are created as images of ourselves."

His body trembled violently. A sliver of saliva trickled from his lip. Again, the question burned through him: *What have I created?*

"The empire is that image of yourself. The image that you didn't have the balls to truly act on and that I do. The empire is mine now."

Each sob brought lightning flashes as the wire bit deeper into the flesh. "Franca...I would have held you..."

"As you held her?" In his ear, her voice seemed to burn like acid. "Your darling Maia? Your beautiful assassin? Tell me, did she struggle when you fucked her? Or did you tie her to your big table and get off on her helplessness? Or just on your own?"

He felt the gush of hot urine coursing through his crotch.

"There is only one path to Omega," she hissed. "Journey down that path now."

Omega forgive her.

He slipped into the long darkness, terrified and then, finally, welcoming it: the silent, infinite peace that he had craved for so very long.

CHAPTER 45

She pushed on the door and waved a cone of flowers through the opening, their plastic wrap imprinted with BETHLEHEM ROYAL. Sanderson's "come in" beckoned her.

Gatsby dashed into the hospital room, skirted around bulky, glowing monitors and panels, and raced to the far side of the bed. She flung the flowers onto the bedside table, stretched her arms toward him, and stopped, panting.

He raised his free arm toward her. As she leaned down for an awkward hug, wrapping her arms around his shoulders, she felt his fingers press against her back.

"I thought I'd lost you."

He whispered, "You'll never lose me."

They exchanged each other's rapid, nervous breath for a moment before she pulled back and slid into a metal chair beside the bed.

Swallowing, he searched her eyes as if preparing himself for the worst. "After I blacked out...what happened?"

She was instantly back in the dark basement, splattered with blood, terrified, seething. Her cheeks flushed with remembered fury. "I could have killed him, and I didn't. He tried to kill himself. I didn't let him. Then police. Handcuffs. Celia was outside, unconscious in her car."

Sanderson reacted in slow motion: eyes widening as his body stiffened and drew back, his mouth yawning open. "My god," he whispered. "Do you want to tell me about it?"

She ran her palms across her thighs, creating wet streaks in the denim. "Yes, but first there's something that you should know."

She described the formula of Logos-Thanatos. Her first taste of using it on him. How it proved deadly in Hyde Park. Then using it on the man that she now knew was named Niccolo Rueke. It all tumbled out in a breathless gush.

His fingers wrapped over each other and then fell inert to his side. "I don't know what to say."

She paused. "This man, Rueke, is the leader of the Omega group. And...that night in Seattle, at the Interfaith Center? It was him. He even admitted to it, asked me how it felt to..." She swallowed as a tear ran down her cheek. "And once I got a good look at his face."

"No," Sanderson moaned, shaking his head.

"Fifteen years ago. It was him."

He dropped his head into his hands. When he looked up at her with blood-shot eyes, he muttered, his voice thick, "You said that you could have killed him and didn't." He waited for her to respond.

She sat back in the chair and crossed her arms over her chest. Her eyes traveled over him: the white hospital gown, the bandage adhered to the left side of his forehead, the line trailing from a monitor to the patch on the back of his hand, the twin peaks of his feet jutting upward under the grey blanket. The furrows and drying streaks on his face.

Her voice deep, she said, "An eye for an eye? Perpetuate a chain of violence? I chose."

She groped in the pocket of her jeans, and the silver chain tinkled as she drew it out and held it up. "I chose to destroy the violence but not the man."

He pulled in a breath as his eyes raced across her face. "You said he tried to kill himself?"

She nodded. "He was going to cut his throat. I stopped him."

"Why?"

She pulled in a deep breath and watched at the swaying motion of the window blinds. "He may worship something that I don't want to know anything about. He can be a Muslim, a Jew, a Christian, a pagan, an atheist. He can pray to rocks or Froot Loops, it doesn't matter. I don't care what myth he chooses to follow—as long as no one dies for it." She paused. "He sobbed like a child and begged for my forgiveness."

Sanderson blinked owlishly. "What then?"

"Then the police were there. The ambulance."

He chewed his lip. "No, what I mean is...did..."

"Did I forgive him? Will I?"

The room hummed: air conditioning, electricity, muffled voices, ticking.

He watched, seemingly patient as the pyramids, while emotions swept through her. At last, he murmured, "Got it."

A sigh moved her. She scanned down his torso to his midsection. "What's the prognosis?"

"Your standard prognosis for a knife in the kidney. Binging, orgies," he added with a puff of dry laughter, "then rest and meditation." He took a slow breath. "I've been probed and scoped and palpated, and I will heal. Slowly but surely."

As she glanced toward the flowers on the bedside table, she murmured, "Slowly but surely," bent to kiss his forehead, and walked out the door.

While wandering down the quiet hallway, she wondered when he would see it. She imagined him fingering through the yellow petals and Ming fern and spotting something tucked deep within the bundle. He would reach in to pull out a red rose to which a card had been attached with a wire twist.

He would read the inscription: *Semantically yours.*

And he would know.

CHAPTER 46

As Singer approached, his stride and uniform imperial, Gatsby rose from the armchair and held the Baber case out toward him.

He took it, eyed her for a moment as if collecting his thoughts, and said, "Any problems repacking it?"

She shook her head.

He nodded toward the hall.

When they had settled in his office, the case stowed in a locked cabinet, Singer cleared his throat and looked at her. "I've been in touch with the Mayfair police. They say that you were very lucky, managed to escape the attack with only bruises. But I hear that your associate wasn't so lucky."

Associate. "He's in the hospital. Recovering."

"Glad to hear that," he murmured. "I want to ask you for two things, Dr. Donovan."

"Yes?"

"First, a detailed report. Everything you've discovered about this book and about the language. We need to learn everything we can about this Omega group."

Everything? Tell him how Woody and I modified the language? Logos-Pax? Her muscles tensed. *Or Logos-Thanatos? A killing language?* The answers were immediate. *Tell him everything. The CIS needs to know that the language can be manipulated.*

"All right." She tipped her chin upward. "What's going to happen to Rueke?"

"That's hard to say. The squad car crashed en route to Belmarsh. Rueke is missing."

Fear jolted through her chest.

"That's the reason for my second request. I want to keep a security watch on your house for a time."

The image of Rueke's tear-streaked face bloomed in her mind, his voice cracking as he whimpered, *Plea...please...oh god, oh god, p-please forgive me...forgive meee, dear god, I...I...I d-don't deserve to live...*

She swallowed. "I don't think that he would come after me a second time." She paused. *Did he repent for his sins— or just want me to* believe *that he did?* "But you, um, can't be too careful."

He nodded. "I'll give you more details when we speak next. Can you have that report to me by next week?"

"I think so."

His face remained stiff, but his tone softened. "Are you okay?"

She stole a glance around the room and smiled. Weary but finally at peace. "Yes. I am."

"Good."

He walked her through the grey hallways and back to the reception desk, where he held his hand out toward her.

"Thank you. I'll be in touch soon." He whirled on his heels and marched down the hallway.

In a minute, folded into a seat on the Tube, Gatsby thought, *What if he did try to find me? I spared his life once—would I a second time?*

CHAPTER 47

Gatsby opened her door to see Celia's face: dark eyes, struggling, lips trembling.

After they embraced tightly, Gatsby herded her into the living room.

Celia dropped into the couch and threw her cape across the arm. Closing her eyes, she muttered, "What a freakin' fool I was."

Gatsby dropped into the loveseat. "You were under the influence of a drug. Just like I was."

"But..."

"You could beat yourself up for a long time, and I might sit here and watch you do it," she shot her a *joking!* look, "or you can be quiet and watch this."

"Watch what?" Celia sat straighter.

Gatsby reached for the remote sitting on the coffee table. "This. I was told that it would make tonight's news."

She pushed the ON button, and the television glowed to life.

The newscaster for BBC News 24 was in the middle of a story on security measures at Heathrow. The story wrapped up, and the copper-haired reporter said, "Back to you, Katy."

Trim in a sapphire blue suit, Katy Shaw looked at the viewers and said in a sonorous voice, "For thousands of years, cultures around the world have looked to holy scriptures for guidance. The Torah, the Bible, and the Koran have offered instruction and inspiration to millions over countless generations. This story exposes one holy book that may have captured the mind to enslave rather than to enlighten. Robert Bruce explains."

Celia's eyes widened.

A man with cropped red hair and a sober face appeared on the screen. "An underground but global religious group is now no longer underground," Bruce said in a deep voice. "Last week, the leader of the group, which is called Omega, was apprehended when police in Mayfair answered a 999 call. Not only had the Omega group developed a very strict code of conduct for the members, but it had created its own bible, written in a complex neo-language understood only by its discipleship. Once the converts learned this language, it appears that they became locked into a slave-like mindset that caused them to cross lines most of us would never consider."

An image of the Gahana faded in on the screen. Celia glanced toward Gatsby, who nodded.

A close-up image of the text dissolved into another image, then the leather cover, as Bruce continued. "One Londoner, who has deferred giving her name, found herself drawn into the state that language effects, a state that seems to mirror serious drug addiction or deep hypnosis. When the group's leader attacked her in a vicious physical assault, she managed to save herself."

As Celia and Gatsby leaned closer to the screen, new images emerged. Gatsby's handwritten syllabary and scribbled notes.

"She reports that she was able to modify the language, restructuring it in a way that brought about a sort of antidote effect. By using this revised language, she was able to escape from her attacker who, she says, experienced a complete transformation of mind."

A female voice floated from the speakers: "Vashla mehi no pa-tahi sho ri-dehi-resu runapai metah shme tah noni..."

Gatsby turned toward Celia and whispered, "Logos-Pax."

Wide-eyed, Celia stared into the images.

As Bruce continued, energy began to build in his voice. "The CIS will continue to investigate the Omega organization, which some have called the world's largest cult, to uncover more details about its purpose and methods. For now, citizens are urged to exercise great caution if approached by anyone offering," he paused, "the word of God. Katy, back to you."

"Now if you..." Gatsby started.

Celia was standing at the kitchen sink.

Gatsby rose and moved up next to her. "What are you doing?"

Celia's shoulderbag lay unzipped on the counter. She clutched a handful of Omega brochures in one hand, a fork in the other. Reaching toward a switch on the wall, she pushed against it with her thumb and, as the garbage disposer growled, she stuffed the brochures into the hole. Feathers of paper flew through the air, confetti-like, until she tugged on the faucet handle. The last snippets of shredded paper slid into the black orifice and oblivion.

Celia flicked the switch off.

Gatsby draped one arm around her shoulder. "Feel better?"

Celia nodded.

CHAPTER 48

Gatsby poured sparkling Perrier, and Sanderson raised his glass. "To the slayer of morphemes and all her grand adventures." He grinned playfully at her, then moaned while fumbling at the gauze and adhesive bandaging under his ribs.

"How is it?"

"It's healing. The stitches come out in a few days."

They watched harried travelers battle their way down the Heathrow concourse.

Gatsby stared out the window at 747s taxiing toward their gates. "The book—will it continue to seduce people, like it did Celia? And have the effects that we saw in Parrish? The delusions," she looked away, shaking her head, "that caused me to accuse an innocent man?"

He pulled in a long breath. "I know that we were able to shed some light on what Omega was doing and how destructive it was to everything it touched. We stopped a vicious man from harming anyone else." He leaned toward her. "And you found a way to transform something intended to exploit into a meme of peace. Who knows how the meme might spread." His eyes sparkled. "Small acts can lead to global changes."

She smiled a little. "Think we'll be canonized?"

He chuckled. "Who knows. But this whole thing has brought me to one irrefutable conclusion."

"What?"

He looked into her eyes. "That the most important thing to me right now isn't the book, or Omega, or what we were able to unearth. It's what I discovered about myself. And what I need in my life more than anything else."

She felt her breath quicken.

He started to reach one hand across the table toward hers, then retreated. "I'm full circle now. I left the place—and the person—that meant everything to me. Now I'm back at that place. Starting again." His eyes softened. "Wanting to start again."

Her gaze slid to the jets on the tarmac. "Woody, I know that it wasn't you that night—it never could have been you."

His eyes darted, and he frowned fiercely as he shook his head. "If that bastard ever tried to touch you again," he smashed his hands against each other, almost unable to continue. "I can't even think about anyone hurting you. I love you."

She sighed. "Woody, I'm not ready to say that. Those old wounds are still there. They still hurt like hell. And the pain that has been part of this whole process, pulling it all up and reliving what we did then? It's a huge shock. We're both astute enough to know just how much of a shock."

He nodded.

"But in the not-too-distant future," she searched his eyes, "I think I could."

A glow moved over Sanderson's face.

"But where is that not-too-distant future? My life is here in London. Yours is at Berkeley."

He threw his hands across the table and grabbed hers. "Listen to me. I lost you once, and I'm not going to do it again." He sighed. "There was a time that I only cared about life after death, but I'm ready to focus fully on life here and now. This is all that matters. And I'll do whatever it takes to be in your life."

His fingers laced through hers as a smile spread across her face. "I like the sound of that."

"My first order of business when I get back to Berkeley is to investigate how I can relocate to London permanently."

She raised her glass, nodded toward his until he picked it up and, as they touched their glasses together, murmured, "Cheers."

"Now seating passengers in Section C," the voice intoned over the PA system.

Sanderson stood and hefted the strap of his garment bag over his shoulder. Gatsby rose and moved closer to him.

"I'm going to call you every day, and write to you, but no letters from Definite Article!"

She beamed. "Aw c'mon. I think I want to keep in touch with Definite Article." She paused. "Woody, you *are* the definite article. I don't believe in fairytale romance, in forever after, in *the one*. But you are *the* one that I am most curious about."

"Curious? I'll settle for that."

She reached into her shoulderbag, pulled out her wallet, and pulled from it the dog-eared photograph. Holding it forward, she watched his look of surprise melt into an ear-to-ear smile.

"Last call for passengers in Section C." A uniformed attendant stepped past them to pull a velvet cord across the boarding aisle.

He wrapped her in his arms.

They held each other tight, breathing in the connection of skin and bone, the wriggling warmth of their bodies. Their old paths, separated, now rejoined. She felt in it a glory that flowed through her body and mind and heart.

I went through my own hell, but this is the only heaven— and it's right here, right now.

He glanced at the boarding ramp. "All this over a book."

She kissed his mouth, murmuring, "Sometimes great things are found between the covers."

EPILOGUE

While Gatsby and Celia watched the news story about Omega, others across London also stared into their TVs, watching the same story.

In the next few days, hundreds, then thousands, of disciples went to their private shrines and gathered their literature.

Millions of pages—all once fervently believed to be the source of highest truth, the infallible word of a higher power—were entombed with no intent for resurrection.

Some disciples stuffed their booklets into garbage bins.

Some fed theirs through paper shredders.

Some packaged theirs in boxes for burial.

Some burned small fires in fireplaces.

Some took an item that symbolized slavery or addiction—a piece of jewelry, a photo, a lock, a letter—and, in the way most meaningful for them, destroyed it.

In their bodies and minds, they felt the healing begin.

THE WORLD OF OMEGA

VOCABULARY

The Prayer of Devotion
Abbah way non push tah non ah meh-gah
("Abba the Blessed Guide to Omega")
Sho day too vashla meed neh-vee von besh garah
("Guide us on the path of eternal truth")
Mem vahla padarah oh meh-ga
("we consecrate ourselves in service to Omega")

Phrases	Translation
Padarah oh meh-ga	Service to Omega
Vash an parate oh me-gah falaji atab raaloh	Belief in Omega (symbol Ω) is service and study
Di-wah nassa bay ah salesh meed neh-vee von besh garah	We reject the lie of lower illusion to walk The path to the Eternal Truth
Keen! Raya keen.	Listen! Stop and listen.
nah-maen	It is truth
Qaz!	Analogous to "Shit!"
pasha-lo	The lower, illusory world, of which a disciple must be stripped

Prayer to Open Damaii

Damaii vash an parate oh me-gah falaji atab raaloh	Damaii belief in Omega is service and study
Mem vahla padarah oh meh-ga	We consecrate ourselves in service to Omega
Di-wah nassa bay ah pash-lo salesh meed neh-vee von	We reject the lie of illusion to pursue the Kingdom of Eternal Truth
Travi ash ahta rom chahava ri-ana ehfaj	This is our holy mission, from this moment until death

Processes and Subgroups

honorum mati	Mandatory tithes, monetary contributions to Omega
val	A word of permission, giving disciples freedom to react without the restraint normally required
dar-chaliid	Open "Q&A" at a gathering; permission to speak freely
hewat	A subcommittee, a "special interest group" within the Dama (the hewat attempting to recreate the Librah Vae-ta is comprised of Rauscher, Isma'il, Polensky, Bunch, Nguyen, Ivan Kuznetsov, Franca Volante, and Maia)
Damaii	The Damaii is the gathering of the inner discipleship, the select members who may attend the services. Dama sit closest to the front, then Shoto, then Dosa at the back. The Habareh at the center leads the Damaii.

ABOUT THE AUTHOR

Ellery Stone is the pen name of the American author Lori Stephens, pNLP, CCP. Stephens earned a BA in English literature and creative writing at the University of Oregon. Her career in the publishing field began in 1988, and she has edited over 200 books on topics as varied as cancer research, dating for seniors, music therapy, Neurolinguistic Programming, software security, and zombies.

The research for the *Paradigms Lost* series was extensive. In addition to visiting England, France, and Italy, she researched Egypt, India, Peru, Australia, Greece, Crete, and Spain. While writing *Deep Structure*, she spent five years learning about archeology (specifically the history of Stonehenge) and quantum physics. *Alpha Omega* required research into the structure of ancient languages, and she drew on her own experience with NLP and hypnotic language. *Viral Glyph* took her into studies of the Phaistos Disk, theories of its decipherment, and the history of cryptography. Descriptions of the world of stage magic were drawn from her association with a professional magician.

The author at Stonehenge (Wiltshire, England)

ALSO BY ELLERY STONE

DEEP STRUCTURE
The Stonehenge Quantum
Where are the mysterious symbols coming from? Why have they appeared in an Egyptian tomb, a Peruvian palace, and a shape created by a fakir's squirming snakes?

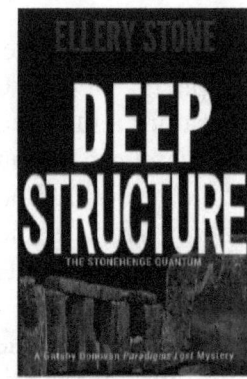

 Dr. Gatsby Donovan's career at the British Museum has made her an expert in decoding ancient glyphs, but solving this linguistic puzzle is the greatest challenge of her life. Will her knowledge unearth the answers, or are they secreted within the very source that she dare not decipher? As she spirals into the universal "deep structure," she finds herself dangling from the edge of everything she once believed about reality.

VIRAL GLYPH
The Rosette Rebellion
When Dr. Gatsby Donovan meets a cocky stage magician, Maceo Affiato, he claims that the most mysterious artifact of all human history—the Phaistos Disk—has been stolen, and he needs her expertise in order to find it.

 If the disk on display in the Heraklion Museum isn't genuine, where is the real one? And how is it connected to a terrible massacre? Finding the answers means outwitting the female-only syndicate called The Circle. Its global network of agents will do whatever it takes to protect the disk and conceal its true purpose and power, no matter the price. Can Gatsby connect the dots—and overcome her darkest fears—before time runs out?

www.ellerystone.com